BARRY WHITE IS STILL ABSURD

ROB HARRIS

Copyright © 2025 Rob Harris

The right of Rob Harris to be identified as the Author of the Work has been asserted by them in accordance with the Copyright, Designs and Patents Act 1988.

First published in 2025 by Bloodhound Books.

Apart from any use permitted under UK copyright law, this publication may only be reproduced, stored, or transmitted, in any form, or by any means, with prior permission in writing of the publisher or, in the case of reprographic production, in accordance with the terms of licences issued by the Copyright Licensing Agency.
All characters in this publication are fictitious and any resemblance to real persons, living or dead, is purely coincidental.

www.bloodhoundbooks.com

Print ISBN: 978-1-917705-00-4

ONE

WE ARE NOT AMUSED

She was more than ten feet tall and looked a bit like Queen Victoria.

The statue of Pearl 'Ma' White appeared overnight from nowhere and with no warning. Now it dominated the village square, towering above the cenotaph that bore the names of Anghofiedig's two lost soldiers: Arwel Jackson, killed by a blunt bayonet through the heart on Juno beach in 1944; and Christopher Davies, bombed out of his skin by friendly fire somewhere near Port Stanley almost four decades later.

Her face was fatter than Ma's, the eyes too baggy, the eyebrows too heavy. She wore a pearl necklace, a silver tiara and a 'we are not amused' expression. Ma never wore a tiara in all her seventy-eight years. She did own a pearl necklace though. The one given to her by Barry Senior during their courting days, which he would make her put on for special occasions such as weddings or rugby club dinners. The demeanour of this cold imposter spoke of entitlement and privilege. However, Ma's privileges in life had been few and far between: a sly glass of sherry before bed on a Saturday night or a few days in Tenby every first week in August.

'What do you reckon she's made of?' said the first council worker. He sucked hard on the roll-up he'd wedged between his front teeth, like all men used to do back in Arwel Jackson's era, especially when sizing up a dash from a flimsy boat to the perilous shifting sands of the Normandy coast.

'Her's pure limestone her is,' said his mate. He was unshaven, gaunt and much younger, but still looked like he'd been chased out of a black-and-white movie by a gun-toting Humphrey Bogart or Jimmy Cagney.

'How she get here?'

'Not a Scooby-Doo.'

'Who do yer reckon she is?'

'Vanessa Feltz?'

'Nah, this old girl's royal. Queen summat. Could be Victoria? Could be Charlie's missus. The new one, who don't smile much. Named after posh tea.'

'Earl Grey?'

'Nah, Chamomile.'

How quickly people forget. That's why Romeo had taken it upon himself to get the statue of Ma commissioned in the first place. He'd kept his plan secret from everyone, including Barry, but Jonah, Pricer and a couple of other ne'er do well pals had helped his cloak-and-dagger placing of the statue in the middle of the night without bothering to ask questions. How they didn't wake up the entire village was anyone's guess. But Romeo wanted the locals to have a visible reminder of who Ma was and what she had done for them all: leaving so much money to wasters who didn't deserve it.

'What d'you reckon she's worth?' said man one.

'Packet.' Man two had his right hand deep in his trouser pocket as if facilitating his side of the conversation by rubbing his own crown jewels.

'What's gonna happen to her when we take her back to the

depot?' said man one, wishing his mate would take his hand out of his pocket.

'Dunno, turned into posh bricks maybe?'

'Shame. She ain't doing no harm.'

'Rules is rules.'

'Suppose. But still a bloody shame.'

Man one stamped out his cigarette and spat. He moved closer to the statue. 'You know what, her looks a bit like Tina Turner if you squint through one eye and stare up from the ground slowly.'

'Who's Tina Turner?'

'Big hair. Long legs. Deep old fag-filled voice. Married to Ike who roughed her up a bit.'

'Ike live round here?'

Man one rolled his eyes. 'Don't fucking worry. Come on let's get the old girl down whilst she's looking t'other way.'

Man two grabbed the statue by the breasts. 'Okay, you cut, I'll hold her steady.'

'Fine but watch where you're putting your hands, I know where they've just been. She's not one of your social club floozies, her's got something about her. A touch of class. The more I looks at her the more I likes her.'

Man two was irritated. 'Get on with it will you, her weighs a bloody tonne. I reckon we're going to need more men. Horse crap, she's slipping...'

And with that, the statue of Ma – twice as tall and twenty times as heavy as she ever stood in real life – fell through the grasp of the council's finest pair of Chuckle Brothers to smash into thousands of tiny pieces, scattering shards and ashes on the wind to carpet the Anghofiedig landscape for years to come.

'You're a real professional, you know that?' said man one, sarcastically.

'I thought I had her.' Man two bent down and picked up a broken foot.

'What we gonna tell 'em back at the yard?'

'Nothing. We'll say she did a bunk before we even got 'ere.'

Man one grabbed his broom and a bucket. 'Let's sweep up the old girl's bones and gizzards and get them in the van before anyone sees us.'

Man two continued to rummage through broken body parts on the floor like he was at a jumble sale. 'Her head's still in good shape. Can I keep it?'

'What for?'

'Dunno. Doorstop or something.'

'You're a strange puppy, you know that?'

'I might be able to sell it to some rich Russian who collects the heads of British royals. What did you say she was called?' Man two held Ma's head by the eyes like it was a bowling ball.

'Hold her nicely, will yer? I reckon this old bird is the sort of gal who won't ever leave you alone, especially if you flog her for peanuts on eBay. Reckon she'll come back to haunt you and bring you a thousand years' bad luck.'

'I ain't got a thousand years, and you bring me more than enough bad luck every morning for one man in one lifetime,' said man two, holding up Ma's head and staring directly into her eyes for obvious signs of damage, life or, at the very least, the portents of a restless and agitated soul.

He rubbed too hard on the glass, attempting to get rid of a grubby mark, and splashed half a pint of frothy lager down the front of his trousers so it looked like he had wet himself. Rex Blunkett and Terry Truman, daytime-drinking wasters on long-term sickness, jeered, laughed and made feeble jokes about incontinence pants and leaky prostate glands. The barman poured the remainder of the pint – which Rex was about to pay for – over their heads and told them it was on the house. Playing mine host did not come naturally to Barry White.

This time a year ago, Barry would have been lying in his bed pretending to work. He'd been happy enough with his life as an idle content creator, comfortable in his position as LesCargo Express Logistics' number two work-shy comms man – only beaten to the top spot by best pal Romeo, a genuine candidate for Wales's all-time undefeated, laziest bastard.

Barry thought back to how he only used to stir from his slumbers for an emergency Teams meeting, or an episode of *The Professionals* on ITV4, or the promise of a plateful of Ma's bacon and mushroom butties slathered in either ketchup or brown sauce, depending on how much spice he wanted in his life on that particular day.

How times had changed. Ma had died in the spring just weeks before Chico – Barry's favourite YouTube gorilla – who choked unexpectedly on a hunk of rotting wood and departed for the great jungle in the sky. Barry thought back to those monumental, life-shifting crazy months, which saw him win a million quid on the horses, give one hundred grand to the church, quit his job, meet Diana and take her round the world on an extended sabbatical. He'd inherited Ma's old house and refurbished it from top to bottom. He'd also bought this pub for the community and given Romeo the deeds, cash, scissors and shavers to half a barbershop. He hadn't had time to think or breathe. He hadn't even paused to reflect on the revelation that his father, local rugby legend Barry White, long deceased, wasn't actually his father. Or that his real dad was John John, the inoffensive, slightly boring owner of the village mart.

All that brought him to where he was today. Skint. Standing behind a bar with a tea towel over his shoulder, listening to the dribble and drivel of irritating know-it-alls, splashing lager about carelessly in the bowels of The Dragon, which was empty as usual. Living with Diana, playing happy families in Ma's old house at 76 Cerys Matthews Heol and trying to act like a responsible grown-up who knew his way around paying bills and fixing broken things. Pretending to be a modern, attentive man who both listened and cared about his girlfriend's small talk. Pretending, too, not to be freaked out of his brain by the sight of a six-foot-plus adolescent with size fourteen feet called Eddie – Diana's fifteen-year-old son – as he strolled from shower to fridge wearing nothing but his mother's pink dressing gown, six sizes too small for him and completely untethered.

Barry sometimes wished he could go back to how things used to be when life was simpler. Before death, money and relationships had complicated everything. Yet he hadn't forgotten how he used to feel whilst in the throes of living that simpler life: yearning to be challenged and more respected, and for new things to come into his days to make him feel better about himself.

He was pretty sure he loved Diana and he certainly liked having her around, but maybe it had been a mistake to ask her to live with him so hastily. He had no idea until she moved in just how much she talked about nothing in particular. It was as if she needed to provide a running commentary on life itself. He'd been unaware, too, of her need to keep moving. Unlike him, she never sat around with a bag of doughnuts on her lap to watch mindless telly. It was tiring to see her in action and it often seemed like she was creating work just for the sake of it, but he would never say that to her face. Ma had never asked or wanted Barry to help out with anything, but Diana wasn't Ma.

In all the years he had lived with his mother, Barry never saw her undies on public display. She manoeuvred them from washing machine to drier to drawer with the stealth of a bodyguard tasked with getting an unpopular South American president over enemy lines and back again before they got assassinated. Diana, by contrast, seemed to revel in teasing maverick snipers, recklessly leaving her knickers on radiators and the tops of open windows for the whole of Anghofiedig to see. Briefs they certainly were: bits of black skimpy material that looked more like top pocket handkerchiefs – ones that cost the price of a small family hatchback yet were too flimsy to hold even one relatively feeble nose blow. Should you wish to, of course. Barry would watch Diana dress each morning with fascination, marvelling at how this so-called garment disappeared within her, leaving just a small perky triangular bit at the front. And every morning, as he witnessed this peculiar rite, along with plenty of others such as the ceremonial removal of every hair follicle from the top lip down with bits of scrunched up sticky tape, or the plucking of eyebrows with tweezers so they could be drawn back on again (in a different place) with a special marker pen, he would think to himself, *Women are truly insane.*

But he would say nothing...

Terry Truman and Rex Blunkett returned from the loos, having dried themselves off the best they could under temperamental hand blowers that threw out less hot air than the two of them. They both tossed Barry dirty looks and, saying nothing, skulked towards the exit feeling sorry for themselves.

Barry threw his tea towel down and held up open hands. 'I'm sorry, lads, I don't know what came over me. How does free beer for the rest of the day sound?'

Rex and Terry looked at each other and nodded. 'It sounds bloody good,' said Rex.

'Aye, you can chuck a pint over my head any day for that kind of deal,' added Terry, sniffing.

And so two of The Dragon's most hardcore beer guzzlers

were effectively paid to sup ale as fast as they could, until they fell down either legless or dead, or their incompetent landlord was forced to struggle to change another barrel of Kicking Kangaroo Super Strength Bitter – the go-to tipple these days for long-distance drinkers.

'By the way, have you heard the news about the reverend?' said Terry to his pal, finishing another Kangaroo and wiping his top lip with his sleeve.

'Who, Hill?' said Rex.

'Aye, him.' Terry belched.

'He's only gone and done a flit with all the church's money. He's vanished like the Holy Ghost into thin air.'

'Surrey oh! Where does a poxy little church like ours get that kind of dosh from?'

'From God, I s'pose.'

'Two more Kangaroos, please,' said Terry, sliding forward the empty glasses to the spot where Barry had been standing, right up to the point where the blood had stopped travelling to his brain and he had temporarily fainted, losing all control of body, senses and consciousness.

TWO
SCOOTING DOWN THE HIGHWAY
TO HELL

There were never usually this many people in church, not even the Sunday before Christmas when the mulled wine was running free.

Today, all faiths came together, including agnostics and atheists, for a good old-fashioned public execution; a metaphorical flogging, the theatre of seeing someone – who wasn't them – hung, drawn and quartered, put in the stocks for a spot of wanton reputation-busting humiliation. Or, in modern parlance, to see Reverend Hill cancelled. Many would have gladly branded him with hot irons given half a chance. No cucking or ducking stool for him and his crimes. He deserved to go whimpering to the God he pretended to worship on knees that had been caved in by blows from their very own second-hand sledgehammers. He deserved a slow, bumpy cart ride to gallows strategically placed in the centre of the village – where Ma's statue had briefly stood just hours ago – to suffer the nip and bite of the noose. No quick drop through a trapdoor, either. Instead, a slow unyielding pressure to make his eyes bulge and his skin run crimson, squeezing the life out of him drop by drop like juice from a lemon. Repent in agony, Reverend Hill, and may God have mercy on your soul. These Anghofiedig villagers could be a barbaric lot when riled.

There was just one problem with all this blood-baying. Reverend Hill was not present to face either it or his judgement. He had scarpered. Fled the parish at speed on two roaring wheels powered by that all-singing, all-dancing Harley-Davidson Milwaukee-Eight engine with the forty-five-degree V-twin configuration that kept many a locked-up convict's dreams warm on a cold winter's night. All that weighed him down was the money tucked inside his sweaty leathers. The money Ma had entrusted into his care for the good of the parish. Or so everybody thought.

Barry felt let down by Jacob Hill but he didn't want revenge. Truth was, he didn't much care about the dosh. He had given the hundred grand to him because he didn't know what else to do with it and because he thought the rev was less likely to waste it. Barry still considered these facts to be true, regardless of whether the rev was cavorting on the world's heavy metal festival circuit, or living it up with Joan Jett's granddaughters, a glass of rum in one hand, big fat Havana cigar in the other, and his dog collar tied loosely around his head like it was Axl Rose's bandana.

Barry alone knew he had given the money to Reverend Hill, not the church. It was an important distinction. However, somewhere down the line, wires had got crossed and the church's suits – accountants, bankers and money men who were no different from any other organisation's accountants, bankers and money men – had steamed in to take charge of the heaving purse for the good of the Diocese. Barry looked around the room and saw loads of familiar faces, all with stern expressions. What was any of this to them? They didn't understand how the reverend had looked after Ma when she truly needed someone to help her come to terms with dying. To get her spiritual and physical affairs in order before it was too late. To drive her to countless secret hospital assessments and treatments and sit with her in waiting rooms for hours on end before and after each painful trip. To hold her hand and talk her through the cul-de-sacs of her limited options. To fetch her cups of tasteless milky tea and persuade her to eat half a tuna and mayo sandwich in order to keep her strength up. To revive her spirits and give her a semblance of hope to hang on to. To listen patiently and carefully, without words of his own. To do all the things that Barry – as Ma's only son and only flesh and blood – should have done himself.

'How you holding up?' said Angharad, sidling along a pew to sit next to Barry. 'Terrible job all this. Not right at all. You shouldn't have to go through this and neither should we.'

Barry had no idea what she was talking about. Or what she was actually going through. More platitudes followed Barry's way from people he didn't give tuppence for.

'This is a bolt from the blue, make no mistake.'

'It's a proper kick in the teeth.'

'Hill should be ashamed of himself.'

'May he rot in hell for the rest of eternity.'

'I hope poor old Ma isn't turning in her grave.'

'Good job Barry White Senior isn't around anymore. He'd have ripped Hill's head clean off his shoulders then stuffed it somewhere the sun don't shine and the missionaries don't tread.'

The murmuring stopped when church treasurer Ralph Kilminster climbed into the pulpit looking solemn, flanked by two men, one pale, bald and thin, the other chubby with curly hair. They looked like the blokes who used to give the teatime Covid announcements during lockdown.

'This is the biggest threat we've faced in decades. You must stay home. Thank you, baked potato.'

'It's with regret we have to inform you that for the

foreseeable future this church will be closed. There is a significant black hole in the church's finances and Reverend Jacob Hill has gone missing,' said Kilminster, shuffling his papers nervously.

'The police have been informed about the matter and are already making good progress with their investigations. They might wish to speak to some of you individually in the coming days and weeks. It appears obvious to all concerned that the financial irregularities of this church and the disappearance of Reverend Hill are intertwined. There is now national and even international collaboration in the search for Hill and we are optimistic a positive solution to this distressing matter will be found. I can confirm there have been sightings of him in both Amsterdam and Thailand, as well as Wrexham, which is encouraging for us, if not for Reverend Hill.'

'How much is actually missing?' shouted Llewellyn Davies.

Kilminster paused and cleared his throat. 'We believe in the region of £93,000.'

'All the money left to us by Pearl White?' asked Alfonso de Costa.

'Most of it.'

'He reckoned he was going to start a bloody foodbank for the so-called poor, not that we've got any of them nowadays with all these rich incomers,' said local curmudgeon Harold J. Jones.

Llewellyn Davies made distorted noises of agreement, as if he were in the House of Commons, before announcing something more discernible. 'Robin Hood? Robbing bastard!'

'And he was gonna fix the holes in the church roof,' interjected Carrie Taylor, younger sister of Swifty and Lazarus.

Rupert Baird appeared, flush in the face. 'He promised me marble worktops in the church kitchen and said he'd mend the leaky bog.'

'He told me he'd fund our music club.' Derry Lee, founder member of the Anghofiedig Over-seventies Teddy Boys Club, looked ridiculous with a big silver quiff, trousers too tight to sit down in, black suede creepers, a yellow drape jacket and a Slim Jim tie.

'Get to the back of the line, Danny Zuko,' teased Clive Clementine.

Derry Lee bristled. 'Gonna make me, daddy-o?'

'You leave him alone, Clementine,' yelled Dot, rocking a look that few seventy-nine-year-olds would ever attempt to pull off, which included a flowing red shirtwaist dress, unbuttoned a little too far down, and a straw hat.

Clive Clementine saw Dot and his jaw dropped. 'Fuck me, Olivia Neutron Bomb's come back from the dead.'

'Watch your mouth, dunderhead, you diss my Judy here and you diss me.' Derry Lee got up and moved in Clive Clementine's direction.

'So what?' said Clementine with a two-handed 'bring it on' gesture.

'Please, everyone, can we calm down and be respectful, this is still God's house,' said Ralph Kilminster, adjusting the gap in his comb-over.

'Up yours, Kilminster,' shouted an unidentifiable voice from the back of the church.

'We trusted you and you let us down,' said Betty Ford.

'We always knew Hill was a liar and a cheat. We could tell just by looking at him,' added Gloria Beaumont.

Maximilius Percival stood on a pew to speak – through the glove puppet of a white cat that now accompanied him everywhere he went. 'He should never have come to Anghofiedig. Miaow.'

'He's too young to be a preacher man,' said Dicky Bridges from Honeywell Farm.

'And too English,' yelled Amy Sharples.

'Too angry and all,' chimed Amy's sister Ena.

'He was pretty scary when he got mad, wasn't he?' Ieuan Drury waved his walking stick in the air, almost hitting those sitting next to him.

Helen Ball stood with her hands on her hips. 'I'm sorry but no vicar should stink of patchouli oil.'

'Fair point!' shouted Derry Lee.

'And what about those leather trousers? Not very godly at all,' said Clever Trevor Peacock, modelling a pair of stained brown corduroys that he bought in a C&A sale in the winter of 1977.

'He was scooting down the highway to hell from the first day he got here.' Gertrude Robinson, dressed from head to toe in matching blue rinse, didn't look like the sort of person who would readily know the titles to AC/DC songs.

'Look, we're all getting a little off track here,' said one of the men flanking Kilminster, the one who looked like Chris Whitty rather than the one who resembled Jonathan Van-Tam with an Eddie Large perm.

Betty Ford was again among the first to react. 'But you knew the books weren't balancing weeks ago.'

'You gave the reverend too much leeway. You let him cut corners, didn't you? You're all as much to blame as him,' said Esme Ilunga, in French.

'You put temptation in his path.' Don the Bastard clasped his hands.

'We took our eye off the ball, yes,' admitted Ralph Kilminster, bowing his head slightly, before realising he was showing off the bald spot he wanted to conceal. 'And for that, I am, and always will be, eternally sorry.'

'So you bloody well should be!' shouted Betty Ford, first again.

'Language, Elizabeth,' said Dot.

'Apologies, Dorothy,' replied Betty.

Barry had seen and heard enough. He pushed past Angharad and started to make his way out of the church.

'Where you going, love?' asked Dot.

'Home.'

'But we're not done here. Miaow,' said Maximilius Percival.

'I am.'

'That's it, run away,' said Llewellyn Davies. 'He don't care about his mother's money getting pissed against the wall by Benny Hill cos he's doing exactly the same thing to us down at The Dragon. The boy's clueless about everything. Always has been. Got dropped on his head at birth if you ask me.'

There was an awkward silence. Barry looked around the room for any sign of an ally but no one was prepared to hold his gaze or defend him so he spoke up for himself.

'It's me who's trying to save The Dragon. You're right about one thing, Davies, the pub is struggling, but that's because of you lot. You want everything for nothing and nothing is ever good enough. It was supposed to be a community pub, with everyone pitching in, but all you do is squabble and bitch and fight. We put up enough cash to cover the first year's bills. We said all along, the pub needed to start paying for itself after that if it was going to survive. It's not going to. So that will be that.'

'No church and no pub,' gasped Clever Trevor Peacock.

'And no more money from me and my family.' Barry pulled out his wallet from an inside jacket pocket, took out his last few notes and tossed them high into the air. He carried on walking down the aisle towards the door, not bothering to turn around for the reaction or to see who was scrabbling around on their hands and knees, trying to get their clammy paws on the crumpled fivers and tenners falling near the cracked font that was only ever used for holding mulled wine at Christmas.

Barry was feeling sorry for himself when he got home, but there was no Diana to put a consoling arm around him because she was working another night shift at the hospital. Eddie was still up, however, weighing a sinister-looking plastic bag on the kitchen scales.

'What you got there, a bag of heroin or John John's out-of-date chocolate drops?' quipped Barry.

'Neither. It's poop,' said Eddie.

'Whose poop?' Barry scrunched up his face.

'Mine of course, I ain't a weirdo.' Eddie's reply was dismissive.

'What you weighing it for?'

'Cos I'm selling it.'

'Who to?'

'Professor Lionel T. Schwartz from Michigan in the good old US of A.'

Barry's face scrunched up even tighter. 'I'm confused dot com.'

Eddie picked up the bag and started fanning himself with it as he talked. Barry was worried it wasn't tied properly and would fly straight into his face. 'I came across him on the internet. He buys poop from all over the world for his medical experiments. Ten dollars per bag. It's all legit.'

'Don't sound very legit,' said Barry, backing off.

'He's a bona fide scientist, he's got certificates and letters after his name. It's nothing dodgy.'

'Nothing dodgy? Secretly buying cack from a fifteen-year-old schoolboy in another country?' Barry's voice accidentally went high-pitched.

'I don't talk to him. Don't even know what he looks like or

how old he is. I just send him poop in a bag and he sends me money.'

'How?'

'BACS transfer.'

'How long you been doing this?'

'Since last Thursday.'

Barry told the boy he had to stop all dealings with Professor Lionel T. Schwartz immediately and flushed his bag and its contents down the loo. He said if he got wind of any more poop dealings, he'd tell Diana and then there would be hell to pay. He said he admired Eddie's spirit of enterprise – even if his moral judgement was questionable – and that if he was serious about finding new ways of earning money, he'd give him some shifts down The Dragon, washing pots, waiting on tables and maybe even cleaning the khazis if he liked working with doodoo so much.

'You've got to be careful, Eddie, there are some serious nutjobs in this world. I know cos I'm friends with some of them,' said Barry.

Eddie confessed that whilst exploring ways of expanding his fledgling export business he'd received a couple of troubling messages from a bloke in Sweden asking him if he had any hair to sell, and one from a white guy in Haiti offering 100 gourdes for every bag of fingernails and / or toenails he could provide (human only).

'Say, your mate Romeo owns a barbershop, don't he? I bet he's got tons of hair he'd like taken off his hands,' said Eddie, excitedly.

'What does this Swedish bloke do with all the hair?' Barry felt the need to sit down.

'Makes jumpers, I think.'

Barry looked at the towering naïve manchild in front of him and momentarily saw a younger version of himself.

'How do you fancy coming rugby training with me tomorrow night? You've got some size about you. I reckon we could use a big lump like you in our pack – and it would get you away from your computer for a bit.'

'Not sure about rugby. It's a bit painful.' Eddie pulled a new loaf of unsliced white out of the bread bin and bit into the end crust as if he was eating an apple. He had not washed his hands.

Barry slipped into salesman mode. 'I'll throw in a couple of pints of cider afterwards, as long as you don't tell your mother.'

'Okay, it's a deal, Uncle Barry,' said Eddie, offering a fist for Barry to bump.

Barry looked at the unwashed hand as though it was something stuck to the bottom of a shoe. 'It's just Barry, not Uncle Barry. And go wash yourself.'

THREE

THE QUEEN OF THE BEAVER STATE

A motley crew of just seven turned up for pre-season rugby training, which didn't include coach Derek. Star player James was there to step in and take charge of mainstays Pricer, McQueen and Jonah, plus Randolph Atkins – wandering postman and even more wandering occasional full-back – along with Barry and Eddie.

'Where's your uncle tonight?' asked James whilst performing star jumps.

'No idea,' said Barry. 'But this is Eddie, Diana's lad. Second-row material all day long if you ask me.'

'How old are you, Edward?' James stopped jumping but still looked like a star.

'I'm fifteen years, two months and seventeen days.'

'Righto. Well, you're welcome to train with us this evening, it'll be mostly general fitness stuff, but you'll have to sit out the contact work. We don't have any junior teams, I'm afraid, but I can put you in touch with a couple of other local clubs who do if you're interested?'

'Nah, don't bother, I've only come for cider.'

After forty minutes of low-level huffing and puffing, James

decided to call it quits and end the session early. Jonah had already departed to mend a barn roof before it got too dark, and Pricer's focus evaporated the moment his missus pushed two kids out of the back of a slow-moving VW Polo and gestured them towards their father because she was late for bingo. Randolph Atkins ambled off towards the woods early into the session, complaining of a tight calf and an early start tomorrow. Even McQueen was seriously off the pace – failing to put any oomph into tackles and lacking all customary bite and snarl in every area of his game.

James scratched his head and turned to Barry. 'He's just not been the same since you sent him on that anger management course. I asked him to hit the tackle bag as hard as he could and I even told him to imagine he was decking you. D'you know what he did? He walked up to the bag and started sniffing it. Really sniffing it. Then he started doing these slow suck it all in and let it out breathing exercises. When I asked him what he was doing, he said "Barry White is not my enemy, my enemy sits within".'

'Bugger! That sounds serious.' Barry was amazed that McQueen had agreed to do the course in the first place. He reckoned it had more to do with the hundred quid expenses Barry had offered him than any desire to control his rages, but whatever the reason, he was a changed man now.

Barry stroked a tackle bag like it was a cat. 'I know we say it every year, but I think the club is in big trouble this season.'

James nodded in agreement.

'Are you going to stick around?'

'Yes, I think so, I don't want to see the club fold without a fight.'

'You know you can count on me every week.' Barry punched the tackle bag and tried not to show the pain flowing through his recently fractured wrist.

'Prop or centre this season?'

'Centre. Unfinished business.'

'But Mum said she don't want you to play no more,' interrupted Eddie, who Barry had forgotten all about. 'She said she wants you to quit cos you're getting too old and Saturday's the only day she gets to see you, cos she's not working.'

'Is that right?' asked James.

'You did well tonight, you must be thirsty,' said Barry to Eddie, changing the subject.

'I'm properly parched, Uncle Barry. Let's go neck scrumpy.'

<hr>

Delores Hamilton stood out in the Anghofiedig Rugby Club's players' lounge for many reasons; most notably her loud American accent, her self-righteous belief that all her needs and wants were a priority to others, and her sparkly blue sequined Dolce and Gabbana dress with added shoulder pads, plus a mink fur coat which she draped over her shoulders. The girl from Oregon 'done good' – Queen of the Beaver State 1984 – had outlived two wealthy husbands: one, an oil baron with a dodgy ticker; the other, some kind of financial hot shot who knew everything there was to know about Dow Jones – the stock market index, not the loner who lived two doors down from Romeo's mother. Now in her early sixties, Delores had left the US and her palatial home in Portland for the greener hills of South Wales in search of excitement. She certainly found it on the arm of her Romeo.

Barry's lifelong best pal met Delores on a visit to Grenville Grayson's racing stables. Delores owned most of the horses in the yard including Brecon Beacon Boy whose unheralded victory at the Cheltenham Festival had earned Barry his million-pound fortune. Delores loved all things quirky, which was why she chose to put her trust and her racehorses in the care of a man like Grayson. Romeo, however, was like no one she had ever encountered before. Delores was fascinated by the way he talked and thought venting forth spontaneous random outbursts of insight, kindness and sheer lunacy amidst gentler spells of introversion and self-doubt. She loved an underdog, having been one herself for many years during her time working as a bunny girl for a wannabe Hugh Hefner in Salem called Lorenzo Montano.

These past few months, following Ma's death and his own whirlwind romance with Diana, Barry hadn't seen much of Romeo. He was surprised to find him drinking in an empty rugby club on a humdrum Wednesday night with an overdressed Joan Collins doppelganger who was dripping in red lipstick and the skins of dead animals.

'Bazzer, I want you to meet my new lady, Delores,' said Romeo, pointing to Delores with both arms as if she was the star prize on an eighties game show.

'Enchanted,' said Barry, for some reason offering a hand to be kissed.

'Heard so many wonderful things about you, Barry White, and so pleased that lil old Brecon was able to make your dreams come true, just like he did for me,' said Delores, kissing his hand.

Romeo furrowed his brows. 'What you talking about?'

'Oh Dewdrop, do the math. If Brecon hadn't – what is it you say, upset the apple cart at Cheltenham – then I would never have met you, my sweet Anglo-Saxon peccadillo hunk of Haagen-Dazs with ripened strawberries on top.'

Delores grabbed Romeo by the collar, pulled him in tight and munched on his face emphatically like he was, indeed, an ice cream being plastered in strawberry sauce direct from the plentiful fountain of her own lips.

'Blimey, she kisses like you eat kebabs,' whispered Eddie to Barry.

'And who's this Willy Wonka golden ticket on legs?' said Delores, dropping Romeo on his haunches.

It was Barry's turn to beam with pride. 'That's Eddie, my girlfriend's lad.'

'Howdy, Eddie,' said Delores, now offering her hand to be kissed.

'Howdy, Delilah.' Eddie put down his pint of cider – his fourth of the night – and took the proffered hand. Unaware of what he was supposed to do with it, he rubbed it gently down the side of his cheek, like he was soothing himself with an eiderdown, before giving it back.

Delores cackled uncontrollably. 'You English brave hearts, I love the goddamn lot of you.'

'But I'm Welsh,' said Barry.

'And Braveheart was Scottish, my love,' chirped Romeo.

'No he wasn't, honey, Braveheart was Mel Gibson, a good ol' New Yorker if ever there was one. Now let me buy you boys some liquor.'

Delores walked confidently up to the bar, sidestepping some chairs and kicking others out of her way as if she was Barry White Senior on a rugby field in his pomp.

'You sure you know what you're doing with that one?' said Barry to Romeo.

'She's a great girl, Baz. She makes me happy.'

Whilst they were alone, Romeo told Barry that he was in the process of selling his fifty per cent stake in the barbershop – which Barry had given him – back to Kenneth Wick. Kenneth's grandson, Olly, was going to return to Anghofiedig to work in the shop, having got sacked from his job in a Somerset slaughterhouse for releasing cows back into the community like he was the lead boy in a beefy remake of *Free Willy*.

Romeo said Kenneth regretted giving up half of his business and wanted Olly to have another crack at it. Olly, by all accounts, had matured a lot and realised which side his bread was buttered after his stint in the abattoir. Barry imagined the fields of Shepton Mallet and Glastonbury – as well as Taunton town centre – full of Herefords with green mohawks and Belted Galloways with wonky fringes.

Romeo tugged at his own hair, a surefire sign he was anxious. He was able to control himself, however, playing with his locks rather than pulling out big clumps.

'It means a lot what you did for me and the trust you showed and all that, but being stuck in that shop, running my hands through old men's bonces is a killer. And once the sale goes through, you'll get your money back. I don't need any money now I'm with Delores. I'm a kept man. She doesn't want me to work, she wants me to concentrate on pleasing her 24/7.'

Barry was pleased Romeo was in a real relationship. Delores Hamilton was not what you would call an easy-going person, she was demanding and high maintenance. However, Romeo seemed able to calm her down. Diana, by contrast, was someone who most people would describe as laid-back and chilled but Barry felt like he brought out the worst in her.

'So you and Delores, do you ever row?'

'Not really.'

'What, never?'

'I mean we disagree sometimes. We just don't row.'

Barry scratched his butt instinctively and pulled a frown like he was solving a complex puzzle.

'But you still do your pacing and daydreaming stuff? Going off to Planet Feelgood to fight the bad dude Wilko and all that?'

'I do. But not so much. Wilko ain't been about lately.'

'Does it annoy her when you fight him?'

'Nope. She says it's adorable.'

'What about your other bad thoughts, the self-harm ones?'

'Not had 'em for a while.'

'You're still random though? I mean, you ain't gone mainstream?'

'Course not. Delores calls me her little space cadet. She says she wouldn't have me any other way.'

'I see,' said Barry. Even though he didn't. Barry was unaware that his butt scratching had not only continued but intensified in pace. Anyone else would have been disturbed by it but Romeo was unfazed. He knew all there was to know about nervous tics and he was well aware this was one of Barry's. He'd seen him do it loads of times, especially when they were kids. Such as every time Angharad showed off her latest boyfriend – or the year Romeo got a new BMX bike for Christmas and Barry got an Etch A Sketch and a Mr Potato Head.

Delores returned from the bar carrying a tray with four shot glasses, each full of a clear-looking liquid. 'This quaint potion is – how do you say it, the dog's bollocks. Romeo tells me it's Irish.'

'What is it? said Eddie, looking scared.

'Holy water,' said Romeo.

Eddie necked the contents of his glass in one before collapsing as if he had been assassinated by a gunman lurking on a grassy knoll.

'What's he just drunk?' said Barry, panicking.

'Potato water,' said an unconcerned Romeo.

'Poteen?'

'Aye.'

'Kicks like a mule, don't it?' said Delores, knocking back hers.

'Ninety per cent proof mules usually do,' said Barry, picking Eddie up off the floor and helping him get to a chair so he could drink a glass of water.

Delores grabbed another shot of poteen and downed it in one. 'Willy Wonka don't look so good, does he? I'm guessing he's one of those home-loving fellas that can't hold his hooch.'

Barry struggled to move Eddie's heavy limp body. 'No, he's one of those home-loving fifteen-year-old fellas that's got school tomorrow.'

'Uncle Barry, I think Uncle Romeo's new woman is trying to kill me,' said Eddie, groggily.

'Your mam's gonna murder me, I know that much.' Barry finally got Eddie upright, though he looked like a Guy Fawkes doll slumped in a wheelbarrow.

Eddie rolled sideways. 'I won't tell.'

Delores grabbed another tumbler of poteen for herself. 'Say, the boy's got soul. More Irish love potion, anyone?'

Barry tried to get Eddie through the front door as quietly as possible, but the loud raucous echoes of his vomiting in the hallway gave the game away. Diana was waiting up in dressing gown and slippers, nursing a mug of hot chocolate.

'Oh my God, Eddie, what's happened?'

'I think it's something he ate, most likely the burgers down the club,' protested Barry, timidly.

Diana stooped to grab hold of her son, ignoring the undigested former contents of his stomach in her path. Being an experienced and highly qualified nurse, it didn't take her long to work out the real cause of her son's incapacity.

'He's drunk!' she exclaimed.

'Is he?' said Barry, innocently.

'Don't play dumb, Barry, you've been with him all night, haven't you.'

Barry said nothing.

'How could you? He's only fifteen.'

Barry tried to blame Delores. 'It was just a few ciders after rugby. He'd have been fine if Romeo's new girlfriend hadn't given him a shot of poteen to try. He knocked it back before I had chance to stop him.'

'I don't want to hear it,' said Diana, showing impressive strength to lift up her son – who was at least twice her size – and usher him up the stairs single-handedly. 'I'm going to sleep on Eddie's floor tonight.' Diana was properly cross.

'No worries. Anything I can do?'

'Clean that mess up.'

'Sure.'

'And grow up!' snapped Diana.

Barry slumped in a chair in the living room where Ma used to sit alone for hours on end. Nowadays, it was his turn to spend long chunks of time sitting on his own in the same room. Eddie had taken over his old bedroom and Diana was mostly out, working all hours at the hospital. Barry couldn't understand how life with Diana had changed so much once she moved in. They'd lived in each other's pockets, seeing the best and worst of each other, on a three-month trip around half the world and they'd had the time of their lives. Diana had perfectly stepped into the void left by Ma's death. She'd made Barry feel good about himself. She'd enjoyed his company and laughed at his silly jokes. She'd even finished off some of his sentences and understood a lot of the mad things that flashed through his brain and occasionally out of his mouth. She hadn't judged him. She'd looked for and seen the best in him and genuinely wanted him to succeed at things. She'd been on his side. She'd had his back.

Now though, back in suffocating Anghofiedig, things weren't the same. Diana didn't smile or laugh as much and she didn't relax as easily. She seemed troubled by so many things and had less patience, especially around Barry. She didn't find him as funny or entertaining. She expected him to do more around the house and got annoyed when he frittered his time away. She fretted about money and bills. And she worried about

Eddie and his wellbeing constantly. She acted like everyone was out to get him – and her.

She didn't trust Barry. Not with Eddie.

And she got defensive when Barry challenged her about this.

She didn't say as much, but it was obvious to Barry that she considered him a bad influence on her son. She had more ammunition for the arguments now he'd brought him home steaming drunk, forcing her to watch him through the night in case he did a Jimi Hendrix and choked on his own puke.

Barry picked up a photo album off the coffee table and began to flick through its glossy pages. The album contained lots of memories of their getaway, much of it crisscrossing Europe in a camper van, Diana giggling behind the wheel, Barry at her side and Eddie on an iPad or dozing in the back. Diana had confidently driven across Spain, France and Italy into Austria to prove herself a real powerhouse. Considering he'd never been abroad before it was a steep learning curve for Barry but Diana was streetwise and looked after him. The world seemed so vast and the people so very different from having all that sun on their backs. Barry liked going places where no one knew his name or automatically put him in a box with a warning label on the front of it. In each new town he could be anyone he wanted to be. His Welshness endeared him to people, except in Madrid where he ran into several Real fans who gave him a hard time over the 'Galactico golfer' aka Gareth Bale.

What he'd give right now to be back on the harbour in Puerto Banus sipping a San Miguel, watching the bronze-skinned locals playing keepie-uppie on the golden sand, or walking around Catedral de Sevilla hand in hand with Diana, pausing at the tomb of Christopher Columbus, or strolling down the winding cobbled streets of Vieille Ville in Nice, pushing Eddie into the lines of multi-coloured laundry hanging in the streets. He looked at the photos of the three of them enjoying a barbecue in Saint Remy de Provence and remembered how they sang Queen songs late into the night until they could rock no more. He stared at the pictures of them hiking through the mountain lakes of Zell am See on their last full day of the trip, none of them wanting to go home.

The holiday had started on a downer, though. Not just because of the death of Ma but also the shock demise of Chico, the charismatic silverback gorilla with the massive global YouTube following who Barry wanted to meet in the flesh. He'd arranged for them all to fly to Rwanda for a few days and trek through damp mountainous terrain to the lodge where Chico lived. He laughed uncontrollably with the other obsessives as their herbivorous idol wooed his girlfriend, Grace, by pulling down branches and breaking off the ends to swallow whole. No one realised Chico's loud throaty exhortations or his manic scratching of armpits weren't part of his 'come and get me' act and that he was actually choking to death. Not even Grace, who looked completely disinterested, no doubt having received countless personal pole dances and parades of strength from him and other suitors far less handsome. Even the Chinese presenter didn't spot anything was amiss as he babbled away at two hundred kilometres an hour in a language every bit as foreign to Barry as Chico's macho courtship routine.

When the giant gorilla stopped spluttering and dropped silently to the ground, the Chinese man stopped talking. Grace wandered over and poked her lover in the chest. She then began to lick and sniff him. She sat as close to him as physically possible, grooming his still body, whimpering occasionally.

· It was the reaction of the tour guide that told the group something was wrong. Hours later, back at the reserve, the same guide sat the party down and told them there would be no more Chico time. Not now. Not ever.

Chico's death hit Barry harder than most people realised. Not as hard as Ma's death, obviously, but it was still a deep, tangible loss to his life that Diana and Eddie did not, and would never, understand. It was akin to losing a much-loved pet – who you considered to be part of the family and might even risk your own life for, but who others regarded as no more important to the health of the home than the fridge freezer.

Diana tried to make Barry feel better by telling him he still had all the old videos but it wasn't the same. He didn't want to look at them anyway. They were too painful.

Throwing the photo album back onto the coffee table, Barry wondered how he had managed to lose a million quid in a matter of months, as if he was Richard Pryor in *Brewster's Millions*. The pub that he hoped would bring villagers closer together was a bottomless money pit and a troublesome millstone around his neck. Few of the locals had stepped forward to offer any help and most bitched and grumbled from the sidelines about those who did. Barry found himself trying to plug gaps in areas he was not equipped to fill. Unable to recruit enough help for staff rotas, he took on more and more shifts behind the bar himself. He quickly realised he wasn't a people person. He didn't have business aptitude. He lacked drive, motivation and vision. He didn't like doing paperwork or dealing with suppliers, caterers and temperamental chefs. He was rubbish at organising and inspiring, and didn't know how to handle disputes. He wasn't a leader. He was a follower. A mid-pack sheep.

His original vision for The Dragon had been one of quiz nights, music nights, theatre nights, and couples' nights – all with reasonably priced top-quality menus showcasing local produce and the finest ales. A proper hub for the whole of Anghofiedig, offering something for everyone, creating a go-to place for people to meet and chat and keep warm, and for clubs to hold their weekly gatherings. Instead, he spent most of his tedious shifts listening to a handful of bores like Rex and Terry spout nonsense about nonsense.

Apart from the pub, Barry had wasted a shedload of money renovating his house from top to bottom. The reality was, he'd done it to help out Angharad at a time when she needed an ego boost and some instant cash for her survival. Now the house looked amazing, but he couldn't help thinking he preferred the place how it used to be. When it was Ma's house, not his.

And then there was his massive investment in the church, or rather Reverend Hill. A cool hundred grand spent who knows where?

How was it possible to get through a million quid so quickly and have so little to show for it?

Even sending McQueen on an anger management course had backfired as it had turned Anghofiedig's second best rugby player – after James – into a gibbering mush of uncertainty and self-doubt.

Dot was happy enough with her collection of posh fifties-style frocks and Jonah was made up with the prize heifer Barry had bought him, but everything else seemed like a total waste of money and good intentions.

The loss of his identity and the fact he was really Barry John rather than Barry White bothered him too. It made Uncle Derek and Aunty Ruth seem more distant. And it soured his relationship with rugby because, in his own head at least, he was no longer the son of a club legend. He'd always dreamed of doing something spectacular on a rugby pitch to earn his rightful place in the White rugby story. It drove him on season after season, failure after failure, and kept him coming back for more, regardless of how many disappointments he had to endure. He always told himself *his* chapter would write itself one day.

But now he hardly cared. He hardly cared about anything. Except his old friend, the grog. And food.

He heard the sound of Eddie throwing up in the bedroom above, followed by the quick footsteps of Diana as she scurried from bedroom to bathroom to empty the contents of his slops bucket. Just like Ma had done for him decades ago when he had come back from the rugby club drunk at a similar age. The same calming voice. The same walk. The same footsteps.

He wanted to go up and check they were okay but thought it would be best if he didn't.

He pulled an old blanket – that used to be Ma's favourite and still carried her smell – from a fancy new cabinet drawer and quickly fell asleep, slouched in an armchair with his rugby boots on; the boots he had worn to training and kept on all night because they were two weeks old and needed breaking in for the season ahead.

FOUR
GIS' A JOB

A heavy rat-a-tat-tat woke Barry from his slumber. He uncurled his back and neck with several loud and painful clicks and made his way from the shabby living-room chair, that had been his bed for the night, to the front door.

'Bloody hell, you look rough,' said Greg, husband of Angharad.

'Ta very much.' Barry sniffed.

Greg stared at Barry's feet. 'And why you wearing rugby boots at this time in the morning?'

'Fail to prepare, prepare to fail.' Barry slammed the door in Greg's face and headed for the downstairs loo because he urgently needed a piss. The studs in his boots made tip-tap noises on the wooden floor.

Barry ignored all further knocks on his front door whilst in the process of relieving himself but returned to see what Greg wanted when he was done.

'Look, can I come in?' said Greg, hopping nervously from one foot to the other.

'No, what do you want?'

'A job. Down the pub. I heard you're desperate for bar staff. I've done a bit of bar work. I know the ropes. Just give me a go.'

'Why?'

'Cos I'm not such a bad bloke.'

Barry laughed out loud. 'How come you're so desperate for work?'

'Cos I want to show Angharad I can be the man she wants me to be. I want to change.'

'Have you told your pecker all this?'

'Told who what?' said Greg, confused.

'Have you told your pecker that you're going to change? He won't like it. He's sure to put up a fight. And how you gonna convince him to change his ways cos he sure as hell don't listen to you?'

'Don't be weird, Barry. Are you going to give me some work or not?'

'I'll think about it.' Barry thought this response was generous in the extreme.

'I won't let you down, I promise.'

'Don't make promises you can't keep.'

'I'll show you; I'll show Angharad. I'll show my John Thomas an' all that he ain't my guvnor, I'm the boss of me,' said Greg, prodding himself in the chest over-enthusiastically.

Barry paused to consider the ridiculousness of both the gesture and the words before shutting the door in Greg's face for the second time.

In the kitchen, scrabbling around for some breakfast, Barry found a note next to the sink and he sighed.

Had to go in early because I'm covering for Angie, didn't want to disturb you. Eddie's okay but not sending him to school today. I'll phone his form teacher when I get chance later and tell her that he's ill. He's got some history homework to do – can you make sure he does it? See you around six this evening, we can talk properly then. Don't worry about food for me, I'll eat at the hospital,

Diana x

Efficient as ever, with stuff left between the lines.

'Didn't want to disturb you' – *didn't want to talk to you.*

'I'll phone his form teacher when I get chance later' – *Cos you can't be trusted to do it.*

'Can you make sure he does his homework?' – *Well, can you, fat boy?*

'Don't worry about food for me' – *I'd rather stay at work longer and eat with people who save lives, as opposed to idiots who encourage kids to get smashed off their tits.*

Signed 'Diana', not 'love, Diana'. Not 'hope you're all right' or 'have a nice day, darling'.

One solitary, lonely kiss at the end of it all, a peck on the cheek, the sort you'd leave on an aunt's forehead without thinking. The sort of kiss that means nothing and carries zero emotion. Just a polite sign off, the kind used by lawyers, doctors and administrators at Network Rail or the DVLA. Just common courtesy, not 'you mean the world to me and I'm sorry for any misunderstanding or overreaction'. Oh no, a single x on the cheek to keep up appearances for the neighbours. A truly British kiss; one to present a united front to the outside world, even though things are falling apart inside these walls and on these shaky shores.

The sort of kiss Angharad got from Greg every single day of her married life, year upon year, never expecting anything better.

Barry ripped up the note into tiny pieces, stuck them in his mouth and swallowed them down with several mouthfuls of Baileys drank straight from the bottle.

'Get a grip, Barry boy, you're bloody losing it,' he said to himself.

When Eddie surfaced around eleven, he felt as right as rain. He devoured the full English Barry had prepared for him two hours earlier, then ate two bowls of Rice Krispies and a microwaveable steak and kidney pie shoved inside an extra-large bread roll to make a heart attack butty.

'Don't suppose you'll be needing an early lunch?' said Barry, sarcastically.

'Cracking night down the club, wasn't it?' said Eddie, drinking semi-skimmed milk straight from the carton.

'Was it?'

Barry told Eddie that he wouldn't let him drink alcohol again, it was strictly soft drinks from now on. He reminded the boy that he'd thrown up in the hallway and explained that his mother had slept on the floor next to his bed because she was concerned he might die in his sleep. He also warned Eddie that his mother was now on the war path – or rather, the assassin path, because she moved much more stealthily, operated as a lone wolf and didn't make a lot of noise.

'I want you to get your history project finished this afternoon before she comes home from work, okay? And you can help clean the house up a bit.'

'Is mum madder at me or you?'

Barry's response was emphatic. 'Me.'

'Sorry.'

'Not a problem.'

Eddie finished off the milk and tossed the carton in the sink. 'It was the firewater that did me in, not the cider.'

'I know.' Barry lifted the carton out of the sink, put it back in Eddie's hand and gestured with his eyes towards the bin.

'I reckon I'd be okay if I just stuck to apples next time,' said Eddie.

'No next time, Eddie.'

'All right. I'm going to get stuck into Martin Luther King, Rosa Parks and Malcolm X now.'

Barry pushed the milk carton Eddie had plonked on top of the pedal bin all the way in.

Eddie stood tall and began an oratory, waving his arms about, pretending to be Martin Luther King Junior, the focus of his history project. 'I have a dream that one day every valley shall be exalted, every hill and mountain shall be made low, the crooked places will be made straight, and the glory of the Lord shall be revealed.'

'We can only hope,' said Barry, still battling with the pedal bin.

'Uncle Barry, why are you wearing your rugby boots?' said Eddie, noticing for the first time.

'Fail to prepare, prepare to fail,' replied Barry, twiddling his toes inside his boots with the assurance of a ballet dancer.

He didn't have to be at work until 7pm so Barry arranged to meet Angharad in the park around the time Diana was due home.

'Had your hubby knocking on my door at silly o'clock this morning.'

'Jealous, I hope. Did he threaten to punch your lights out if you ever went near me again?'

'Afraid not. He asked me for a job.' Barry stopped to sit on a bench overlooking the pond. Angharad sat next to him.

'Doing what?'

'Barman.'

'What did you say?'

'That I'd think about it.' Barry threw a pebble into the pond, forcing a duck to duck. He reasoned that was where they got their name from.

Angharad pretended not to notice the wayward throw. 'He never said anything to me but that's not unusual.'

'So what d'you think?'

'About what?'

'Giving your husband a job. Would it help?'

'Help who?'

'You.' Barry noticed the duck he had annoyed moving towards him.

'It doesn't make much difference one way or another.'

'Well, you decide. Yes or no?'

'Yes,' said Angharad, standing and clapping her hands to scare the onrushing duck away. 'It'll keep him from getting under my feet. Everyone thinks we're back together because we're living under the same roof but we're not. He's sleeping in the spare room and that's how it's gonna stay until he moves out or finds another bimbo. Truth is, I've forgiven him so many times over the years but he's just a liar. I don't trust him. Not one bit. And without that, well, we've got nothing, have we? He'll never change. He wants to, but sooner or later some woman will come along, flash a smile or a big chest his way and off he'll go again. Doesn't really matter who she is or what she looks like. That's just him. It's in his DNA. Do you understand?'

'Yeah, in the DNA. I get it,' said Barry.

For the second night running, Barry failed miserably at trying to creep in through his own front door without making a noise. For the second night running, he was greeted by the waiting Diana, in dressing gown and slippers, nursing a mug of hot chocolate between two hands.

'Hello, stranger.'

'Hey, Diana.'

'I'm sorry for overreacting last night.' Diana stared into her mug to watch the froth of chocolate spin clockwise.

'I'm sorry for the bad stuff I did. And all the things I keep getting wrong.' Barry wasn't actually sure what he was apologising for, but thought it best to cover all bases. He knew he could be irresponsible and selfish. However, he felt like he was really saying sorry for being a crap boyfriend and an even worse stand-in father figure.

'You're not so bad. You bought me flowers last week. And ran me a bath on Sunday. And you bring me a cup of tea most mornings and evenings,' said Diana.

'But I'm going to let you down again, even though I don't want to.'

Diana said nothing but leant forward and took his hand. 'Let's go to bed.'

'In a bit,' said Barry, breaking away.

He sat alone in the living room and helped himself to a brandy large enough to transform Eddie into a human Niagara Falls. He picked up the pile of condolence and sympathy cards he'd never really had time to read after Ma's funeral and went through them all, one by one. So many cards, so many kind messages of support. People who he barely knew and who had barely known Ma spoke of their deep loss. Like the lollipop man who stood outside the primary school. A couple of days per week, when she went to the Darby & Joan Club, he'd escort Ma across the road with the kids and they'd have a laugh and a joke about it being time for her to move up to big school. A fleeting albeit regular acquaintance but memorable enough for this man – whose name was Alan, not Lollipop – to go to the trouble of buying a card, filling it with lovely words and posting it first class, even though he only lived two streets away.

Barry thought back to the day of the funeral and how he had lay on the sofa for hours on end watching *Cash in the Attic* and *Homes under the Hammer*. It had all been a bit surreal. He hardly saw a soul in the morning. He showered and dressed slowly around lunchtime. Then came a loud knock on the door from Uncle Derek.

'Time to go, boyo.'

Derek had marched him military-style to a car waiting to take him to join the rest of the family. They later sat in Derek and Ruth's living room and drank tea like it was a Sunday afternoon get-together. Cousins and nieces looked relaxed and chatted amiably about holidays past and future.

Their joviality was shattered by the official knock on the door from the undertaker. Michael was pleasant and professional as he marched them, military-style again, down the long path and up the drive to the waiting limousine. In front of them was the hearse with Ma's body inside a wicker coffin dressed out in green and white lilies and irises. Her favourites.

Barry had started to shake. They crawled towards the church and other motorists showed the kind of courtesy he had never noticed on a British road before. If you want to get somewhere in a hurry don't flag down a police car with flashing blue lights, get a hearse and drive a bit slower.

His senses went into overdrive once they stopped outside the chapel and four pals gently lifted the coffin from the back of the black car and raised it onto their shoulders. She was only seven or eight stone when she died but they seemed to struggle. Maybe it was the wicker.

Head bowed, Barry followed the bearers inside, refusing to make eye contact with anything or anyone bar his own shiny black shoes that were stepping steadfastly towards the end of Ma's rainbow. He wasn't sure, but he sensed he was surrounded by sympathetic faces. Hearing others cry heartened him.

The theme of Uncle Derek's eulogy had been simple acts of kindness. That was Ma. Leaving bars of chocolate on people's doorsteps, collecting groceries from the shops for the 'old folk' (who were usually younger than her), giving money and frothy cappuccinos to desperate street beggars, donating soothing words to those with fragile egos. Like her son.

And so they went on to the wake at the rugby club.

If it had been anyone else's wife or mother, Barry would have stepped up to the plate to send them off in a sea of lager and he'd have called it a good night.

The booze took the edge off his emptiness but it didn't put its arms around him when he later turned off the lights in a pathetic drunken state. And it didn't shout a cheery 'see you in the morning, son' either. Barry wasn't worried if that morning came or not but at least no one was going to march him anywhere like a squaddie. Returning home after the funeral, he remembered sitting on the stairs and looking around. Everything was different.

Back in the now, Barry put the pile of cards inside a Tesco carrier bag and tucked it in the sideboard.

He switched off the lights and made his way up to bed, feeling his way in the darkness. The brandy had taken the edge off his restlessness but he couldn't wait for the warmth of Diana's alive but sleeping body to bring him properly back into the present tense.

FIVE
IT'S SHOWTIME, NAPOLEON

Over the border, the one separating Wales from England, or more specifically, Anghofiedig from the Forest of Dean, a big night was planned at The Buck. And some of the locals were getting edgy.

More than 150 years had passed since, according to Forest legend, a few Frenchmen and their dancing bears had been chased into hiding by an angry mob. A false rumour had spread through the trees that the bears had mauled a woman and killed a child. The Frenchmen feared for their lives. The shame of the pursuers lived on through families and generations.

On becoming a millionaire, Barry, egged on by Romeo, hired The Parisian Prancers to turn up at The Buck and put on a show with their dancing bear. The confused Prancers duly arrived for the gig – only to be sent packing by an angry landlord who hadn't booked them and thought they were taking le piss. The Prancers headed back across the Channel vowing never to set foot in *L'Angleterre folle* (crazy England) ever again.

However, a new landlord was now ensconced at The Buck, one who was determined to keep pro-European alliances alive and let bygones be bygones. Marcus Armstrong was a sweet, gentle dreamer who looked for the good in everyone and was usually happy to give those who fleeced him second, third and even fourth chances to do so again. He had a string of failed relationships and businesses behind him that bore evidence of this, but he still walked through life's travails with a bizarrely upbeat demeanour.

Marcus thought it was time for his customers to forget about past mistakes and the guilt of their forebears. He also thought it was time for a fresh glass of *entente cordiale*, and for his pub to reach out to both the Prancers and France itself in a true spirit of friendship. He invited the Prancers to return and perform at The Buck but they declined immediately in a flurry of agitated *sacre bleus*. He would not accept *non* for an answer and kept messaging them, increasing the number of euros on the table with each email. Eventually, the Prancers found themselves with an offer they simply could not refuse. So they squeezed back into their vintage Citroen H-types and headed over the Channel with their amazing world-renowned showstopper Napoleon – the talented dancing brown bear who moved and grinned like a young Anton Du Beke.

They were unloading their stuff in the pub car park, ready to set up for the show, when a group of lads spied them and shouted 'bear'.

Napoleon got spooked by the noise, slipped free from his cage and ran into the woods.

The Prancers cursed 'crazy Englanders' under their collective breaths. The lads just laughed and walked away.

Marcus Armstrong called the police and said he hoped he wasn't being too much bother.

He then told the waiting audience in his pub that there really wasn't anything to get too hot under the collar about but... a large brown bear named after a revolutionary French commander just happened to be exploring the beauty of their rugged countryside and enjoying his new-found freedom, deep amongst the Anglo–Welsh woods where he would not and could not be restrained by metal chains or the commands and demands of a Latin Salsa.

Of all the quacks to be on duty today, it had to be Doctor Humphreys. Barry had avoided him like the plague since being told by him that he was a fat alcoholic heading for an early grave. The doctor hadn't used those exact words but the sentiment of his message was clear enough. However, needs must and nowadays, when it came to seeing a GP, a beggar couldn't be a chooser. It was Doc Humphreys or no one. A closer run thing than you might imagine, but Barry wisely listened to the urgings of Diana's voice in his head rather than any of the others.

'So, Mr White, what is it today?' said the doctor, peering above the rim of his spectacles.

Barry explained his symptoms, chiefly achy muscles, headaches and a feeling of restlessness. Along with, curiously, a few pimples on his chin and very tender breasts.

'Hmm, are you still necking the equivalent of the River Wye in beer every week?'

'No, sir.' Barry tried to look indignant and hurt but Humphreys wasn't even looking at him.

'What about your diet?' Doc Humphreys picked up a banana off his desk and waved it in Barry's direction like it was an offensive weapon.

'I'm not on one anymore.'

'No, what do you eat? Are you still stuffing your face with too much processed rubbish? How do you get your fibre?' The doctor put down his banana like he was laying it to rest.

'Oh no, Doc Humphreys, I've got a woman cooking for me these days – a nurse. I've never eaten so many greens, reds and yellows, well, not since I swallowed a snooker table,' said Barry.

'Is that a joke?'

'Yes, sir.'

'Well, I'm never quite sure with you.' The doctor was irritated. 'What medications are you currently taking? Just the blood thinners that I prescribed last time?'

'I stopped taking them.'

'Why?'

'Because I figured my blood was thin enough now. Like the rest of me. I still take a vitamin C tablet every day.'

The doctor's face reddened. 'Enough! See Nurse Roberts outside, we'll take some of your chunky blood if we can get it out of your body, run a few more tests and go from there. All right? Good day, Mr White.'

Barry feigned an abbreviated bow and walked out of the surgery backwards, as if exiting the presence of King Charles III.

'Man's a fucking buffoon,' muttered Doc Humphreys to himself under his breath, before reaching for the top drawer of his desk and pulling out a packet of pills of his own.

On his way home from the surgery, Barry called in unannounced on Uncle Derek and Aunty Ruth and found his aunt curled up in a ball, crying on the living-room floor.

Ruth told her nephew that Derek hadn't been his old self for some time. She explained how his mood swings had become more pronounced, and how he would suffer days of the 'black dog' as Winston Churchill used to refer to his bouts of depression. She described how her husband sometimes became confused by the simplest of things going on around him, forgetting the names of people he had known for years, or repeatedly asking the same questions over and over. They'd put it down to old age, but a couple of days ago he went out for a walk and couldn't remember how to get home. It came back to him after a while, but it scared the life out of both of them.

'We've seen a specialist and had all the tests done and they think it's CTE: chronic traumatic encephalopathy,' said Ruth, tears still streaming down her face.

'Is that bad?'

'Yes, it's bad.'

'Can it be cured?'

'No. It's dementia.'

Ruth told Barry that his uncle would become more disorientated and more confused, until eventually he would no longer know who he or anyone else was. She picked up a cushion bearing the emblem of a rugby ball and hugged it tightly to her chest as if she was going into contact.

'Mr Bhari at the hospital reckons it's the rugby. All those bangs on the head over so many years, they mount up. Stupid bugger used to come home concussed, drunk or both every single Saturday night without fail. Him and your dad. They stuck their heads in amongst all those flying boots cos they wanted people to see how big and tough they were. Well, go and take a look at your uncle now, upstairs rocking himself in his bed. He doesn't look so big and tough, I'll tell you that for nothing. All that macho White brothers rubbish. For what? They were selfish, both of them. Stupid and selfish.'

Ruth began sobbing again, squeezing the cushion even closer to her stomach. Barry took it off her and held his aunty in his arms. 'He seemed all right when I last saw him.'

'Mostly he is,' said Ruth. 'But you don't see what I do. The day's coming when he won't be able to hide it no more. It's me who cops the worst of it: the frustration, the temper tantrums, the anxiety, the daft decision-making, leaving the front door wide open, putting the remote control in the oven, turning the taps on and letting the bath overflow, putting plates in the washing machine. I've been covering for him, but it's getting too hard. They reckon he's stage two, firing to stage three. Stage four, well that's when they stop counting.'

Barry pulled away but still held his aunt's hand. 'I'm so sorry. Can I see him?'

'Yeah, go on up, he's having a lie down. Maybe you can cheer him up.'

Derek was lying on his side, with no top on, just a pair of grubby blue Y-fronts poking out from under the duvet. He looked so old. His body looked frail, covered in wispy bits of weedy grey hair, not like Barry remembered at all. He preferred to hold on to those memories and imaginations of the all-conquering rugby player, muscular, fearless, hoisted shirtless and smooth-chested on the tops of teammates' shoulders following another big cup win. The Whites were the leaders of a pack of everyday Goliaths. Anghofiedig giant-killers one and all.

But that Derek White died years ago, along with his brother.

Truth was, Barry never saw Derek or his father play rugby in their absolute pomp. He was a child of the eighties, raised on rugby all the same, but introduced to the song just as the final chorus was fading out. He was a witness to the rugby-playing White Brothers in their thirties, not their twenties. Still destroyers, but on the slide. Less ruthless. Forward-stepping, cunning and battle-heartened, but without the natural power and spring of step loaned to them by youth.

Nevertheless, Barry grew up with all the tales and stories,

the legends and the photos, and he received them whilst they were fresh in other people's minds. Since then, he'd watched these stories evolve and take on lives of their own, becoming richer and more exaggerated with every retelling, usually in beer-fuelled clubhouses and pubs, narrated by the gravelly voices of forlorn men – always men – who took their cuts from unspoken deals, their ten per cent of the respect and glory. They gestured and pouted with feigned authority in their comfy lounge courts with imitation leather three-piece suites.

'I was there.'

Well, so was everyone.

They were hangers-on, but they couldn't be blamed for wanting the great times to last or for the White boys and their talented peers to stay young forever.

Barry knew who the bullshitters were and who he could rely on for a few grains of truth. He remembered the older versions of the stories. Told by men, now dead, who he mostly trusted. Men who fought in world wars so gave it to you straight.

'Aunty Ruth told me the news,' said Barry.

'I heard her,' said Derek, sitting up, making sure to cover himself.

'Can I do anything for you?'

'No, there's nothing anyone can do for me now, lad.' Derek's words were meant to sound stoic but his voice cracked on the word now.

'What's it like? Scary?'

'It is. I won't lie.'

'What's the worst bit?'

Derek's head flipped back and hit the headboard before rolling forward again more softly. 'Having to talk about it all to the likes of you and Ruthy. Feeling like I'm letting you down.'

Barry sat on the bed, physically dominating his uncle for once. 'You were the brave one, not my old man, everyone says so. Everyone says you were the one who made him look good. You did his donkey work.'

'Not sure that's true.'

'You're twenty-five points down with ten minutes left on the clock, but you've got to keep battering the oppo to let them know you think you can win. That's what makes you, you.'

'I'll try, but pretty soon I'm going to forget who "me" even is.' A small unformed tear escaped from Derek's right eye, but was abruptly swatted away as if it was an annoying fly by a rough, calloused hand.

'We won't ever forget you, Uncle Derek.'

The words touched a nerve somewhere deep in the confused electrical connectors of his punch-drunk brain; a brain that he'd willingly propelled thousands of times into the hearts, bones, guts, heads and barrelled torsos of anyone foolish enough to stand in his way or think they could stop him.

And there was a twinkle in Uncle Derek's moist right eye.

A sparkle, even.

Or perhaps, it was just another runaway tear?

The legend, as told by Barry and then others in the years to come, would ultimately decide which one.

SIX

EVERYONE HAS A FEMININE SIDE

Barry had succumbed to temptation. He'd flicked on an old video of Chico, alive and well, sucking a pineapple and making dramatic playful noises as he scooped and ate, seemingly in one movement, playing up to the crowd like only he could. Or did.

Before this, he'd watched a dozen videos or so on a channel called Cats Wearing Helmets but it did nothing for him. He hated the canned laughter and the sad faces of the cats who were mostly wearing helmets made out of melons, and all looked like hostages being made to tell the world at gunpoint that they were doing great and their owners were really looking after them. Barry wasn't a cat lover and lately had even less time for them on account of Maximilius Percival and the cat glove puppet he wore everywhere he went and talked to endlessly. Max never used to be so strange. He used to drive buses and play snooker. However, these days he would come into the pub of a night and order a pint of Kangaroo beer with one hand and a saucer of milk with the other.

Barry had also idled an hour or so away watching old clips of the 1970s Welsh rugby team during their golden era: Mervyn Davies, J.J. Williams, J.P.R. Williams, Phil Bennett, Ray

Gravell, John Dawes, Barry John, all gone, God rest their souls. At least they'll stay young and fit and strong in people's minds. Like Chico.

And what of Uncle Derek? Yesterday's news still troubled him. Another golden era was coming to an end.

'What you watching, Uncle Barry?' said Eddie, bursting into the lounge as if arriving by genie's lamp.

'Bit of old Chico,' said Barry, hiding his screen.

'Ooh, not the vid of him choking to death?'

'Course not.'

'My biology teacher told me I share 98.3 per cent of my DNA with gorillas.' Eddie beamed.

Barry nodded. 'That's exactly right.'

'She also said I was just as charismatic and twice as inquisitive.'

'Sounds like a smart lady.' Barry shut his laptop and put it on the arm of the chair.

'She is, though a bit too squeamish to be a biology teacher in our school,' continued Eddie. 'I asked her about women's periods, but she went red and told me to google it.'

'Wise advice.'

'I wasn't that bothered, I didn't want to know the ins and outs of it all – sounds disgusting if you ask me – but Che Johnson bet me £2 he could drink a bottle of Pepsi through a tampon and I thought she could give me a steer on whether to take the bet or not.'

'You can always talk to your ma,' said Barry.

'Not about that I can't,' replied Eddie, frowning.

Barry shrugged. 'Well, don't come to me for tampon know-how, I'm as baffled by all that stuff as you.'

'It's all right, I took a punt and it came off. He was well short – bit of a pathetic attempt really, he never got down to the string.'

'Good to know,' said Barry.

'In the old days, who taught you about sex?' Barry had hoped Eddie would go away but the boy pushed on.

'Gavin Gonzales. Boy in my class. Half Spanish he was. Still is, I suppose. Knew loads. Or thought he did. His dad ran a newsagent's so sometimes he'd get his grubby mitts on a few jazz mags and bring 'em in. We called him Speedy because if he said he was bringing summat in on a Monday he wouldn't actually do it until Friday.'

'So, with no internet, where did you go to see naked women moving around?' blurted out Eddie, his filter off as usual.

Barry tried to play it cool like a man of the world. 'Romeo had a Betamax tape called *The Stud*, in which Joan Collins got her kit off.'

'Was Joan Collins a porn star?'

'Wouldn't say so.'

'I like women, but I'm glad I'm a man. I definitely wouldn't want to spend a quarter of my life menstruating,' said Eddie, pulling the face he usually saved for eating asparagus.

'Amen to that.' The phone rang, rescuing Barry from further unwanted tangents of conversation. Barry answered with trepidation because few people called the landline these days, not with good news at any rate.

'Hullo...'

'Mr White? It's Doctor Humphreys here. Got the results of your blood tests. Think I know what's been causing your latest problems.'

'Am I dying?'

'Afraid not. I mean, no. There is something very odd though, your oestrogen levels are extremely high. Well, for a man.'

'What's oestrogen?' Barry looked at Eddie but got no clues from him.

'A group of female hormones,' said Doc Humphreys.

'You saying I'm turning into a woman?'

'No, but you also have very high levels of progestins, which is a synthetic progestogen, also found in women.'

'Cut to the chase, doc, I don't understand.'

'Okay, tell me, these vitamin pills you say you take every day, what are they called?'

'No idea.'

'Can you check, please?'

'What, now?'

'If you could, please.'

Barry went to the kitchen cupboard and returned with a box from the Tupperware container where an assortment of different pills, potions and tablets lived. He looked at the label and read the name back down the phone.

'They're called Rigevidon, one a day,' said Barry in a slow, loud voice.

'As I suspected,' said the doctor.

'Are they a bad batch?'

'For you, yes. I want you to stop taking them immediately because they aren't vitamins at all. They're contraceptive pills. For women.'

Barry dropped the phone temporarily and said nothing. He recomposed himself and returned to the call to find the doc still talking.

'What on earth made you think they were vitamin tablets?'

'They were in the place where Ma always kept the vitamins,' said Barry.

'And you never thought to read a label or check what you were taking?'

'Never needed to. Not when Ma was around.'

There was a long pause before Doc Humphreys began speaking again. 'Come back in for another check-up next week. I would expect things to improve immediately, especially your blood pressure, which was plenty high enough to start with. However, I want to keep an eye on you if that's all right.'

'Will do,' said Barry, having no intention of going back to Doc Humphreys' surgery this week, next week or ever again if he could possibly help it.

'Barry, I keep saying this to you but it's time to grow up and, if you'll excuse the pun, be a man,' continued the doctor. 'Your health issues won't go away unless you face them head on. I understand you've got more responsibilities these days, new people in your life, but only *you* can make the changes you need to make to improve your life chances. Not me, or your new girlfriend or even your family. You understand?'

'Thank you, doc, I'm hearing you loud and proud.' Barry put the phone down emphatically.

'What was all that about?' asked Eddie, who had been sitting patiently on the sofa, listening to one side of the peculiar conversation and trying to join up the dots that linked vitamins to high blood pressure and the chances of Barry turning into a woman and suddenly getting pregnant.

'It's just man stuff.' Barry started piling the pills into a black bin liner.

'Have all those vitamins gone past their sell-by date?'

'Yes.'

'Can out-of-date vitamins turn blokes into women?'

'These ones can,' said Barry, before holding a single finger to his lips and lowering his voice considerably. 'But mum's the word, got that?'

'My lips are sealed,' said Eddie, who couldn't wait to go to school the next day so he could announce his bombshell of a discovery to Che Johnson, who would surely want to try 'Rigevidon one a day' for himself, just to prove to all of Class 10C that Eddie Fenwick was a complete and total bullshitter.

Barry was home alone when an earthquake struck his world and all its certainties. It came via another sharp, impatient intrusion, this time, a demanding knock at the door, wanting 'in' right away.

'Hey, Barry, got a few minutes?' said Sergeant Sargent.

The sarge was flanked either side by men Barry had never met before, dressed smartly in crisp shirts, expensive jackets and shiny shoes. Both smelt of overpowering expensive aftershaves. One was small and had curly hair and weak sideburns. The other was tall, muscular, decades younger than his boss and didn't smile much. His shirt was a distinctive shade of dark purple and he wasn't wearing a tie. His cufflinks were golden. Barry didn't know anyone in Anghofiedig who wore cufflinks, let alone gold ones.

The sarge introduced the two men as Detective Inspector Craig Willard and Detective Sergeant Duncan Burrows from the Serious Crime Squad.

'Barry, these men want to chat to you about Reverend Hill. Is that okay?' said Sergeant Sargent.

'Sure, come on in.'

They started with some easy throw downs on a standard length: When was the last time you saw Reverend Hill? What was the nature of your relationship with him? Were you aware that he planned to leave the village so suddenly? Do you know where he is now? Do you know where he might have gone? Did he mention details of any personal problems to you? Do you know if he had any debts or money worries?

But then the questions got harder to fend off.

'I understand you recently gave Reverend Hill the sum of £100,000 in cash?' said Detective Purple Shirt.

'Not exactly, my ma left it to him in her will. She died recently.'

'That's an awful lot of money for a little old lady of seemingly limited means to leave to someone who wasn't family.' Detective Curly Hair's tone was warmer. Barry had watched plenty of crime shows these past few years and knew how the good cop, bad cop routine worked.

'Did your ma leave this money to Reverend Hill or did she leave it to the church?' Detective Purple Shirt began nosing around the living room, looking at photos of young Barry on the wall.

'Because, you see, there's no mention of any of it in her actual will,' said Detective Curly Hair.

The detectives kept up the pressure, taking it in turns to fire short one-liners at Barry so he hardly had time to think.

'Your ma's legal instructions upon her death were actually very vague.'

'As are all details about where she got such vast sums of money in the first place.'

'She didn't actually have a will at all, did she?'

'And we've looked into her bank records.'

'Very sketchy.'

'We just need a few simple answers to clear this mess up,' said Sergeant Sargent, trying to reassure Barry. Detective Purple Shirt scowled at him for interrupting their flow.

'What we have right now is something of a gigantic fiscal black hole,' continued Detective Curly Hair.

'A black hole that seems to have swallowed up Reverend Hill along with a whole load of cash,' said Detective Purple Shirt.

'An almighty supernova explosion.'

'You could call it a collision of the stellar kind.'

'This place is looking very stellar.'

'You've had an awful lot of work done in a short space of time, haven't you?'

'Like I said, stellar.'

Detective Purple Shirt picked up Barry's prized elephant ornament and held it upside down. 'We understand your mother wanted you to pump a considerable sum of her money – or rather, your money – into The Dragon pub?'

'Strange request, don't you think? A pub investment? For a woman who didn't really drink?'

'Or even go out that often?'

'Unlike yourself.'

'You like a drink, don't you, Barry?'

'Nothing wrong with that, so do I.' Detective Curly Hair laughed at his own feeble joke.

Detective Purple Shirt found a mirror and admired himself in it. 'Got yourself half a barbershop too, eh?'

'How's that all going? I could do with getting these curls trimmed.' Detective Curly Hair ran his fingers through his own hair as if they were tongs.

'We'd like a little look at the shop's books if we may. Tomorrow will be fine,' said Detective Purple Shirt, still admiring himself in the mirror.

'And your uncle's driving a nice new set of wheels these days.' Detective Curly Hair walked towards the window and fingered the curtains. 'Hot to trot.'

'How was Europe?'

'And Rwanda? Funny place to go, no? I mean, the last government couldn't even persuade desperate refugees to go there.'

'What was the nature of your business out there?' Detective Purple Shirt held Barry's furtive expression in his own firm stare.

'Monkey business, wasn't it?'

'What time is it?'

'It's Chico time!' shouted both detectives together.

'Is there anything else you'd like to get off your chest whilst you have this opportunity?' asked Detective Curly Hair.

'Much better to tell us now and be up front about everything.'

'Better for us.'

'Better for you.'

'Stop!' shouted Barry.

He told the officers that Ma had squirrelled away a lot of money that neither he – nor anyone else – had ever known about. He told them she had gambled big time whilst looking for kicks when bringing up a small child on her own, following the death of her husband, and won on the horses back in the 1980s or 1990s. However, she felt ashamed of what she had done and had stashed the cash away secretly and tried to forget about it. Until she knew she was dying. Then she let Barry in on things and moved the money from wherever she'd been keeping it to the loft. Barry told the officers that all Ma wanted in death was for him to be secure and for the community to benefit from her stroke of good fortune – or misfortune, call it what you will – all those years ago. He told them she didn't trust banks that much. And that she never gambled once, to his knowledge, in all the years he had known her.

'Sounds like a hundred per cent, bona fide, solid gold Mother Theresa your ma,' said Detective Purple Shirt, sarcastically.

'She was,' said Barry, holding his ground.

'So back to Reverend Hill, just to clarify because I don't think you actually did so before, did your ma leave the 100k to him or did she leave it to the church?' asked Detective Curly Hair.

Sergeant Sargent huffed in irritation. He had little time for the detectives or the games they played with people. 'Barry, you told everyone that the money was for the community; for a new foodbank and building repairs and other local causes.'

'It was,' replied Barry.

'So not for Reverend Hill's own personal use?' Detective Curly Hair sat right beside Barry, invading his personal space for the first time.

'No,' said Barry, directly.

'That's great.' Detective Curly Hair inched back.

Barry had had enough. 'Am I in trouble? Are you going to arrest me for anything?'

'Don't think so,' said Detective Curly Hair.

'Providing you've told us the truth,' added Detective Purple Shirt.

'The whole truth.'

'And nothing but the truth.'

'I have,' said Barry.

'Then having a rich mother isn't a crime.' Detective Curly Hair got up again and Barry watched the way he worked the room and all its space like an actor on a stage.

'Nor a lucky one,' said Detective Purple Shirt.

'Or even a dead one who can't talk.'

'Mind if we take a little look around the joint while we're here?'

'Go ahead, I've nothing to hide,' said Barry.

'Fabuloso.' Detective Curly Hair was off towards the door. 'You must let me know who did all the design work on this place, they've a real eye for quality and a flair for space. I'm considering sprucing up my humble crib, though I'm probably on a much tighter budget than you. I might be able to give them some more work though, if they need it. If we were able to come to some sort of mutual agreement.'

'It was my friend Angharad,' said Barry.

'Yes, of course, sister of the dude who you bought the barbershop for?'

'That's right,' said Barry, rattled by how much they actually knew about him.

'Tell me, Mr White, where exactly is the loft?' enquired Detective Purple Shirt.

'Upstairs, second bedroom on the left, there's a hatch.'

'Okay if I take a look?'

'Fill your boots. Just watch that nice shirt don't get dirty.'

'Any more cash up there?' said Detective Curly Hair.

'Not a penny.'

'What about any Jesus-loving preachers gone AWOL?' Detective Purple Shirt nodded and walked off towards the stairs with his colleague, the pair muttering as they went.

Sergeant Sargent sighed with relief now they were out of the room. 'Sorry about all this drama, Barry.'

'Not your fault.'

'You've nothing to worry about, they're just doing their job. Which is tracking down the reverend and the missing loot.'

'I know.'

Sergeant Sargent was a humble village policeman, an old-time bobby waiting for his pension, more at home giving directions and returning lost dogs than catching criminals, but he knew his patch and its people. 'You would tell me if you had any problems, wouldn't you? I mean, we go back a long way, don't we? I'm on your side.'

'Of course,' said Barry.

'I know I'm a copper but I live here, like you. I'm not like them.'

'No, you're not like them at all.'

'It's just, I never had Pearl down as a risk-taking heavy gambler,' said Sergeant Sargent. 'I knew her. I knew her well. I knew your old man too. And I thought I knew you.'

'Then you'll know that Ma took the biggest gamble of her entire life the day she walked down the aisle with my dad, thinking she might change him.' Barry remembered he had a glass of orange squash on the table and drank it down in one.

'Never thought of it like that,' said Sergeant Sargent.

'She went all in on that one and lost big time.' Barry confidently slammed his glass back down.

'She did.'

'Listen, sarge, I don't want anyone to find out where Ma's money actually came from. I just want people around here to see and feel the good she's doing, even though she's gone,' said Barry.

'What's in the loft, Barry? Any skeletons?'

'Nope, it's all as shiny as a detective's suit up there.'

'Glad to hear it,' said Sergeant Sargent, putting both hands behind his head, sitting back and closing his eyes to cat nap.

SEVEN

ANOTHER BOARDER BITES THE DUST

Having Detectives Curly Hair and Purple Shirt turn up unannounced at his front door had spooked Barry and he was struggling to think clearly. He told himself he wasn't a criminal and hadn't done anything wrong – quite the opposite, he'd given Reverend Hill a whole lump of cash out of the goodness of his heart. But now he was lying to the police and he knew nothing positive would ever come from that. The best thing to do would be to call them back and come clean – letting them know that *he'd* won the money gambling and given 100k to the rev – not the church – with the vague and simple instruction to 'do something good with it'.

However, he still wanted people to believe that the money had come from Ma. He wanted her to continue having this amazing legacy that actually meant something. Since she had died and seemingly left all her savings to locals and local projects, she'd taken on this status of cult hero – as if she was part Cinderella and part Princess Diana – and somehow, this made it feel like she was still alive and moving around the community. People talked about her with fondness and appreciation in coffee shops or post office queues. They were proud to have their stories to tell, to prove they once knew her. Her gifts and her own story would outlive all of them. There was no way Barry was going to throw all this aside unless he absolutely had to.

And what's more, there was no way he wanted every local busybody to know he was rich. Or used to be. He didn't want to be dragged above anyone's radar. He liked being in a crowd, preferably middle to back. No pressure there. No spotlights. So he decided he would keep on lying to the police. And keep on lying to those he lived with and amongst. If anyone asked him, he would reluctantly agree that Reverend Hill was a thief on the run who had stolen from the church and from Ma's legacy.

However, Barry couldn't forget the overriding good the reverend had done for Ma in her final days and weeks. And he was confident the rev would forgive him for any public or private betrayals once the dust had settled.

Right now, though, everyone in the village needed Reverend Hill to be caught and brought to face natural justice in handcuffs – to pay the price for crimes against Ma before a living, wheezing judge, with human flaws just like them, dressed in a big red robe and a silly long wig that resembled the natural locks of Detective Curly Hair in his wild glam rocker phase.

As for what happened next between Reverend Hill and God, that was entirely up to them.

And what about Barry and the same God he still believed in?

He decided he would put that relationship on hold for now. He'd cross that bridge of reckoning when he got to it.

Barry picked up the phone and rang Dot. He told her about his visit from the police and asked her if she would do him a small favour.

'If anyone official asks, will you say that Ma won a small

fortune on the horses sometime back in the eighties or nineties –
you decide when? And will you say that she didn't tell a soul,
apart from you. And that she hid all the money, you don't know
where, and didn't spend any of it because she was ashamed of
her gambling?'

'Oh love, what you gone and got yourself into?'

'It's nothing, honestly,' lied Barry.

'How much did Pearl win back in the day?'

'A million quid,' said Barry.

'That's a whole lot of nothing.'

'Will you do it? No one is likely to ask you. Just, if they do…'

'Dunno. If I do, it won't be for you, it'll be for Pearl –
because she would want me to put my head on the block for
you, because you were all that mattered to her.'

Napoleon was doing his best to enjoy his new-found freedom in
the woods but he was an inexperienced forager. He stumbled
upon the contents of two grey wheelie bins near a remote
Forestry Commission hut, which included a large pot of leftover
potato salad and some out-of-date chicken curries. He had also
come across the carcass of a dead deer but his true comfort zone
was parading onstage like Anton Du Beke, not sliding through
the English / Welsh forests as the powerful assassin he was born
to be. He preferred his fish to come from supermarkets,
hypermarkets and the Intermarché rather than fresh out of
streams and rivers, and for his meat cuts to come handed to him
by his generous French masters in porcelain bowls, neatly
butchered and squared into chunks.

He wasn't used to this fend-for-yourself life in the wild. His
claws were too manicured for stripping bushes of fruit or bones
of beating flesh. His were show nails, they were even painted

silver. He'd walked right by a singular of wild boar, including piglets, without knowing they were there.

Meat wasn't even his go-to staple. He much preferred to feast on cured salmon or delicate mushrooms or even pine cones and grasses, which surrounded him in this ancient woodland he now called home. However, he was too civilised, too humanlike to know what was staring him in the face or where it had come from.

The smell of something good filled his nostrils from somewhere in a distance he could not yet see. He followed the scent to discover a small cabin in the middle of an enclosed clearing. He could hear someone moving around inside and the sounds of sizzling and frying on a stove, and he recognised the aroma of sausages and onions because he had tasted them both before. Of course he had, he was called Napoleon and he was French. He looked through the window and saw the figure of a man. It wasn't in his nature to make enemies of people – he was a showman, born to entertain audiences, not eat them. But needs must. This was all about survival. Bear versus Bear Grylls. He smashed the window with his giant paw and heard the shrieks, shatters and spits of dropped pans, knocked pots and human shock expressed in high frequency yelps and deep throaty grunts.

'Fuck off you scavenging beast, you hear? Else I'll pump your brain so full of lead you'll be shaking hands with your creator long before sun-up,' came the cry from the bristling red-eyed man inside the cabin.

The man dispatched two loud shots from his semi-automatic bolt action rifle with locking lugs through the roof of the cabin into the still night air. It was enough to scare the life out of Napoleon, who turned and ran for the cover of darkness and a recently discovered cave in the buried, almost untouched undergrowth. His instincts rightly told him a few well-seasoned sausages were not worth dancing his last tango for.

He watched the bear turn and run but knew his cabin hideaway was no longer safe. Even if the bear was too chicken to come back, insomniac Foresters – or those staggering home from a Buck pub lock-in – would have heard his gunshots ring out through the slender-gapped silences of sleeping oaks and their paper-thin cottage walls, stuffed with asbestos and old copies of *The Dean Forest Mercury* from yesteryear, used by hard-up miners in the pre-Hitler age as cheap wall cavity insulation. And they would be sure to explore the woods come light of day, because they – unlike Napoleon's dancing lineage – were a naturally nosy breed with a genetic strut in their DNA.

The man packed his meagre possessions into a small rucksack and scrubbed away his tracks and trails so no one would easily see where he had been.

A pocketknife, a sleeping bag, a length of rope, a compass, a box of matches, some tins of baked beans and one of Spam, his gun and not much else. He finished the sausages and onions off straight from the pan and put the utensil into the top of his rucksack without cleaning it.

He put on his boots and all the clothes he had with him and stepped out into the fresh air, walking in the opposite direction to which Napoleon had bolted.

As he walked, the man hummed 'Onward Christian Soldiers' under his breath for motivation and inspiration.

Hearing a branch on the forest floor snap hard, he stopped to listen.

'Pull yourself together, Jacob, remember who you are,' muttered Reverend Hill to himself, unshaven, unrecognisable and wearing six-day old underpants that would have smelt like fresh doughnuts to a large terrestrial lone mammal, a long way from home, be that the coastal mountains and woodlands of

British Columbia or Alaska, or the creaky well-worn boards of Parisian theatres such as Le Petit Casino, le Grand Rex or Theatre de la Hutchette.

The man was in his forties or fifties, overweight with a big beer belly, wearing faded over-washed shorts, ill-fitting flip-flops and a cut off T-shirt that carried the 1980s philosophy message 'Frankie says relax'. He gestured and shouted to those below him, many of them children, some of them his own, to get out of his way. The kids looked up to him in more ways than one. He stood on the roof of a moderately sized house, about fifty feet above ground level, somewhere hot, sunny and idyllic with blue skies and palm trees in the background. Underneath his right arm was a skateboard. In front of the house was a half-filled family-sized paddling pool. Once he was happy with the movements of everyone beneath him, the man flexed his biceps, just like Chico used to do, safe in the knowledge he had his audience's full attention.

He tentatively took to his skateboard and steadied himself. He began to skate down the roof, gathering speed as he went, in a direct line with the paddling pool. However, as he was about to leave the roof the skateboard caught on a tile that was sticking up, which fired the board into a different direction. The man was hurtling alone now, without wheels, and there was no way his own steam would carry him to the safety of the lukewarm water in the pool. He tried in vain to apply his own brakes, his ankle twisting at right angles in the guttering, and a look of terror took over his face as he realised what was coming next. Abject failure and the stark realisation, all too late, that arrogant middle-aged men full of bravado and beer make lousy stuntmen. His stiff, flabby frame flopped tamely onto the concrete pathway between house and pool with an almighty thud, his face smashing into the ground first. Well, he wanted to go viral and now he would. A burst of Queen's 'Another One Bites the Dust' signalled the end of the short video that more than six million people had 'liked' and left cruel comments on.

'What the...?' said Barry.

Eddie stuck his chest out. 'There are loads more like that one on 'ere.'

'Did he die?' asked Barry.

'Don't know.'

'Is that what you spend all your time watching?'

'Not all, but a lot.'

Barry looked away. 'I don't like it.'

'Don't you find it a bit funny?'

'Not if he died, no.'

'You're overthinking.'

'I just wanna know he got up, that's all. He had kids.'

Eddie, like most of his generation, had an inbuilt ability to separate internet fact from fiction. 'It's left open-ended. Like in fairy tales, the ending is what you want it to be.'

'Fat guy skateboarding off a roof and headbutting concrete at forty mile per hour ain't no happily ever after,' said Barry.

'Want to watch another one?' Eddie pressed a few buttons on his device.

'Don't think so.'

'This one's funnier. Look at this skinny bloke dressed as Captain America, he's riding pillion on a really fast motorbike.'

'But he's holding on to a cow? Is that animal actually steering the bike?'

'Cool innit?'

'Do they crash?'

'What do you think?'

Barry winced. 'Do all these vids end with Queen's "Another One Bites the Dust"?'

'Yes.'

'I feel dirty.'

'Wait until you see what happens to the cow!' Eddie laughed.

Whilst they were talking, Diana had walked in unnoticed from her shift at the hospital. She'd said 'hello' to both her life partner and her son but neither had acknowledged her presence. She sat in an armchair opposite them and kicked off her shoes. She fixed her eyes on them, watching them laughing and giggling contentedly in each other's company, like a pair of naughty adolescent schoolboys. The tag applied to one of them but not the other.

She'd had a wretched day. The son of a friend – who was only a year younger than Eddie – had been knocked off his bike by a car that failed to stop and he was now fighting for his life. When he arrived at the community hospital – in the back of a passer-by's car – no one realised the full extent of his injuries. The passer-by thought he was being a Good Samaritan by refusing to wait ages for an ambulance that might not even show. He thought it would be better – and quicker – for everyone if he bundled the boy into the back seat of his Toyota Corolla, laying him on a crumpled dog blanket, and drove to the nearest hospital he could think of. Diana thanked him for his efforts out of politeness, and to spare his feelings, but the reality was he had probably reduced the boy's survival chances by at least thirty per cent.

Diana spent the rest of the day trying to relay scant information and numerous cups of sweet tea to her stricken friends, Tara and Alvin, before a couple of female paramedics whisked them all off to St Andrew's Hospital, where they should have gone in the first place.

There was nothing Diana could actually do or say to reassure her friends. At best, their fourteen-year-old son Rhys – their only child, their whole world, the apple of their eye, their absolute everything, the glue that held their relationship together – would spend the next year or two of his life in and out of different hospitals or recovery wards or rehab units scattered across the whole of Wales or the south of England.

At worst, however, Tara and Alvin would find themselves shopping for new black outfits from Next or River Island and talking in hushed tones to undertakers about funeral arrangements.

From across the living room, Barry and Eddie smiled and sang out in accompaniment to the tinny *duff, duff, duff* of 'Another One Bites the Dust'…

Barry looked up and finally noticed Diana was in the room. He also observed that she wasn't smiling and looked tired. Eddie scanned her face too but said nothing, oblivious to anything his mother might be thinking or feeling.

'Sorry, love, didn't see you come in. Did your day go okay?'

'Yep, all good,' said Diana, fighting hard to hold back tears.

'What's for tea, Mum?' asked Eddie without breaking his gaze from his iPad.

'Fish fingers and oven chips with mushy peas sound all right for everyone?' Diana got up and moved to the kitchen.

'Lovely, but can I have baked beans instead of peas on mine, please?' said Barry.

'Extra chips and extra fingers for me, I'm proper Hank Marvin, plus two rounds of bread and butter and can I have garden peas, not mushy ones? Oh and baked beans as well on a separate side dish?' added Eddie.

'Coming right up.'

'Need a hand?' asked Barry, unconvincingly.

'Nah, it's okay, you carry on with whatever it is you're doing. I'll manage on my own just fine.'

EIGHT

DATE NIGHT DOWN THE BUCK

Diana had made a real effort: showering and shaving her legs and armpits, plucking her eyebrows, spending time on her hair, putting on her face and her trusted favourite little black dress that had served her so well over so many important nights of her past. She polished her statement-making silver-heeled shoes and donned her best costume jewellery. She hadn't been on a date night in months and was looking forward to it, dressing up and having Barry all to herself for a few hours, rather than sharing him with Eddie, or the customers down at The Dragon. She needed this quality time with him to remind her of why she was making so many sacrifices in her life and why she was investing so much of herself in him.

During their trip across Europe, she fell in love with the best of him. The gentle, kind, trusting listener with a big heart who showed an innocent curiosity in most things; the naïve and vulnerable charmer with an adventurous urge to explore what was hidden inside people. She enjoyed staring at shared horizons together and thought they'd do that forever, even when they got back to South Wales and those horizons were colder, bleaker and full of rusting steel. Lately, however, she had found herself living alongside someone she didn't really know or understand and didn't always like. His negative influence on Eddie was her biggest concern. Eddie was easily led as it was, without having his own personal Uncle Buck take him by the hand and pull him over cliff edges. When Eddie came up with stupid teenage-boy suggestions he needed the guidance of a firm but fair male to nudge him back in the right direction, not someone to fist-bump him and scream 'boom, let's do it'.

Diana was sure Barry possessed most of the qualities she longed for in a man but his immaturity was irritating. Tonight provided an opportunity for a reset, where she could focus on the things that mattered without being knackered or emotionally drained from an overcharged twelve-hour hospital shift or from cleaning, cooking and wiping up after her two loveable but frustrating dependents. She needed a night where there wasn't rugby training or some old cop show from yesteryear to watch on the telly.

'So where you taking me?'

'We're having a bite to eat at the place where we first met.'

'Er, The Black Pig in Monmouth?'

'No, silly, The Buck.'

'The Forest Buck?'

'One and the same.'

Diana was cross. Again. She never used to get angry so easily or so often. She'd always regarded herself as something of an expert in defusing conflict. Now she was a living, breathing landmine, lurking in plain sight, just beneath the ground, waiting to erupt once Barry came clumsily marching through her pastures, whistling and singing as he went.

'And you watched me get dressed up like this? Knowing full well we were going there?'

'You look a proper picture,' said Barry, still oblivious to the dangerous territory he was now stomping all over.

'But a bit overdressed for The Buck, don't you think?'

'Not at all.'

'But you said we were going out for a surprise meal?'

'And we are.'

Diana rummaged in her handbag for tissues. 'So what's the surprise? Don't tell me, are we eating pickled eggs with our pork scratchings?'

'No, my love, it's a double date.'

'Who the hell with?'

Barry continued to read the room disastrously. 'Romeo and his new lady friend, Delores Hamilton,' he announced boldly.

'The rich American?'

'That's right.'

Diana wanted to swear and curse and thump Barry with her handbag. 'The woman who thought it was all right to pour poteen down my son's throat?'

'Er, let's not dwell on that. Romeo's smitten by her,' said Barry.

Diana let vent with her handbag against the wall. 'Well, whoopi-fuckin-do for Romeo.'

Delores and Romeo arrived at The Buck in a chauffeur-driven car like they were going to the Oscars. Inside the pub, there was a red carpet, albeit a sticky one. Delores wore sunglasses, a tiara and a sequinned, puff-sleeved orange dress that screamed for attention, especially in The Buck, where everyone else was in crusty jeans and bomber jackets. Romeo looked like a not-so-young Don Johnson in an off-white suit with the sleeves rolled up. Barry wore his favourite red Anghofiedig rugby shirt with a pair of ill-fitting black trousers and white and black trainers.

Diana said he looked scruffy. Barry corrected her and said he was shabby-chic.

'Sorry we're late, I took Delores to see the rusty pole – by street light,' said Romeo.

Barry was impressed. 'Romantic. Pretty spectacular, isn't it?'

Delores grunted like a wild boar. 'You think so? You Brits are something else. It's just big rusty pole. In a sheep field. Next to a sewer vent.'

'People come from all over the world to marvel at it,' said Romeo.

'Well, America mostly.' Only Delores picked up on Diana's personal barb.

'It's not actually a rusty pole at all. It's a stink pipe.' Barry went into amateur tour guide mode.

Delores cackled with laughter and threw her hands about wildly. 'You guys kill me. You're so twisted and warped but you get my juices flowing every time. It doesn't change the simple fact, however, that your rusty pole is just a rusty piece of shit. Unlike this place. Say, this joint is – how d'you boys say it again? – the dog's bollocks.'

'Told yer you'd like it, they've got original Space Invaders and everything.' Romeo caressed Delores' back. Diana looked on jealously, wishing Barry would do the same to her.

Delores purred. 'It's like a war room. I could imagine Churchill plotting to destroy Adolf Hitler and smoking fat cigars in here, whilst whistling *Moonlight Serenade* under his many chins.' She turned to Diana. 'Say, we ain't even been formally introduced and you don't say much, but I'm guessing you must be Lady Di?'

'That's me.'

'Enchanted to meet you and your peekaboo lover boy again. He's a whole hunk of Welsh beef, ain't he? You gotta love him, don't ya?'

'What's not to love?' said Diana, her British irony lost on her dining partner.

'If I wasn't so goosey for my own slice of cherub cheesecake over there, I might just have rolled the dice for yours,' said Delores.

'Good job you're so goosey then,' said Diana, with more delicious irony.

'Say Romeo, Romeo... where for art thou, my handsome lothario?'

'I'm over here, sweet pea. Me and Barry are just having a quick go on the Pac Man then we'll be right with you.'

'Okey dokey, cutie patootie,' cooed Delores. 'You might be a Romeo but don't leave me on my owneo, you hear?'

'Oh for fuck's sake, stop it,' said Diana without a moment's pause, as if stricken by a lightning bolt of Tourette's.

'Geez Louise, did Cupid's arrow miss your heart and get you in the tits?' fired up Delores.

'Something like that,' said Diana, sheepishly.

Things got easier after that. Diana instantly felt bad for responding so childishly and made more of a conscious effort to be polite. The food was better than expected too, thanks to a new chef called Pierre who had discovered untapped culinary skills deep within himself whilst on a twelve-year training sabbatical in Brixton prison. Landlord Marcus was always happy to take a chance on an ex-con and this one seemed to be working out – with customers flocking from far and wide for Pierre's Madeira braised beef cheeks on a bed of turnip mash, his black pudding, pork and apple pie with celeriac, and rugged, delicate classics such as the Ultimate Wye & Welsh Rarebit, and builder's tea ice cream with Earl Grey and strawberry shortbread.

Barry opted for the wild boar surprise. 'The surprise is

there's no boar in it, just French bear,' quipped Romeo, whilst in the midst of ordering for himself.

Two tables along, renowned Anghofiedig scrote Freddie Truman – son of Dragon regular Terry – was shouting at Marcus, whilst Freddie's dining companion, Gerald, did his best to ignore them both. Gerald was a seventy-something, part-time photographer for *The Bugle* newspaper and Freddie, on work experience at the ailing weekly, had come along with him to write a food review for next week's edition. Barry knew Gerald well and called him over.

'Wos the problem, Big G?'

'Truman's young 'un is an A1 idiot, that's the problem,' said Gerald. 'He ordered the whitebait for his starter but sent it back cos the fish were too small. Now the chef is starting to twitch.'

'Ooh, are they too small?' said Romeo, straight-faced.

'No, they're just whitebait, that's all.'

'Right size then?'

'Right size.'

'What yer gonna do? I mean, he's making a bit of a scene, ain't he?' said Barry.

Delores waded into territory she didn't understand, like her brother Beau once did in Vietnam. 'Want me to smack the dork?'

'No, I've got this,' said Gerald. 'The boy can't hold his beer, he's a bloody embarrassment to his family cos they're all renowned pissheads, as you know. He's on his third free pint as things stand so it won't be long before them whitebait are swimming around in the bog.'

'Gross.' Diana acted squeamish though she really wasn't.

'Give dork boy a shot of the holy Irish water, it's dope,' said Delores, her volume dial still cranked up to max.

Gerald was apologetic. 'Sorry for disturbing your meal.'

'No problem, Big G,' said Barry.

The drama certainly broke the ice at table number five, giving Delores and Diana something they could finally agree upon.

'The way that kid spoke to his senior? Well, I wouldn't stand for it.'

'I want my boy to show more respect to his elders than that.'

'He will, sister... your kid's a candy cane dreamboat.'

'Thank you.'

Delores poured Diana a glass of red wine. 'We're lucky we've landed on our feet with this pair of doozies, aren't we?'

'Yes, I suppose we are,' said Diana, sipping her Merlot.

'They know how to treat a girl right, don't they?'

Diana nodded and looked across at Barry, who was having his own semi-animated conversation with Romeo.

'What's wrong with kids today?'

'It's bloody outrageous, make no mistake.'

'We weren't like that, were we?'

'Hell no.' Romeo accidentally knocked over the salt shaker.

'Poor Terry, can't be easy for him, having a lightweight like that in the family.' Barry brushed spilt salt into the palm of his hand and tossed it over his shoulder for good luck without casting a glance behind.

'Feel for him. The lad's an out and out shandy drinker.' Romeo watched an inoffensive middle-aged man behind Barry, in a distinctive dark green blazer and baggy fawn trousers, wipe salt out of his eyes with a damp serviette.

Barry ploughed on, oblivious. 'Young Eddie's exactly the same, you know. Maybe it's 21st century gene mutation or the fallout from global warming?'

'Could be.'

'What you saying about Eddie?' said Diana, hearing mention of her son's name.

'Oh nothing, love. We were just wondering why young people today can't hold their beer anymore.'

'It's one of modern life's mysteries and that's the truth,' chimed Romeo.

'They don't start 'em early enough, that's what it is,' said Delores. 'I mean, I was necking brandy in the womb and my granddaddy, Ol Grancher Rancher, used to give me a splash of bourbon on my Lucky Charms every breakfast time when I used to stay at his and Grandma Betty's place in Prairie City. It gave me my constitution. Built some physical immunity. Made me the woman I am today. Stopped me being so goddamn lilywhite. Kept me from turning Democrat with a capital D. If you ask little old me, strong liquor and the Ruger GP100 revolver are the last two surviving bastions of what makes my country great.'

'Reckon you're right, buttercup.' Romeo caressed her back some more like a lovesick physio.

'You're the man, rebel,' bawled Delores.

NINE

AN UNWANTED SLICE OF HISTORY

It was a club record no one saw coming. Admittedly, things had been bad for a while but no one expected this. The Wappers were a team Anghofiedig played twice a season and usually beat comfortably. They were no great shakes, so to lose to them 103–0, with the ref blowing the whistle ten minutes early out of pity, was embarrassing.

There were some mitigating factors for the heavy defeat. Anghofiedig started the game with only twelve players and lost Jonah, twenty minutes in, to cow milking duties. Star player James pulled a hamstring in the second minute of the match and couldn't run, so went off injured with the score at 0–0. There was no Uncle Derek to cajole or inspire from the sidelines. McQueen was still massively out of sorts, being too nice to people, like the rest of the team, lacking bite, snarl or even a desire to be out there.

Barry started the match in the centre but was so off the pace, so terrible in the tackle, that James moved him back to the front row for the second half – where he was just as slow and just as terrible, but it didn't show up as much. Maybe Barry had been one ambitious project too far for James – his face certainly said as much as he limped up and down the touchline, ruffling his already tousled hair and scratching at his cheeks. Failures like this didn't drop at James's door too often, if ever, so this defeat, with him at the helm, was a significant shock to his system.

The dressing room after the game was Halloween quiet. Most of the players just grabbed their kitbags and clothes and went straight home without showering or saying goodbye. In the end only James and Barry were left in the sweaty, mud-filled, liniment-stinking box of a room where so many memorable drunken parties of yesteryear got kick-started.

James, naturally tanned, young, athletic and wise for his years, sat on a bench in nothing but Calvin Kleins, rubbing the backs of his thighs. Barry sat opposite him, still in his full kit: boots, shirt and all. For several minutes both men stayed silent, locked in their own private thoughts and self-interrogations. Barry's thoughts weren't for himself, he imagined the crestfallen look on Uncle Derek's face when someone, probably Aunty Ruth, told him the score. Maybe there was an upside to onrushing dementia if it made him forget what she had told him only a few minutes later.

'Uncle Derek's not well,' said Barry, breaking the silence.

'I figured as much,' said James, pausing. 'I didn't want to ask. Is it bad?'

'Dementia. He's still himself at the moment, mostly, but we all know what's coming.'

'Sorry.'

'Not your fault.'

'Not yours either.'

'Don't say anything to anyone for now.' Barry flipped off his muddy boots and instantly regretted going to the trouble of wearing them around the house to break them in.

'I won't,' said James. 'Puts 103–0 into perspective, doesn't it?'

'Don't it just.'

Barry opened up and told James things he hadn't told anyone else. That he was struggling to adjust to life with Diana and Eddie and do the right things. That he didn't want to work in the pub. That he didn't really want to be responsible for anyone or anything because he felt like he was always going to let people down. He missed his old simple life. With Ma. He missed her more than he, or anyone else, realised. Some days, he even missed working for LesCargo and sparring on a daily basis with Juliet and Bish. He felt let down by Reverend Hill. He confessed that rugby didn't mean as much to him these days. Searching for his place in the White legacy, which had driven him on through so many years of setbacks and failures, seemed like such a pathetic waste of time now.

'Funny thing is, I'm surrounded by more people than at any other time in my life yet I've never felt so alone,' said Barry.

James stood up and like a proud, unashamed Scandinavian removed his Calvin Kleins innocently, but at completely the wrong moment. 'You've been through a lot in a short time. Maybe you should take a break from rugby.'

Barry blushed at the sight of James's manhood. It swung rather than dangled in front of him at eye level. 'Maybe we all should?'

'Won't be much left in this village if we do.' James scratched his butt with both hands and stuck out his torso.

Barry didn't know where to look. 'Is that a bad thing?'

'Yes,' said James, slapping his own butt cheeks.

'What you going to do?' asked Barry.

'I'll be moving on soon enough. My work here was only ever going to be for a couple of years max. But I've met so many good people, I want to do right by them.'

'So shall we keep going?' Barry began undressing nervously.

'Yes, I think so,' said James.

'No one would blame you for walking away, you know. You don't owe this club anything.'

'Ditto.'

The two men walked side by side towards the showers: James stark naked, carrying a wash bag; Barry still wearing his underpants and holding a bottle of Matey bubble bath.

Barry turned on the taps, still in his underpants. 'I don't want to play centre no more. I want to go back to prop.'

'Fine,' said James, now lathering his groin area with something yellow out of an expensive-looking glass bottle.

'How do we make things better?'

'We just keep turning up.'

'Even if we lose 200–0 next week with eight players?' Barry turned to face the wall and slid off his pants, whilst James continued to soap his own manhood with pride.

'Yep.'

'Okay.'

'I reckon I could pull in a few more players through my contacts at LesCargo. I know some guys like me, who've relocated here and played a bit in the past.'

'Do it.'

'They're English though.'

'Good. We gotta find a way to make McQueen angry again.' Barry squirted his armpits with Matey. The pirate on the front of the bottle appeared to be laughing at him.

'So, shall we face the music? Pint in the clubhouse?'

'Shit!' exclaimed Barry, dropping his Matey. 'Llewellyn Davies and his clubhouse cronies.'

'You can handle them, you're a White.' James kicked the bottle of bubble bath, shaped like a smiling seafaring child, back Barry's way.

The clubhouse was almost empty and it was only five o'clock. Llewellyn Davies and his cronies sat beneath photos of themselves from the days when they were a lot more muscular and had hair and teeth. The poses were still the same; stern looks and folded arms, like a gathering of the Soprano family just before a hit. James and Barry strolling in laughing and singing to themselves was too much for some of them to take – but there was no audience for the committee men to play up to bar themselves, so they seethed and simmered in quiet.

The two players sat at a corner table with pints of lager. Llewellyn had expected more players to crawl into the clubhouse, desperate to throw themselves at the committee's mercy for bringing shame on them and the village. He expected adult men to come sneaking in apologetically on their bellies, begging like snakes for his forgiveness. Eventually, Llewellyn could keep council no more. Finishing his beer, he wandered over to the table Barry and James were sitting at and slammed his empty glass down in front of them.

'Reckon you fellas owe a drink to me and every single person in 'ere who has ever pulled on the red shirt of Anghofiedig,' barked Llewellyn.

James eyeballed Barry and Barry stared back.

'Sure, I'll buy you a pint if it helps,' said Barry.

Llewellyn looked smugly across to his cronies as Barry walked to the bar and ordered the beer. He also handed over a wad of notes so each of the cronies could get a pint too. He returned and stood directly in front of Llewellyn, holding the beer. 'Before I give you it, I want you to know this isn't just from me, it's all from all eight or nine of us who were out on that field today doing our best.'

Llewellyn loved performing to his own crowd. 'I've never seen such a shower of shit in all my days.'

'I agree,' said Barry. 'But the thing you've got to remember is that your time has gone. The glory days have gone. Most of your old teammates have gone. Most of those fellas over there, looking down their noses at us and judging us, didn't even play in the glory days, well, not for the firsts at any rate. Weird, ain't it? How they've all become much better players since they hung up their boots and the likes of my dad, who knew the truth, are no longer around to remind them of it.'

'Aren't you ashamed of what happened out there today?' snapped Llewellyn.

'Actually, no. But on behalf of all of us – Anghofiedig's class of 2025, the shower of shit generation – I'd like to present you with this pint, for all your staunch support and for turning out each week in all weathers to watch such crappy schoolboy rugby. If I were you, I really wouldn't bother. I'd go and watch Pontypool or Pontypridd or maybe even Cinderford instead.'

And with that Barry handed Llewellyn his pint and walked out, with James following like an eager to please PA.

'I honestly thought you were going to tip that glass straight over his head and make those gammons' blood boil,' said James once they were alone in the car park.

'I changed my mind at the very last moment,' said Barry.

'How come?'

'Because I've tipped a few pints over people's heads lately and I don't want it to become my thing. And I looked into his eyes and all I saw was a feeble old man with not much time left and not much else to live for. And I felt sorry for him.'

The plan had been to go on to The Dragon and get a bit less sober, just the two of them, to forget the rugby woes of the day. Barry wasn't sure about drinking at The Dragon – in case someone had gone down sick and he found himself working behind the bar instead of drinking from it, but James persuaded him it was the best option. James always instinctively knew the best options and he was right; it was the closest boozer for two men who had already had a few and weren't looking to drive, walk, waste time with taxis or stay out all night.

Inside the pub, Barry spied Angharad sitting alone at a table. 'Not like you to come here solo.'

'Greg was here until a minute ago. There were a few things we needed to sort out but he started whining and doing my head in so I told him to shove off.' Angharad played with a beer mat. She'd already ripped half of it into confetti.

'Greg's the hubby,' said Barry to James, who still hadn't been introduced.

'Ex hubby to be,' replied Angharad, emphatically.

'Nice to meet you anyway, I'm James.'

'Likewise. I'm Angharad.'

Within half an hour, Barry felt like a gooseberry as his two friends hit it off like bangers and mash. Angharad told James all about her lifelong friendship with Barry, through her brother Romeo, and her frustrations of marrying and trying to maintain a relationship with a man with a roving eye. James responded with details aplenty about his very different upbringing, his experiences of boarding schools and his burgeoning career as a LesCargo Logistics high-flyer.

'It's fine for now but it's not my forever job,' said James.

'So what is?'

'Not sure, probably something to do with property development – I've dabbled a bit in the past. Still got a bit of a portfolio.'

'I'd love to do something like that,' cooed Angharad.

'Make it happen then,' said James with the authority and ignorance of a man who completely believed all doors opened the same way for all people.

'Easier said than done,' said Angharad, picking up a handful of confetti, having now destroyed the whole beer mat.

'Why?'

'Because I'm a soon-to-be-divorced woman with a soon-to-be-ex who won't take no for an answer, living in a place offering fewer career opportunities than the moon. On top of that, I'm not getting any younger and I don't have any money.'

James looked sympathetic. 'I'm happy to provide you with some pointers and a few connections to get you started.'

'Really?'

'Of course. Any friend of Barry's is a friend of mine.'

Barry recognised the look in Angharad's eye because he'd seen it before, that night he went round to hers for Greek stifado and she'd tried to lure him into her bed.

As for James, Barry wasn't sure if he really understood what he was getting himself into or not. He still didn't understand how Anghofiedig and its people ticked.

Barry got up and brushed the confetti into a neat pile. 'I'm gonna head off home, wanna be there for when Diana finishes her shift.'

'No problem, go steady, big man. And thanks for all your support today – you were awesome in the clubhouse,' said James.

'If not on the pitch,' said Barry.

'You don't have to rush off do you, James? No lady waiting at home for you?' Angharad fluttered her false eyelashes.

'No, I live alone.'

'Wonderful. Then stay and have another drink with me and let me pick your brains some more,' gushed Angharad.

James nodded. 'Sure but it's my shout. What would you like?'

In her head, Angharad answered the question with 'I'd like

you, handsome, sitting on my lap and whispering sweet nothings in my ear all night long.'

'Rum and Coke, please, if that's not too much trouble?' she said, tilting her head to one side and holding James's gaze longer than he expected, before flicking her hair back with a casual stroke of a right hand that ran through and rested to a gentle stop on the soft fleshy nape of her neck.

TEN

SLAYING DINOSAURS WITH A FORK

Uncle Derek was sitting in his favourite battered armchair, wearing Aunty Ruth's gigantic headphones that masked his large cauliflower ears, which had turned purple with age and ailing capillaries. John Fogarty's Creedence Clearwater Revival pumped some hope, energy and loud guitars into his otherwise sedate day.

'How's he been?' enquired Barry.

'Oh today's a good day,' said Ruth.

'No tantrums?'

'Nope, quite chilled. Even when I told him about your thrashing yesterday.' Ruth waved Barry and Diana through to the lounge whilst she carried on sorting and folding laundry. They found Derek rocking back and forth as he played air drums on 'Fortunate Son'.

'Nice work, John Bonham. How are you diddling?' Barry sat on the sofa.

'It's Creedence not Led Zep. And I'm diddling a bloody darn sight better than you, I reckon,' said Derek, way too loudly, removing his headphones.

'You know the score then?'

'A hundred and summat to nil? Bloody disgraceful.'

Barry leant forward. 'We played most of the game with ten players and James got crocked early.'

'Still disgraceful.'

'I'm sorry.'

Derek laughed. 'Bloody rugby. It's killing my brain cells but I can't let it go. Don't make sense, eh?'

Diana had grown up watching rugby but her love of the game had been soured by having to stitch up and plaster wannabe local heroes every Saturday afternoon. 'Aren't you bitter?'

'No,' said Derek, not understanding the question.

Diana pushed on. 'But would you still play rugby if you knew what you know now and had your time all over again?'

'Yes, of course.'

'Surely you wouldn't?' Diana's tone was serious.

Barry didn't like where the conversation was going. 'Go easy, love.'

'It's all right, let her speak her mind,' said Derek, waving a big hand in Barry's direction.

Diana paused and leant against the arm of the sofa. 'I feel like a hypocrite cos I actually enjoy watching rugby but I don't want Eddie to play no more. And I want Barry to quit. I told him so again this morning.'

'I've been telling him to pack it in for years, love, but he don't listen to me,' said Derek.

'But the club needs me now more than ever.'

Derek snorted. 'Don't fall into that old trap.'

'See...' said Diana.

'You should knock it on the head, boy. For your health and your good lady.'

'Like you did?'

'We didn't know any better. We worked down the pits in the dark and we stayed in the dark when we came up.'

Barry felt under attack from both sides. 'I don't go looking for trouble on a rugby pitch. If it comes my way I usually step backwards, not forwards.'

'That's true enough,' said Derek, laughing.

'But you've had concussions over the years?' added Diana.

'Some...'

'How many?'

'Dunno.'

'Pack it in. Please,' pleaded Diana.

'She's right, it's time,' said Derek.

'I will.' Barry loosened his shirt collar.

'When?'

'Soon.'

'How soon?' Diana was not stopping now. Barry could hand her off, but he couldn't sidestep her and Derek teamed up together.

'Soon, okay. Don't nag,' said Barry, more forcefully.

'This season?'

'No, not that soon.'

'I won't nurse you. When you can't remember my name or the fact that you ever played rugby in the first place. When you don't know who you are or where you live,' yelled Diana.

Ruth had walked through to the lounge from the kitchen and was standing a couple of yards in front of the doorway. She paused to listen to what was being said but added nothing. Eventually, she straightened herself up and put on the fake smile she'd been wearing a lot since realising the true direction of travel for her and Derek in their autumn years. She'd always dreamt of filling these days with slow hand-held walks along beachside piers, and long leisurely drives into the countryside to mooch around curious antique dens adjoined by undiscovered tea shops run by large red-faced ladies who made and sold delicious home-made cakes and pastries with secret recipes. She had always told herself days like that would make up for all those lost weekends when Derek was off playing rugby and drinking with his pals, and she was on her own.

'I've put the kettle on. Cup of tea anyone?'

Eddie came across Harry's café whilst shuffling through his TikTok feed. Harry's aorta-sapping Supersaurus Breakfast was advertised as 'Wales's biggest brekkie for Wales's biggest beasts' with an Arnold Schwarzenegger doppelganger from Caldicot pictured saying 'Don't push me' and 'I'll be back'.

Harry's Café, fifty minutes away in Chepstow, was nothing to write home about. It was a greasy spoon stop-off for unfussy truckers before they drew breath to cross the Severn Bridge into Bristol.

Romeo, Barry and Eddie took their places at the largest and filthiest of booths where a pencil-thin man with a blotchy face, wearing a whitish apron heavily stained with either blood or ketchup, approached them with a sticky laminated menu.

'What's it to be, boyos?' said Harry himself.

'Three Supersaureses, please,' replied Eddie, excitedly.

'How old are you?' asked Harry.

'Fifteen.'

'Sorry, son, you gotta be eighteen to tackle the Supersaurus.' Harry wiped ketchup from the table on his apron.

'Pants,' said Eddie, thumping the table.

'What can he have?' enquired Barry.

'The Brontosaurus – it's two down from a Supersaurus. One down from the T-rex.'

'Okay, we'll have two Supersaureses and one Brontosaurus.'

'Make mine a Brontosaurus as well,' piped up Romeo.

The Brontosauruses came out first on two huge white trays, carried separately by a pair of young female assistants who looked like twins. The girls strained all of their sinews to deliver the food to the table, dropping them down like they were fifteen-kilogram dumbbells.

'Thunder lizard?' said assistant one.

'Nah, I ordered the Brontosaurus,' said Eddie.

'It's the same thing,' said assistant two.

Eddie's eyes enlarged as they filled with blood and trepidation.

Before him was a mountainous pile of fatty foods, enough to keep his mum going for a month. Harry sidled up to the side of the booth to give the duo the instructive lowdown.

'Okay, boyos, what we have here is a true American classic of a breakfast, The Brontosaurus, AKA The Thunder Lizard, a dinosaur with its paws firmly fixed Stateside, hence the French fries with mayonnaise, the four-stack of prime Texan beefburger, plus streaky bacon, cheese, beans, sausages, plum toms, three eggs and for a nice Yankee Doodle Dandy twist, three pancakes and four side waffles with their own pot of golden syrup. You'll see it's all draped over a plate with a shorter neck and a longer tail, which is a feature of the mighty Brontosaurus. It weighs in at a mighty six and a half thousand calories so I suggest you skip the fish and chip drive-thru on your way home. It's going to cost you fifteen quid a pop unless you finish every scrap inside an hour – then you'll get it for free with a special "I slayed Harry's dinosaur" T-shirt. Happy chomping, Bronty sisters.'

Typically, Eddie jumped in like the proverbial twenty-tonne Jurassic reptile at a swamp party, whilst Romeo took the time to roll up his sleeves, don an apron and work around the periphery of the plate looking out for things that he wasn't too keen to put in his mouth.

'Wish I'd gone for the T-rex now, this ain't a breakfast, it's a gooey, sugary pick and mix,' he whined.

The two put their heads down and got stuck into their challenges, but it wasn't long before both were feeling the heat from the monsters in front of them. They came up for air when one of the female assistants threw the kitchen door open to allow a couple of broad men, both with moustaches, to burst through. They carried a sleeping creature from another world's lagoon on an imitation silver platter. Harry beckoned Barry with a crooked finger to move over to the next booth.

'Ladies and gentlemen, I salute one big, butch, brave Welshman and one badass mother that roamed the Colorado plains in days of yore looking for innocents. Five storeys high and the weight of seven elephants, the Supersaurus was born to lend his name to a predator such as this. You should know, no one has ever tamed the Supersaurus. Many have tried to defeat her, travelling from far and wide, but this is a Diplodocus that won't be swallowed whole without a fight.

'If you silence the Supersaurus you'll leave here with the contents of your wallet intact, plus a T-shirt saying "I slayed Harry's dinosaur" and your face fossilised for possible eternity in a framed photo above the booth where you now sit. If you lose, however, there's every chance you'll exit this joint with electrodes stuck to your bare chest, carried aloft by head-shaking paramedics. You'll be 19.99 lighter in the pocket too. God speed. Have courage, proud caveman. *Pob lwc.* You have one hour to kill the beast, starting from now.'

All three men stared in awe at the spectacle laid before Barry.

'Dude, that's death on a plate,' said Eddie.

'Have you got your will in order?' quipped Romeo.

The platter groaned with some fifteen thousand calories of fried and processed foods, enough junk to clog the digestive system of a living Supersaurus. A dozen jumbo sausages, ten fried eggs, a couple of large tins of plum tomatoes, three large tins of baked beans, a packet of bacon, eight hash browns, a hill of mushrooms, a dozen slices of black pudding, a handful of Spam fritters, half a loaf of buttered toast, and a large pot of strong tea to wash it all down with.

Romeo quit his Brontosaurus and pushed it aside just fifteen minutes in, saying he felt like he was going down with a cold and wasn't in the mood for food.

Eddie fared better, but barely got halfway through his plate and never even touched the syrupy waffles. He pulled up the front of his hoodie and patted his aching bare belly. 'Gonna need the toilet soon.'

All eyes turned to Barry, who was sweating heavily but seemed to have the bit between his teeth and a steely glint in his eye. Other diners in the café could see this and left their booths to gather around him as he stuffed his chubby face at a lightning pace. The café proprietor – dubbed 'Dirty Harry' by Romeo – stood over him with a ticking stopwatch in his right hand.

'It's a fair effort, son, but I still don't think you're going to make it,' said Harry.

'Us Whites don't quit,' said Barry, slurping brown tea from a chipped mug as a couple of befuddled onlookers raised eyebrows and tried to make sense of his words, hoping above all hopes that his proud boast did not carry racist connotations.

Most of what was on Barry's plate slid down easily but what tested him was the starchier stuff, the hash browns and the toast. The runny eggs too. His body groaned at what it was being asked to do. His stomach, which had been conditioned and stretched over the years, was more like a cement mixer than a balloon and could handle fifteen to twenty pounds of food being carelessly thrown into it. His gag, burp and vomit muscles had been to school too, and knew how to relax their reflexes in the face of adversity. Barry couldn't actually remember what it felt like to feel full. His vagus nerve – the one that usually sends those high priority WhatsApp messages to the brain to tell you to stop eating – had been shorted and overridden. His body instinctively knew how to jump and twitch and move to prevent food backing up in the oesophagus. Gravity mattered. However, he was venturing into the unknown in terms of what he was doing to his 'don't mess with me' organs such as the pancreas. Nurse Diana Fenwick would have despaired at what he was doing to his blood glucose and insulin levels. Nurse Diana Fenwick would have despaired at what he was doing, full stop.

As he frantically chewed the last slice of toast more than twenty times before forcing it down his cavernous throat with the help of a tired squat and the dregs of his builder's tea, all around him whooped and hollered and cheered and clapped. Eddie shouted the word 'awesome' over and over and had tears in his eyes. He'd been filming it all and said it would send Barry global.

'Bearded Meats can shove over, there's a new king in town,' he said from behind his recording camera.

Barry stuck out his tongue to prove to his new-found fans that his mouth and airways were clear. Harry emerged with a camera of his own for celebratory photos and handed Barry his XXXL 'I slayed Harry's dinosaur' T-shirt. All of his life Barry had dreamt of receiving hero adulation such as this, but in his dreams he was usually scoring the winning try to earn Anghofiedig Rugby Club an important league title or a famous cup success.

He looked around at the grim faces and his grim surroundings and felt nothing but shame. Not only were there people starving in the world, there were people going hungry in

Chepstow. How would all this look to them? What about the friends he had made in Rwanda and Europe? The families who had shared so much of the so little they had with him?

He eyed the wasted food on the plates that had been so quickly discarded by Romeo and Eddie. He wanted to run. From this place and his own embarrassment.

He didn't want to be famous for being a fat git. He didn't want to be Wales's most famous greedy bastard. He didn't want people to think that he didn't care about no one or nothing. Not even himself.

When they got outside the café, Barry discreetly tossed his T-shirt into an open wheelie bin.

'Can you walk, Uncle Barry?' said Eddie, putting his arm around his shoulders.

'Want me to bring the car round?' asked Romeo.

'That was amazing! You are amazing!' said Eddie.

'Yeah, pretty impressive, champ,' said Romeo.

Barry pushed Eddie's arm away. 'Eddie, please don't tell your mum what I just did.'

'Why not? She'll be mega proud of you.'

'No she won't. Just promise me.'

Eddie huffed. 'Fine...'

'And will you delete that video off your phone? I don't want you to show it to anyone or post it anywhere.'

'Really?'

'Yes, really.'

'But you've just done something incredible.'

'No, I haven't.'

Eddie threw his arms up to the heavens. 'The world's got a right to know what you did in there.'

'Please, Eddie. Will you delete it?'

'My friend Bertie Rostron's dad has got over five thousand followers on Facebook and all he ever does is post pictures of every pint he drinks and every fry-up he eats, which is like, every day, with the same words... "oh go on then".'

'Eddie, just bloody delete it will yer?' snapped Barry.

Eddie sighed in frustration, the way only teenagers can, and slammed his fingers onto his keypad.

'Binned,' he said, sulkily.

'Thank you,' said Barry, softly.

Within seconds, the theme tune from the James Bond films began to play and the trio froze and looked at each other.

'Hullo?' said Eddie, answering his phone.

Romeo and Barry soon worked out who the caller was from Eddie's guarded responses.

'I'm in Chepstow with Uncle Barry and Romeo ... No, Mum, I'm fine, I'm not in any trouble ... He's fine too ... Yes, honestly. Promise ... We're just exploring a bit ... The castle, it's wicked ... No, I'm not lying to you ... We're coming home now ... Uncle Barry's really looking after me like a proper grown-up ... Oh, have you? Thing is I've arranged to meet Che tonight ... Er, not sure ... I'm pretty sure he'll be fine with that ... I know, but ... Yes, Mum ... Okay, Mum ... Sorry, Mum ... See you later, Mum ... Love you too, Mum.'

Eddie's eyes filled with terror.

'What did she say?' said Barry.

'She wanted to know where we are, what we're doing and when we'll be home.'

Romeo rubbed his chin. 'We've just got to lie like we're Harry off *The Traitors*.'

'I can do that. I told Mum we've been sightseeing around the castle,' said Eddie.

'We heard. Did she believe you?' asked Romeo.

'Don't think so.'

'Anything I should know?' said Barry.

Eddie nodded. 'Yeah, I'm not coming home, can you drop me at Che's house?'

'Why you suddenly so keen to see Che?'

'Cos Mum says she's cooking a roast beef dinner and I can't face it.'

'Bugger,' said Barry, folding his arms.

'What's your plan?' said Romeo to Barry.

'Can't let her down if she's cooking a roast special, can I?' said Barry, shrugging.

ELEVEN
THE GOOD, BAD AND VERY UGLY

Friday night was skittles night down at The Dragon. Clever Trevor Peacock, captain of the predictably named Fiery Dragons, took the game seriously and expected the rest of his squad to do the same.

Like the rugby club, The Dragons were often a player or two short. However, recruiting people to roll a few balls down a wooden lane was much easier than asking them to run around and get their head kicked in on a rugby pitch. Age was no barrier for one thing. All Clever Trevor and his trusty lieutenant, Swifty Taylor, had to do to gain new signings was twist someone's arm with the promise of a free pint or two plus a share of the post-match grub, which usually consisted of bread, cheese, cold black pudding, chips and as much wife repellant (raw onions in vinegar) as you could eat.

Barry roped Eddie into playing when they were desperate because he was there anyway as the 'sticker up'. It was his job to stand the pins up every time they got knocked down and slide the balls back down the chute. For an hour's hard graft, he got £13.50 and as much Pepsi Max as he could neck (as long as he didn't need to go to the loo too often during a game). James would help the team out occasionally, though he was reluctant to commit because beer, even when free, wife repellant and the game of skittles itself held no charms for him. He would cite various excuses for not being able to make it, which Pricer translated to mean 'the boy's got a life, unlike us sad bastards'. Uncle Derek used to play, until Aunty Ruth switched their cinema night to Fridays. McQueen just stopped turning up without explanation. As for Reverend Hill, Clever Trevor would wait until the last possible moment to write his team up on the chalkboard just in case the AWOL clergyman made a dramatic reappearance.

'He might, you know... the Lord works in mysterious ways. And he's our Gareth Edwards, our best player, our little talisman – Hill I mean, not God – so if he rocks up, he's in. He's a thief and a lowdown swindler – Hill I mean, not God – but I don't care about any of that on a skittles night – he's tidy on a Friday and if he helps us crush The Mighty Bush then all's fine and dandy with me.'

Greg, who was working his first shift in the pub, was signed on just minutes before the match, having been told by Barry that playing skittles was part of his job description. Romeo took exception to this on two counts: firstly, he didn't think it fair that Greg should effectively be a professional player who got paid to play; and secondly, he couldn't stand being around Greg on account of how he had serially mistreated his sister.

Clever Trevor wore a leather waistcoat, tracksuit bottoms and an open white shirt that flashed grey and ginger wisps of curly hair. He jangled when he moved, due to the big bunch of keys he kept tied to the outside of his belt, as if he had walked in straight from a shift at Shawshank. He fancied himself as the Pepe Guardiola of the skittles world; the Warren Gatland of the pub backroom alley. He would sometimes turn up wearing cowboy boots but change into black and white Adidas pumps before the game got underway. He also liked to carb up before a match. Two cereal bars and a packet of scampi fries from the bar would ensure there was plenty of oomph behind his right arm when it was his turn to bowl.

Having announced his team to the world on the pub chalkboard, Clever Trevor rallied his troops together for their customary pre-match team talk. It was a rude awakening for new boy Greg, who didn't have a clue what was going on. He had expected to spend his first shift learning how to work the till, acquainting himself with colleagues and customers (including a few ladies), taking food orders and changing barrels down in the cellar. Listening to Clever Trevor thump tables and bang on about the importance of 'percentage shots' and 'hard wood' left him dazed and confused.

'Greg, I'm putting you into bat in the middle order so there's no pressure. Have you ever skittled before?' said Clever Trevor.

'Nope. More of a skater,' said Greg.

Clever Trevor jangled his key belt. 'Do you understand what you've got to do?'

'Chuck three balls down and knock the planks over.'

'They're called pins, Greg. Pins. Got that?' Clever Trevor was beginning to think he'd made a tactical selection error.

'Got it,' said Greg.

Singing was a big part of Clever Trevor's motivational tactics. He had a personalised song, shout or jingle for every player and every situation. When someone floored eight pins to leave only one standing, Clever Trevor would begin a frenzied demonic chant of 'nine, nine, nine, nine, nine' – as if he was at some German rally in the 1930s – encouraging all and sundry to join in, followed by handclapping and back slapping for a hit, or a shake of his head and despondent tuts for a miss. He lived every high and low. He masked no disappointment in others.

He would scream instructions at comrades in random streams of consciousness.

'What do we want? Six!' he cried, with a refraining chorus of 'But seven would be nice'.

The more worked up he got, the more his keys jangled.

When Greg took to the alley and recorded five consecutive ducks in a row – a feat that had never been done before in the history of the skittles league – the whole of Anghofiedig seemingly fell silent. Except for Greg, who simply laughed it all off and refused to show the slightest bit of remorse or contrition. Greg bowled like a wild man, flinging the balls down at terrific speed but with no accuracy whatsoever. Most of his deliveries failed to stay in the alley. He struck three different walls and hit Eddie the sticker-up twice. The rest bounced halfway down the alley and flew right over the top of all of the pins.

Clever Trevor's face grew redder and redder as he implored his new signing to slow down and look where he was aiming.

Barry and the rest of the Fiery Dragons couldn't watch. They stared at their shoes and averted their eyes from all possible gazes. They knew a perfect storm was brewing in which Clever Trevor's simmering rage would hurtle out of control when it met Greg's laissez faire 'I couldn't give a shit, this is a stupid game anyway' attitude head on. The impending collision would be made ten times worse by the smirks, quips, giggles and piss-takes of the cocky Mighty Bush players, who couldn't resist an easy opportunity to wind Captain Peacock up.

'Oi, Trevor, open the fire escape, will you – your star bowler is on again.'

'Quack, quack, oops! Who knew Donald Duck was a Dragon!'

'You must have got up at the quack of dawn to sign this bloke, Peacock.'

'Hey, lads, leave old Clever alone – no more wise quacks.'

'This guy getting all the zeros is actually called Cinderella – cos his coach over there is a right pumpkin.'

'Nah, mate, he's called homeless – cos he spends half his life in the gutters.'

'It's so quiet in here you could hear a pin drop. Oh sorry, Trevor!'

Clever Trevor seethed and bristled until he could hold it in no more. When Greg sent his final ball hurtling towards a skylight – and the Mighty Bush captain made one joke too many about it being a night of pane – Trev picked up a flimsy wooden chair that had held some of his paperwork and cracked it right over the head of the Bush skipper, who fell to the floor clutching his skull as the chair snapped into multiple pieces around him.

For a split second nothing happened. Time stood still and people froze, unsure what to do next. The Bush skipper, who was called Monty, slowly got to his feet and brushed away a small drop of blood from a cut above his left eye. He posed like Clint Eastwood's Blondie character, with hands on his imaginary holster, eyeing Eli Wallach's Tuco in *The Good, The Bad and The Ugly*. Monty wandered over to Eddie and without any words, demanded a pin. Without words, Eddie obliged. Monty sauntered back towards Clever Trevor, who had not moved an inch and stood directly in front of him like they were gunslingers. In a single movement, Monty lifted the pin up and crashed it down on Clever Trevor's head.

What followed next was a chaotic scene right out of the Wild West as normally mild-mannered men brawled, fought and wrestled with other normally mild-mannered men who they did not know and had no beef with. More chairs crashed over heads and tables got flipped or buckled under the weight of falling torsos. Pint glasses were smashed and curtains ripped off their hooks and used to lasso victims. A stairway banister collapsed like a pack of Swan Vesta matches Blu-Tacked together under the weight of Romeo's flying body. Pools of beer collected in the hollows of ripped up floorboards. Old men punched young men and vice versa. Some bit, some slapped, some shouted, some swore. Some, too breathless to land blows, wheezed and threatened pretend fisticuffs with bits of furniture as make-do shields, like pumped-up terrier dogs barking at passers-by behind the safety of their front gates.

Drinkers from the main bar heard the commotion and poked their heads around the door, quickly backtracking from the carnage once they saw what was going on.

Barry lay in the pit at the back of the skittle alley under a tarpaulin, holding on to Eddie for dear life – until the boy broke free of his grasp to join in the fun and smack Pricer, one of his own teammates, flush in the face with a right-hook that had been intended for a fifty-something Bush player called Perry Armstrong. Barry knew Perry from his time at LesCargo Logistics and was surprised to see him join in the fighting. Perry had always hated conflict, especially when it came to arranging the unplanned movement of recyclable cardboard boxes from one obscure depot to another.

It wasn't long before both teams had run out of steam and everything fizzled to a limping standstill. No one had chance to gather their breath because Sergeant Sargent and his merry boys in blue burst in waving batons and holding aloft Tasers and cans of CS spray. Paramedics followed in after them as some men were taken away in handcuffs – Clever Trevor and Romeo amongst them – whilst others headed for Diana's minor injuries unit to have cuts stitched and strains bandaged. A lucky few blended back into the night or the main bar as if nothing had happened. No one was seriously hurt but Eddie would soon be saying 'hi' to his mum, having dislocated the pinky on his right hand whilst thumping Pricer.

When all was quiet, Barry came out from playing dead beneath his tarpaulin to survey the true impact of the tsunami.

The room was destroyed and would cost a fortune to fix. Barry sat on the metal box that usually housed the skittle balls and wondered what he ought to do first: assess the true scale of the damage and start the clean-up, go to the hospital to smooth things over with Diana and Eddie, or just go home to bed.

His priority was decided by a mini commotion that had spilled over in the main bar.

Barry found Greg at its epicentre, gesticulating and shouting at a corner table where James and Angharad had been having a quiet drink together.

'We're still married, how could you?' said Greg.

'Not for much longer,' yelled Angharad.

'It's not what you think, I was just giving Angharad some business advice,' said James, ever the peacemaker.

'I'll give you some bloody business advice, mate, and it starts with mind your own,' said Greg, pulling his right arm back to deliver a blow he hoped would make a dent in James's devilish good looks.

Barry grabbed the arm before it had a chance to be propelled forward towards its intended target. He swung Greg, who was already off balance, off his feet and watched him hit the floor as if he was Jackie Chan. Greg lay on his back groaning.

'You're sacked,' said Barry, surprised at what he'd just done, before summoning over a young constable who had been taking statements about the brawl. The PC was so wide-eyed and innocent that he would surely have snuggled up to Barry under the tarpaulin had he been here thirty minutes ago.

'This is your ringleader, he's the one who started all the trouble next door,' said Barry to the constable.

'You little liar,' yelled Greg.

As the young man escorted him away, Greg continued to protest his innocence – shoving the young PC in the chest. Two older, more streetwise coppers saw what was going on and rushed to the aid of the young recruit. They lifted Greg clean off his feet and carried him out of the door like a second-hand carpet to one of their waiting vans, which was now choc-a-bloc with remorseful white-haired skittlers – their sanities restored by the cold night, the stark yellow lights inside the vans and the prospect of having to explain their out-of-character actions to unsympathetic partners and offspring. However, Greg hadn't learnt his lesson and continued to struggle. He slipped the grasp of the two policemen holding him, pushing one into the path of the other. Both policemen tumbled backwards into their own van, so Greg quickly slammed the door shut, with the policemen on the inside, and ran for the hills.

'Quite an evening,' said James, inside the pub, still shocked by what he had witnessed, even though he had grown up with fagging and initiation ceremonies involving dead pig heads.

Angharad giggled. 'Who won tonight?'

'Not your hubby,' said Barry, oblivious of the fact that he had now assaulted two more policemen and turned himself into a desperate fugitive on the run.

'Skittles, eh? Who'd have thought it?' said James.

'Only in Anghofiedig,' said Angharad, still laughing to herself.

Beneath the main bar, in the dank depths of the unused rear part of the cellar – away from the area where the barrels were housed and the fat, dozy, drunken rodents played kiss chase of a night – an unkempt bearded man stood on a rickety chair with his ear to the ceiling, trying to listen in on the conversations taking place above his head. He recognised all of the voices. He knew all of the people. He strained to hear any snippet of news or gossip that might help him evade the long arm of the law, for another night at least.

The fight had thrown him off kilter. It made no sense to him; he had no idea what it was all about. For all he knew, the Russian Army could have just invaded South Wales to commence the start of World War Three. He was scared. He needed to make a new plan but was fresh out of ideas and options. He was tired of surviving on crisps and cans of Fanta and doing his business in an old toilet that didn't flush properly unless he poured out-of-date cider down the pan. He hadn't washed for days and stunk so badly that even the rats gave him a wide berth. He missed being 'tidy on a Friday' and the star of Clever Trevor's skittles team. He missed standing up in church on a Sunday and seeing his parishioners turn to him for leadership and spiritual guidance.

Where was his God now?

Reverend Hill climbed down off the chair and sat on the floor against a wet wall.

'Oh Lord, show me a way out of all of this.'

TWELVE
NOT EVERY TREVOR IS CLEVER

It took Sergeant Sargent and his team a couple of days to process all of the pub arrests. The majority got sent home with stern warnings and police cautions, but Monty and Clever Trevor were distraught to discover they faced ABH charges on each other. Greg was in the hottest water, his whereabouts still unknown and multiple warrants out for his arrest.

Angharad knew from personal experience the kind of chaos her husband was capable of wreaking – but even she marvelled at the fact that he had managed to start a job and get sacked from it on the same night he also assaulted three police officers and received a lifelong ban from a sport he was playing for the first time, having simultaneously set an all-time league record for being its worst ever player.

The demise of The Dragon's skittles team was just another sign that everything was falling apart in Anghofiedig. The pub business was collapsing, just like the rugby club. Barry also felt like things were falling apart in his own life and wished he had never won a million pounds. It had brought nothing but bad luck and misery to all it had touched. The pub, the church and the rugby club had previously been reliable pillars that held his life together. Ma was gone and Uncle Derek was fading. His relationship with Diana felt like it was at a crossroads. Diana was far from impressed to see her son pitch up unannounced at her A&E unit unsupervised when Barry was supposed to be looking after him. When she learnt that Eddie had damaged his hand in a pub brawl, she was fuming.

'It's not Uncle Barry's fault, Mum, honestly,' insisted Eddie.

'Don't defend him.'

'I got carried away by everything going on around me. It was exciting.'

'I tried to stop him,' said Barry.

'Not hard enough.' Diana caught her own words as if someone else was saying them and inwardly chastised herself for being so grumpy lately.

'It was crazy. We couldn't avoid the trouble cos it was in our faces,' said Barry.

'That's right,' said Eddie. 'Uncle Barry didn't actually lamp anyone until much later. He played dead under a blanket thingy and tried to make me do the same.'

'Will you stop sticking up for him?' said Diana.

'But none of it was his fault.'

'It never is.'

'That's true.'

'Tis,' said Barry, lamely.

Diana ignored Barry and faced Eddie. 'I'll tell you what's true. Before we moved in with Barry you didn't get into any trouble at all, either in school or out of it. Now, it's just one thing after another – and every single time, just look who happens to be with you.'

'That's coincidence.'

'Bullshit.'

'Don't swear, Mum. I don't like it when you swear.'

'Tough titties,' said Diana, really hating herself now but unable to stop the demon force within from bursting out.

'I tried to look out for the lad,' said Barry.

'So why didn't you come to A&E with him? He's only fifteen.'

'That was a mistake. I'm sorry.' Barry bowed his head.

'You're always sorry afterwards.' Diana was in no mood to let him off the hook easily.

'I can't do anything right, can I?' whined Barry, still searching for pity.

'Seems not.'

'Mum, please...' said Eddie.

'Eddie, go to your room. This is grown-up stuff.'

'No, I won't – cos you're not being fair.'

Barry tapped the boy's arm. 'Don't raise your voice to your mum, Ed.'

'Sorry, Uncle Barry.'

'He's not Ed, he's Eddie – and he's not your bloody uncle, I've told you that a hundred times. He's just Barry, got it?' screamed Diana.

'Okay,' said Eddie, scared because he'd never seen his mum like this before.

Diana turned to face Barry. 'And he's my son, not yours. I'll tell him when he's got to lower his voice, not you. Is that clear?'

'Crystal.' Barry walked away.

The pub opened as usual on Monday morning but Barry wasn't behind the bar serving session ale to faithful but annoying alcoholics. Instead, he was in the back room, sweeping up glass and loading the skip that sat out the front. Most of the chairs and tables that got smashed had been cheap and cheerful. None of it was worth much on its own, but collectively it all added up to a sizeable total. More expensive to fix would be the two large smashed windows. The room's infamous sticky carpet was now a darn site stickier but it would live to fight another day (unlike the skittles team) once they'd scrubbed out the worst of the blood and beer stains.

Barry had asked Angharad to go through the pub's insurance documents, which he didn't understand. He sighed at the amount of paperwork he needed to fill in just to get a few hundred quid back. His mood – which was funereal to start with following his row with Diana – suddenly got a whole lot blacker. When he cut his hand on the jagged edge of a broken bottle, he swore out loud and threw the bottle in frustration towards the door, just as Clever Trevor was making a sheepish entrance.

'Guess I deserve that,' said Trevor.

'Sorry, it wasn't aimed at you. It's just...'

'It's all right, I can see. Go and sort that hand out.'

Trevor had come to apologise to Barry in person and lend his services to the clean-up operation. He also offered to pay something towards the repairs, though no exact sum was discussed or agreed. He was ashamed and embarrassed by the way he had behaved, smashing a chair over Monty's head to start the ugly mass brawl. He hadn't fought anyone since he was twelve and had never been in trouble with the police. Worse than the public and private humiliation he was now facing was the realisation he'd no longer have his beloved skittles in his life.

'I live for my Friday nights, what am I going to do now?'

Barry's head was swimming with problems of his own. 'Stay in with the missus and watch romcoms?'

'She's not talking to me cos of the ABH. I don't even know what ABH means.'

'Actual bodily harm.'

'Oh. Why do they call it actual?' said Trevor.

'Cos it happened.'

'As opposed to what?'

'Not happening, I suppose.' Barry picked up a piece of wood and realised it was half a skittle pin. 'Thought you were supposed to be clever, Trevor?'

'Nah. Not every Trevor is clever, just like not every Dan is the man. My old mum, God rest her soul, used to say that in my case people were being ironic – but I never knew what she meant by that and I still don't.'

Barry smiled. 'She meant people were saying the opposite of what is really true, in an attempt to get a laugh.'

'I see.'

'For what it's worth, I think you're quite clever, Trevor,' said Barry.

'Is that ironic too?' asked Trevor.

Barry handed Trevor his half a skittle. 'No, that's sympathetic.'

When Trevor left, Barry found himself completely alone in the pub. He couldn't be bothered to do any more clean-up work so sat with a pint of lager, contemplating the meaning of his life.

His silence was broken by the sound of something falling beneath his feet. Maybe a box from a shelf in the cellar below? Bloody rats.

Barry cautiously got up and walked towards the noise. He tiptoed through the cellar but could see no evidence of vermin. The room was full of old junk, the ghosts and relics of the pub's past, which were far from haunting. There were beer towels, old kegs and leftover promo merchandise stained a smoky yellow, paying homage to yesteryear's pub songstresses: Double

Diamond, Watney's Red Barrel, Younger's Tartan and Worthington E. The balladeers to a thousand hangovers, not to mention all those life-changing pregnancies and vicious arguments, outscored, thankfully, by the countless glows of drunken warmth that had made people forget their woes and sorry miserable lives, for a few hours at least.

Barry sensed he wasn't alone.

The dank, dark cellar had a set of rickety stairs with a broken banister leading down to two neglected rooms. The first was stuffed floor to ceiling with crates, barrels and boxes. The air was cold and musty, thick with the smell of drains and old beer. Gas cylinders, casks, random bits of humming machinery and an old fridge freezer – still working – blocked pathways and vents. On top of the fridge freezer lay a random bald and naked female mannequin.

Barry noticed a concealed trapdoor in the floor, close to where the original pub exit would have been more than a century ago. He had no idea the trapdoor existed. He paused and leant down, listening for signs of life.

Slowly, he pulled on the lever, which creaked like an old footballer's knee cartilage moving up a flight of stairs.

A shaft of light broke into the hatch but Barry couldn't see a thing. He opened the door wider. An old sack twitched. Ever so slightly, but it was still a twitch. Barry did nothing. The sack did the same. After half a minute or so, Barry bent down and ripped the sack away in one swift motion. Barry gasped.

'Hello, Barry boy, fancy bumping into you down here,' said a barely recognisable Reverend Hill. He was lying on his side like a fetus, speaking through the open slats of a twisted plastic beer crate that he had perched upon his head in a pathetic attempt to conceal himself from both prying eyes and daylight.

THIRTEEN
BEWARE SUE, AND OTHER RUNAWAYS

After taking his first shower in months and shaving off enough hair to make Delores a warm winter fur coat, Reverend Hill put on a clean bright red season 2015/16 Anghofiedig rugby club tracksuit of Barry's, which was worn at the crotch and at least two sizes too big. He combed his hair, brushed his teeth, sprayed himself with cheap deodorant and devoured two reheated lasagnes while Barry cleaned the filthy bathtub. Barry then went to the pub kitchen and returned with a couple of mugs of extra sweet hot chocolate. He handed the largest one to the reverend.

'There are real life bears in the woods, did you know that?' whispered Reverend Hill.

'I heard.'

'A big brown 'un came right for me.'

'Probably just lost and lonely and wanted to tango.'

They skirted around the houses with long pauses and snippets of chit-chat about the kind of creatures who inhabited the Forest and what it was really like to camp out in the wild. It was as if the reverend was catching up with an old friend after a weekend excursion. Barry said nothing and went along with it,

115

until his patience finally ran out and he cut through the baloney in the simplest, kindest way he could think of.

'Vicar, what the bloody hell have you done with my hundred grand and why were you hiding in my cellar?'

'It's a long story,' said Reverend Hill, startled by Barry's directness.

'I got time.'

Reverend Hill pursed his lips and sipped his hot chocolate. 'Are people angry with me?'

'I'd say so.'

'Who exactly?' Reverend Hill's tone was serious but he looked ridiculous, sporting a newly acquired chocolate froth moustache.

'Pretty much everyone.'

'Who's everyone?'

'Well, the OAP Teddy Boys are screaming blue suede murder for a start.'

Reverend Hill held his nose like he was about to dive under water. 'I strayed from the path.'

'You strayed a lot further than that, to be honest, considering where I found you.' Barry sighed in exasperation. 'Look, there are people who want to see you jailed with the keys thrown away. Or worse, Llewellyn Davies wants you crucified and your head put on the spikes of the church gates as a warning to other renegade clergymen. There ain't much sympathy for lying, swindling preacher men around these parts. It's not just the Teddy Boys and brown bears after your hide, there are detectives with curly perms and purple shirts hunting you down too.'

'Crikey, was all that fuss in here last night because of me?'

'Nah, that was the skittles. It got rowdy. Clever Trevor Peacock had the hump cos we were losing and started an almighty war with Monty from The Mighty Bush.'

'Oh Lord,' said Reverend Hill, shaking his head and playing with the metal cross that dangled loosely around his neck.

'Proper riot it was. Greg thumped three coppers and went on the run same as you,' said Barry.

'I've been away from my flock for too long.'

'I'm inclined to agree with you.' Barry scratched his head and paused to consider his next line of attack. 'Anyhow, back to what really matters. Where's my hundred grand?'

'Is it technically yours, seeing as you gave it to me?' Reverend Hill soon realised he had walked straight into a minefield.

Barry raised his voice. 'Where is it?'

'Gone.'

'Gone where?'

'Welsh Mafioso.'

'Who?'

'Black Caracal.'

'Who?'

'Black Caracal. They're a biker gang. Bad dudes.' Reverend Hill looked around for anyone who might be listening.

'Why have they got my hundred grand?'

'Cos I gave it 'em.'

'What for?'

'To stop them from dropping my brother in the Bristol Channel with lead weights round his ankles.'

'They wouldn't do that,' said Barry, softening just a little.

'They would. I've seen 'em do it.' Reverend Hill again looked nervously around the room for eavesdroppers.

'When?'

'When I was one of them.'

'You were a Caracal?' Barry could hardly believe what he was hearing.

'I was.' Reverend Hill bowed his head.

'How long ago?'

'Yonks. Before I saw the light, obviously. Before I was born again.'

Barry put his empty mug down on the floor. 'You're a walking surprise party, you know that?'

'Don't wanna be.'

Reverend Hill explained that his brother, Morgan, had been caught skimming thousands of pounds off the top of various crime rackets he was responsible for – mostly related to money laundering. He said his brother was too soft and sensitive to be a gangster but didn't know how to get out. Reverend Hill had tried to help him, but his brother didn't have the guts to walk away from people who were not used to being rejected.

'God provided me with a way out of that lifestyle but Morgan wouldn't – or couldn't – hand over the reins of his life to the Lord,' said Reverend Hill.

'He's a good lad really. I mean, he didn't even steal the money for his own gain – he used every penny to pay our mother's nursing home debts, God rest her soul. He looked after her for years. The fees were outrageous, an insult to common decency if you ask me – far worse than anything the Caracals could threaten you with. Anyway, he got careless and stopped covering his tracks as well. Probably when Mum's health took a turn for the worse. He loved his mum, he was a proper mummy's boy, bit like you. But he took his eye off the ball.

'It was his so-called best mate, Perfect Dai, who worked out what he'd been doing and dobbed him in. Morgan came to me, scared, saying there were crazy people out to do him serious mischief. He didn't know who else to turn to. I'm his big brother. I'm supposed to look out for him but I was the one who led him astray in the first place. I got him into the gang when he was just a snotty-nosed kid who wanted to go to college to study accountancy. Me! I did that! I asked God to provide a way out for him. And then you came around, with a whole load of cash seemingly wired straight out of heaven's bank vault. It felt like an answer to a prayer. It felt like a gift from above. Do you understand? You do understand, don't you?'

'Where's Morgan now?' asked Barry.

'Conwy, little place called Llansannan. Free as a bird.'

'It's a proper pickle you've put me in.' Barry patted his belly, seemingly for inspiration.

'I know and I'm sorry. And if you call the law on me, I'll understand and accept my fate with good grace. I'll forgive you.'

'Big of you,' said Barry.

'Not at all,' said Reverend Hill, missing the sarcasm.

'I need time to think.'

'Yes, you do,' agreed Reverend Hill, sensing a reprieve.

Barry gave his belly a big final tap. 'Are you going to scarper again if I leave you here?'

'No, I'm done with running. I'm in your hands now. And God's.'

'Okay. You can go back down in the cellar for a bit. I'll bring you what you need. Make it cosy.'

'I kept my promise. I did something good with the money,' whined the reverend, like a simpering politician.

Barry had heard enough. 'Tell that to Derry Lee and his rocking rebels.'

'No, my friend, you tell it to Pearl when you're alone in contemplation, just the two of you. She'll understand. She always went out of her way for an underdog.'

'Yes, she did,' said Barry.

* * *

God was truly working in mysterious ways.

Having settled Reverend Hill back in the cellar with a load

of provisions, including a sleeping bag, fluffy pillows, a deckchair, a portable heater, biscuits, a flask of tea, newspapers – both local and national – and a Gideon's Bible, Barry got a visit out of the blue from a distraught Pricer. Jonah was a couple of footsteps behind him. Pricer's wife had grown tired of her 'pathetic loser husband' and kicked him out. In a stream of rambling, semi-literate texts, which Pricer attempted to show Barry, she cited diverse reasons for her love growing cold and her decision to terminate their stop–start relationship, most notably Pricer's recurring testicle infections – and the impact on their love life – plus his ridiculous mohican haircut, which he'd never asked for, but had decided to keep. She also complained about his annoying habit of playing Tammy Wynette records way too loud at all hours of the day and night, and his lack of regular income. A painter and decorator by trade, Pricer hadn't lifted a brush in weeks because his van was on the blink and he couldn't afford to get it fixed. No one within walking distance wanted his services.

Mrs Price also bemoaned her husband's substandard parenting skills, particularly the way he allowed the kids to 'treat him like shit'. She was hardly Mother of the Year material herself. Her texts gave notice of the fact that she'd reactivated and updated her Tinder profile and was already getting plenty of attention from young and eager Forest lads, as well as their dads. She was loving life out on the dating scene 'searching for real men who could get her juices pumping again'. With nowhere else to go, Pricer had bizarrely sought the help and advice of Jonah of all people, a confirmed bachelor who liked to go AWOL for months at a time from his work on Eric's farm. When he wasn't off wandering who knew where, Jonah lived in a ramshackle hut in the middle of the woods. With no mod cons and only two rooms, he was unable to put Pricer up. However, he knew there were rooms going spare at The Dragon.

Barry agreed to let Pricer stay until he sorted himself out and also offered him Greg's shifts behind the bar.

He told him to stay out of the cellar at all costs.

<hr>

Less than half a mile away, Derry Lee and Dot had hired the village hall for an hour to practise their jive for the upcoming 'Glad to be Grey' dance-off in Berry Hill.

Derry's tight trousers were playing havoc with his troublesome prostate so Dot sat alone in the hall, slapping her own thigh and twirling her skirt whilst Dion sang to warn other fellas about the antics of Runaway Sue and Derry Lee sorted himself out in the disabled loo.

Dot was not alone though.

Napoleon the bear, a runaway himself, heard familiar music in the distance and it drew him closer. He considered the jive the king of all the swing dances and loved to twist and flip to Runaway Sue.

Many people, particularly outside his French homeland, considered his keepers cruel for making him dance in public for money. How wrong they were. Napoleon danced because he was born to do it. No one forced him. He was a free spirit, probably placed in the wrong body. He sometimes wondered if he was Fred Astaire reincarnated.

Napoleon stood unseen at the window of the village hall for a couple of minutes, watching Derry Lee and Dot huff and puff their way through some laboured swivels and underarm turns in a truncated slowed down jive. Today, they just weren't feeling it. They needed more bounce, more lifting of knees, more rocking of their semi-arthritic hips. There weren't enough kicks. Not enough energy, darling.

Napoleon knew nothing of the perils of tight trousers but

couldn't help but think that Derry's timing was all out and he ought to vary his tempo a bit more. Surely everyone – even ageing humans – understood that the jive's steps are built around a simple six beat sequence? You start with left foot back, then chasse on the count of three, four, five, six. Four beats to the bar. Easy-peasy. Even a bear could do it.

Dot had been friends with Derry Lee most of her life and had even dated him through much of 1961, until she fell for the rugged earthy charms of her rugby-playing, hard-drinking, coal-mining late husband Lionel.

Derry Lee shared Dot's lifelong passion for old-time rock and roll and that kept them connected through the ensuing decades. Both had been raised in simple homes without televisions or cars and with parents who regarded Elvis Presley as the devil's chief whip. Growing up in Anghofiedig in the late 1950s and early 1960s there wasn't a lot of space or time for teenage angst. There weren't any phones, very few drugs and the highlight of the week was the Saturday night dance in this very village hall. Little had changed around the place over the years, except that only a handful came to dance now. The records she loved to shock her parents with no longer shocked anyone.

Dot reflected that she'd been dancing in this hall to the same songs for most of her life. Why did she still dance? For romance? Or nostalgia? Or was it because she didn't know anything different? What would she do when her limbs no longer allowed her to move?

She liked to pretend she was still young and pretty and sometimes the music had the power to take her right back to the times of her youth when it was thus so. But not today. Today, she felt old, ugly and pathetic. She regretted the fact she'd not progressed with the times. Anghofiedig always was – and still is – ten years or so behind the rest of the world, but she'd never departed from her love of Little Richard, Cliff and the Shadows, and of course Dion, even when Lionel and his pals were bigging up the beats of swinging London, with its Beatles and its Stones and its slim fitting suits with skinny ties.

Rock and roll, she vowed, was the one thing she'd always remain faithful to.

Napoleon, through big brown eyes watching at the window, could tell Dot longed for more excitement in her steps, some danger to make her feel like she was listening and moving to these records for the first time. So he breezed through the open door, took her by the hand and began to lead her around the wooden floor.

Of course, she was terrified at first. However, she soon relaxed and went with the music and her partner's knowing paws.

She even forgot she was dancing with a bear. Instead, she imagined she was in the strong powerful arms of Fred Astaire himself.

The dance couldn't last beyond the song's running time of two minutes thirty-eight seconds. Derry Lee spied Napoleon through a crack in the door after finally sorting out his problematic trousers. He called Sergeant Sargent who dragged the Parisian Prancers from their B&B and led them to the hall under the speed of a blue-lit escort.

Napoleon immediately recognised the friendly Gallic call of his favourite keeper – coincidentally, also called Dion – and went to him willingly, but only after his dance with Dot was over and he'd bowed a gentlemanly 'thank you' in response to Dot's dress-held curtsy.

Dot, Derry Lee and the sarge waved *adieu* from the pavement as Dion drove away slowly with his contented show bear sleeping in the back of the van.

Bound for Paris, they'd be on the ferry home within a couple of hours.

So too, their stowaway Greg. He'd hopped into the back of the open van when he feared his hideaway was about to be turned over. Having dossed down in the shed at the back of the village hall for the past couple of nights, he wet himself when he saw Sergeant Sargent walking around the courtyard that linked the two buildings.

Greg would wet himself twice more before the day was out. Firstly, when he emerged from beneath a pile of blankets in the back of the moving van to find a large brown bear staring right at him, from just a couple of feet away.

And secondly, when he saw the large welcome sign saying *Bienvenue à Cherbourg* – confirming he was lost in France, without a passport or even a single euro to his name, wondering how best to give himself up and why there was never a bloody gendarme around when you really needed one.

FOURTEEN
A DAY AT THE CRICKET WITH
JOHN JOHN

People liked him, trusted him, relied on him, confided in him. Older women especially. He wasn't considered a threat by anyone except for a few greedy supermarkets, determined to rule the world via all-conquering two-for-ones and BOGOFs. He didn't see life quite like other people. He lived to work; all day, every day, regardless of how he felt or what else was going on around him. He knew the value of just turning up. He also knew everything going on in the village, behind the closed curtains and the shut doors. His customers frequently mistook his simplicity for simpleness – sharing whatever was in their heads before their thoughts manifested into real-time deeds and actions. He'd stopped plenty of virtual destructive storms from causing actual carnage. He'd curtailed potential relationship pandemics. Rescued marriages. Prevented crimes. Saved lives, even. He was part shrink, part angel of hope, part agony aunt and part old-fashioned emporium owner, selling every bargain under the sun. His brand was simple and clean, like his white apron, and built entirely on him and who he was. It had taken him years to get to where he was now, a thread running through generations of families on every street of Anghofiedig. His prices were fair. His deals were fair. He was fair. He knew what you needed and what you wanted to buy before you did, and he worked it all out without any computers or all-powerful algorithms. He wasn't on social media. His mart didn't have a website. He could walk into a room and stay invisible. People looked past him and through him. He was constantly underestimated. He was Lieutenant Columbo behind a solid oak counter. 'Just one more thing...'

Younger people laughed at his out-of-date mannerisms and attitudes behind his back but he usually had the last laugh. To many, including Romeo, he was Anghofiedig's most boring man, if not Wales's. He liked it when people thought of him that way. He deliberately bought friends the same birthday gift every year to keep the ruse going. It gave him room to manoeuvre. A licence to roam. A screen to work behind. You don't create the most profitable and enduring business in the district by being wholly one-dimensional and unable to change with the times. The games he played were long and patient. He knew how to adapt and make it look like he didn't. He was John John. Everyone's favourite shopkeeper. Pillar of the community. Salt of the earth. Say no more.

John John had been surprised to receive anonymous gifts of a Glamorgan County Cricket Club season ticket and a series of extremely rare, framed butterflies – including a black, red and white Bhutanitis lidderdalii and a Vietnamese female Teinopalpus aureus – shortly after Pearl's death, but he knew immediately who they were from. His son. Not the legitimate one he had raised with his late wife, Thelma – Sidney, the letdown with wacky tastes, who showed no interest in taking over the mart or working honestly for his living. John John frequently thought about disowning Sidney but his conscience wouldn't allow him to do so. He cared about public appearances, which is why he often felt like cutting Sidney loose and also why he didn't.

Lately, Sidney appeared to be getting his life together; he'd changed his first name to Elton and landed himself a job on a cruise ship performing as a tribute act to the great singer who shared the same surname. Sidney 'Elton' John possessed a decent singing voice and the right receding hairline. He also liked wearing giant spectacles, bright tank tops and golden boots with enormous platforms.

When Elton came round to share his cruise ship news with his father, John John looked across the kitchen table and told his son he was proud of him. Elton, not used to making anyone proud, beamed. However, when the meal was done and his son tottered precariously down the road in his shimmering shoes, John John closed his front door and poured himself a large whisky in which to drown his true feelings. He was glad to see the back of his embarrassing offspring for a while. He wasn't bothered if things went well for him or not and didn't understand how you could call pretending to be Elton John 'real work'. Truth was, there was much more going on inside John John's head than anyone ever knew. He never really loved his bossy wife and was glad she was dead. He'd always loved Pearl White though.

John John had suspected for years that Barry White Junior was his secret son. Pearl had never said anything to him but he instinctively knew. He knew people and how to read them. And the dates corroborated the evidence: a nine-month gap between Barry's birth and the one time he dropped Pearl off at home following a rugby club dinner and ravished her on her bedroom floor to bid her goodnight. Barry Junior, he concluded, couldn't possibly have swum from the loins of Barry Senior because they were too different. The fat, bumbling lad was too sensitive, too insecure and too frightened of life to be cut from the jib of a hard-nut rugby-playing coal miner. Barry White Senior had also suspected as much. He'd confronted John John once because he noticed a physical resemblance. However, he doubted John John's capacity to have an affair with anyone, let alone a married man's wife – especially the wife of a man like him. Still, he bust John John's lip with a single punch as a precaution. To warn him – and others – off, just in case. John John told no one about the incident and said to Thelma that he'd walked into a door.

No one in the world knew that John John collected butterflies apart from Pearl. He'd grown more interested in them after Thelma's death; when people told him he needed a new hobby and she wasn't around to pour scorn on the idea. Even now, when he got his precious butterflies out and laid their cases neatly around the kitchen table, he could hear Thelma talking in his head, plain as day.

'Don't you think they're wonderful, Thelma? They can see colours that you and I cannot. There are more than 180,000 different types in the world and they live on every continent, save Antarctic of course. Such beauty – you wouldn't believe it could all come from a humble caterpillar. Isn't metamorphosis remarkable, Thelma?'

'I'm still waiting for you to metamorphosise into a real man, John John. It's been a long wait.'

Pearl must have mentioned the butterflies to Barry Junior. Perhaps when an Attenborough programme about them was on the telly? Sidney 'Elton' John certainly wouldn't have noticed or grasped these things. He'd never given his dad a single birthday, Christmas or Father's Day card because he was far too preoccupied shopping for white suits with feathered trims or singing 'Crocodile Rock' in his pants, in front of a full-length mirror.

Maybe Pearl had mentioned John John's passion for cricket to Barry Junior too? He'd loved the game since his early twenties, from the time he saw Sir Garfield Sobers smash six sixes off a single Malcolm Nash over at the St Helen's ground in Swansea in August 1968. The ground was near the coastline and it was like Sobers was trying to hit the ball out to sea. One blow destroyed some pub guttering. For the unfortunate bowler Nash, it was five minutes that would ultimately define the whole of his life and career. Of course, he didn't know that at the time.

Same as John John's fifteen minutes on the bedroom floor with love-of-his-life Pearl White.

Barry didn't really understand cricket. He'd played it a bit at school – badly – getting hit in the face with a ball in a house match and losing a tooth in the process. He'd never lost any teeth in all his years of rugby, despite being on the wrong end of countless hidings in hundreds of matches. Cricket seemed like a game for the middle classes because even the violence was polite and well-mannered. It was okay for a deranged lunatic to deliberately propel a hard rock of leather at your head at 85mph in an attempt to knock you out, or even kill you. However, because the lunatic spoke nicely, wore white flannelled trousers and applauded your survival every now and then, he was somehow considered less murderous.

Cricket called for co-ordination. The art of bowling a ball, as opposed to throwing it, from one end of a pitch to another required the kind of balance and timing that Barry did not possess. Different limbs had to move in different directions yet somehow remain in sync, otherwise nothing worked at all. Similarly, when batting, eyes, head, hands and feet had to move in unison to create a successful stroke. Fielding also irked and made no sense: standing around for hours on end, waiting for someone to hit a ball to you so you could run after it, fetch it and throw it back like an obedient dog.

And yet, when John John stopped him in the mart one day and asked him if he fancied joining him for a Sunday outing to Cardiff to watch Glamorgan versus Middlesex at Sophia Gardens, Barry said yes without really pausing to think things through.

Barry reasoned that the offer had come because of Ma. John John had carried a torch for Pearl White throughout his life and now she was gone, he was simply looking out for *her* boy. He was just being a mate. It had to be innocent. John John wasn't the kind of man to have ulterior motives. Why? Because he was John John, that's why.

What Barry didn't know was that John John did have ulterior motives. Lots of them. He knew Barry was his illegitimate son and wanted to spend some time with him to find out if he shared his passion for well-ordered, well-stacked shelves, butterflies, hard work and whiter than white aprons.

'Why are they all walking off the pitch?' enquired Barry.

'They're going for lunch.'

'Really? You mean they interrupt the game to go and eat? How long for?'

'Forty-five minutes.'

'Wow. What do they eat?'

'Normal things,' said John John, unzipping his own cooler bag. 'Pie and chips, curries, roast lamb, plus desserts too. They stop for tea at twenty to four as well, just before the evening session of play.'

'That's so English,' said Barry, accepting a piece of the pork pie offered to him.

'Are you enjoying the game?' John John applied thick yellow mustard to his own piece of pie via a plastic knife.

'I'm enjoying sitting here having a picnic and beers in the

sun but, to be honest, I don't really understand what's going on out there.'

'It takes time to get your head around the laws. Do you think this is something you might like to do again?'

'Not sure. I'm more of a rugby man.' Barry swallowed half of his pie in one gulp, as if to prove the point.

'Of course.'

'Do you like rugby?' said Barry, speaking with his mouth chock-full of processed meat and congealed jelly.

Somehow, John John knew what he was saying and answered. 'No.'

'You're Welsh though?' said Barry.

'I am.'

'What don't you like about rugby?'

'Er, it's just not my thing. People say cricket is a complicated game but compared to understanding the fine arts of rucks, mauls and scrums it's an absolute breeze.'

'If you say so.' Barry helped himself to a second piece of pie.

'How you coping on your own? Without your ma?' John John handed Barry the mustard knife.

'I'm not on my own. I've got Diana and Eddie now. We're doing fine.'

'That's great. Did your ma ever talk to you about me when she was alive?'

'How d'you mean?'

'Well, did she mention me. Did she mention our friendship?' John John stared outwardly at the field, as if the game was still being played.

'Not really,' said Barry.

'We had a fling once,' said John John, bowling the kind of unplayable ball the Glamorgan bowlers had struggled to deliver in the morning's session of play.

'Did you?' Barry pretended he didn't already know and kept a straight bat.

'Yes. It was a complete one-off. It shouldn't have happened.'

'Cos you were married to Thelma?'

'Yes.'

'And Ma was married to my dad?'

'Yes.'

Barry put down the knife, aware he'd been accidentally brandishing it. 'Was your marriage unhappy?'

'I wouldn't say unhappy. But I wouldn't say happy either.'

'Ma wasn't happy with my dad.'

'I know,' said John John.

'Did you love Thelma?'

'No.'

'What about my ma? Did you love her?'

'Yes, I did.'

'Did you like my dad?'

'No, I did not.'

'Were you jealous of him?'

'No.'

There was an uneasy silence. Barry delved into John John's cooler bag without being invited to do so and pulled out a Pink Lady apple. He crunched into it. 'Do you think I'm like him? My old man?'

'Not at all,' said John John.

'Do you think I'm more like you. Is that it?' Barry took another noisy bite of the apple.

'I can't answer that. I don't really know you.'

'I'm going for another pint. Want me to bring you back more sparkling water?' said Barry, tossing the half-eaten apple back into the bag.

'Thank you, that would be nice. Here, take some money.' John John pulled a couple of ten pound notes out of his wallet.

'No, put it away. I'm good for a bottle of water.'

'The players will be back out soon, don't be long,' said John John, returning his wallet to his jacket pocket and tidying the contents of his cooler bag, making sure to remove the apple and put it into a small green bag he'd brought with him exclusively for food waste.

'Not bothered if I miss a bit to be honest. I mean, do we have to stay all day?'

'No, we can leave whenever you want.'

'I think I'd like to go after a couple more beers, if that's all right with you?'

'Absolutely.'

Barry got up and put some more space between himself and John John. 'It's just it's a Sunday and I've not seen much of Diana and Eddie all week. I'd quite like to spend some time with them if I can. They're my family. You understand, don't you?'

'I do,' said John John. Right now, his youngest son seemed stranger and even more distant to him than his bespectacled, pot-bellied, platform-wearing half-brother, Elton.

FIFTEEN

WILL YOU THROW IN THE GHOST FOR FREE?

There was so much time to sit and think and pray.

Reverend Hill would typically wake around 5am, when the central heating system spluttered noisily into action like a morning smoker. He'd fold his sleeping bag away and reluctantly use the old stinking cellar toilet that didn't flush properly. He'd wash and shave his face in the grubby sink next to it and dress in whatever clothes Barry had laid out for him the night before. Then, he'd settle down on his deckchair to read his Bible for a couple of hours.

Usually, he'd go straight to the Psalms. One hundred and fifty poems across five books. All of life captured within these verses: the highs and lows, the trials and tribulations, the celebrations and the solemnities. In his morning vigils he would thank God for the dawning of another day and the survival of another night – a night in which drunken men (mostly, though not exclusively) above his head swore and cursed and drank and sang to forget their miserable lives. They told bawdy jokes to each other and shouted out their badly timed punchlines so they could be heard above the din. So much noise, so much laughter. So much life. Ten or fifteen years ago, when he was just plain old Jacob Hill, the reverend would have slotted comfortably into their midst, a fag in one hand, a pint in the other and an F-bomb never far from the end of his lips. Ogling the ladies as they squeezed between tables in their short skirts and stockings. Undressing them with his eyes. The same eyes that now looked to God and scriptures for crumbs of hope and a semblance of forgiveness. Oh thank God for redemption's bittersweet song.

His current existence was that of a monk in a boozy monastery, switching from Bible to prayer to mental walks with the Lord. A flask of tea, some ham rolls and a packet of biscuits for sustenance. The mornings were the quietest time when he could get closest to his creator. A chance to hear the word and receive correction and encouragement until Jackie broke the silence with her temperamental vacuum cleaner and tuneless whistling around ten o'clock. Give or take whatever time it took her to get to The Dragon from dropping the kids off at school and popping round her mother's to make sure she hadn't fallen into the fireplace again.

Stuck in this cellar, Reverend Hill was also forced to confront his own demons. He didn't much like what he saw. He would scare himself sometimes when he caught sight of his own reflection – the one staring back from his soul rather than from his face.

The monastic day beneath the pub was long and tedious. The reverend looked forward to Barry's brief visits because he made him laugh and always brought him nice food and a few books. He gave him Denis Johnson's *Jesus's Son* yesterday, thinking it was a Christian text rather than a collection of short stories about lost souls, junkies and social misfits. Or perhaps he knew all along? The reverend devoured its 133 pages in one sitting and loved it. Another reminder of his past.

Reverend Hill couldn't sing or play music or listen to the radio to pass the time of day because he had to keep deathly quiet in case anyone heard him. He had to suppress coughs, farts and sneezes, else release them whilst buried in his sleeping bag.

In the afternoons he'd sleep or read his magazines and papers. He might crack open a bottle of beer and a packet of crisps to take the edge off his loneliness, though this wasn't a new experience. He'd been lonely for years.

On and off throughout the day he would force himself to pray, for the company if nothing else. Wrestling with the Spirit inside him, straining to hear His voice, wanting Him to speak louder and clearer so there could be no misunderstandings or confusion. Other voices would try to impersonate this voice of conscience but they could only do it for so long before they gave themselves away. The reverend could tell if the Spirit's voice was true or not by the way it castigated him – demanding he hand over much more of self than he was comfortable with. The Spirit wanted Jacob Hill to disappear completely.

'*Make every effort to add to your faith, goodness; and to goodness, knowledge; and to knowledge, self-control; and to self-control, perseverance; and to perseverance, godliness; and to godliness, mutual affection; and to mutual affection, love.*'

'*But Lord, that seems like an awful lot of adding? Can't we discuss a bit of subtraction? I've got a few issues I'd quite like you to take away.*'

Reverend Hill wished his mind was stronger than it was, strong enough to hold out under stress and physical duress. He had read and marvelled at the stories of Terry Waite – the Church of England envoy chained to a radiator by his Lebanese kidnappers from 1987 to 1991. Held in solitary, beaten and threatened with mock executions. He saw no daylight, save for a small occasional shaft through a shutter – yet not once did he lose his faith. His hope stayed strong, his mind remained his own, regardless of what his captors did to him. He put his whole being into God's hands. The sympathy he had previously held for people on the outer margins of life morphed into empathy. He even viewed being imprisoned as a gift.

Four years in prison. Four bloody years! Jacob Hill could not do time like that, not even in a pub cellar. He'd managed six nights so far and was already going crazy. He contemplated grabbing his bag and taking his chances in bear country once more, fleeing back to the sanctuary, space and clean air of the woods.

But he had promised Barry he wouldn't run again.

He didn't want to break another promise. If he did so, how would anyone trust him ever again?

He'd leave everything up to God, like he had agreed.

And Barry.

Having said all that, he was only human.

And a weak one too – definitely no Terry Waite.

Humble flesh and blood. Mortal. Vulnerable.

Capable of pretty much anything, really. Including flicking the bird at sanctimonious law-abiding do-gooders and hopping on a fast Harley Davidson to head for the hills at 175mph.

Right now, escaping captivity was all he could think about. That and evading justice.

<hr>

'Did you hear that?'

'What?'

'Coughing.'

'Only you and me here.'

'Oh. Okay.'

Romeo sat across the pub table from Barry, eating sandwiches bought from John John's Mart. Barry chose coronation chicken, Romeo a BL (bacon, lettuce and tomato with the tomato taken out). They swilled them down with pints of Fiery Fred (nine per cent cider) from the bar.

'How are you doing for cash?' said Romeo, munching lettuce like he was a rabbit.

'Not great, I could probably sub you a twenty,' said Barry, chewing on a lump of chicken gristle.

'You can do better than that.'

'I'll push it to thirty. Tops.'

'Try again,' said Romeo with a grin.

Barry recognised that grin. Self-satisfied and mischievous, he'd seen it hundreds of times over the years. He got out his phone and tapped into his bank app. 'You've paid me fifty grand!'

'Yep, you're filthy rich again,' said Romeo, proudly.

'I don't know what to say.'

'Don't say anything then.'

Romeo's sale of his half of the barbershop had gone through and Kenny Wick was now the sole proprietor of Anghofiedig's only male salon once more. How long this would last was anyone's guess, seeing as Kenny had put his useless grandson, Olly, back in sole charge of day-to-day business. In no time at all, Olly would surely destroy everything that grew on any man's head as well as all that Kenny and his father before him had sweated to build. That's family for you. Kenny wasn't a fool; he knew what Olly was like and what the future held. However, more important to him now, at his ripe age, was being seen to do the right thing by his own daughters. Kenny comforted himself with the knowledge that, with any luck, everything would tick along for another two or three years at least, by which time he might be cold in the ground and oblivious to any fallouts shaking the soil above him.

Romeo pulled the crusts off the second half of his sandwich.

'I've got another proposition. One that's gonna make you even richer.'

'You want some of your money back?' said Barry, deflated.

'No, I want to give you more. Well, Delores does.'

'How come?' Barry slurped at his Fiery Fred.

'She wants to buy this pub off you.'

Barry was sick of trying to keep The Dragon afloat and wanted shot of the place. It was bloody hard graft and the hours never ended. It had been a mistake to try and do something nice for the community that involved money and alcohol. The recent skittles night fiasco was the final straw and Barry didn't see why he should be out of pocket and have to fork out for all of the repairs. Down in the dumps with the whole saga, he had confided to Romeo – over a few jars – that he was thinking of cutting his losses and putting the pub up for sale. Romeo had gone home and told Delores that she couldn't possibly miss out on the deal of the century. Delores had more money than she knew what to do with and the thought of getting her hands on a proper British pub excited her. She was keen to lay down roots in Anghofiedig. She told Romeo to negotiate a deal with Barry on her behalf and get the wheels rolling.

'Name your price, she'll pay you fair. She's no rip-off merchant,' said Romeo.

Barry thought he was dreaming. 'You've landed on your feet there.'

'Not a bad day's shift for either of us.'

'No, a good day's work all round.'

Romeo glanced at the clock. 'Racing's on the telly, from Kempton Park. Want to watch some?'

'Yep.'

'Few bets?'

'Why not?'

'You sure you can't hear noises? Definitely sounds like someone coughing.' Romeo turned his ear to the floor.

Barry put on his best serious face. 'Did I tell you this pub's haunted?'

'No you did not. That's fantastic. Delores will be revved up to know she's getting her own free ghost thrown in. Who's ghost is it?'

'I think it's my old man's.'

'No way! How's he doing?' Romeo helped himself to more cider.

'Dunno, we don't talk. He just glides around with a rugby ball for a head, tucked under his arm.'

Romeo stopped pulling his pint abruptly. 'Why's he got no head?'

'Cos it got sliced off in the motorway accident.'

'Holy crap. Have you told anyone else?'

'No, only you.'

'Mum's the word,' said Romeo, spilling his drink.

Barry knew Romeo wouldn't be able to keep a secret. That's why he couldn't tell him who the mystery cougher really was. Romeo was his best pal in the world but when it came to keeping schtum, even Greg was more trustworthy.

What Barry hadn't considered was that by the end of the day, half the village would be interested in the shadowy headless figure, performing stepovers and selling dummies to barrels of ale down The Dragon in the dead of night.

'If he's got no head, how come he coughs so much?' said Romeo after much quiet contemplation.

'Pit dust,' said Barry without hesitation.

'Poor old goat. He's proper hacking it up. Can hear it clearer now. Will he be doing that for eternity?'

'Not my call.' Barry shrugged.

'Why's he here? In the pub?'

'Cos he's lost his way.'

'Never good with directions your old man. Tell him to steer away from motorways.'

Barry cleared the table of sandwich wrappers and made for the Fiery Fred. 'Like I said, he can't talk and I don't listen.'

<hr>

She walked around and bounced her eyes from floor to ceiling like she was tripping on acid. Looking at everything yet seeing nothing. She was dressed in tight pink jeans and a pink sweater, separated by a large golden belt. A sixty-something woman with dyed blonde hair, cherry red lipstick and a crease-free forehead, thanks to well-administered Botox given to her by an expensive Oregon consultant whose neat handiwork allowed her to keep most of her facial expressions. These days, she was doing her damndest to turn the heads of sheltered pale Welshmen in the home stretch of her life. Turning heads was all she knew; it was her proven go-to strategy. Was she glamorous? Most definitely. Attractive? Yes. For her age. Three derogatory little words that no former beauty ever wants to hear. At least Romeo was infatuated.

'So why are you selling up, honey? Can't just be for cash, my Romeo's already given you fifty Gs.' Delores scratched at peeling wallpaper with her long talons.

'Just had enough.'

'Your woman been bitching in your earlobes?'

'No. I've not even told her I'm selling yet.'

Delores froze and looked at him. 'Ouch. You need to address that.'

'I will.'

'Probably too late anyway to save you,' said Delores, flicking her nails and blowing on them to get rid of the dirt from the walls.

Delores seemed smaller and less outlandish walking around The Dragon with her business head on. She didn't get to where she was today by being cute and ditsy. She could play hardball when she had to. She'd won a ferocious divorce battle with an arrogant oil baron, a man with a personality slicker than one of his oil wells who she'd driven to the grave prematurely. She had also defeated a fancy-dan financier in the US courts. He thought his hefty bank balance, strong book of contacts and even stronger head for numbers could insure him against anything. He found out the hard way that it could not.

Plenty of other men besides those two had underestimated Delores Hamilton and come unstuck. She wasn't a lady you could charm into bed then get rid of easily once you'd had your fun.

'Where's the ghost?' she asked.

'He don't come around so often.'

'I don't believe in ghosts.'

Barry smiled. 'Good, cos neither do I.'

'Why you putting crazy nonsense stories in my Romeo's head then?' Delores stopped smiling and Barry sensed this woman's bite could match her bark.

'It's just something we do.'

'Why you gotta tell him it's your own daddy, though?'

'Made a better story.'

Delores poked a long fingernail Barry's way, so he could see the sharp end of it. 'You hurt my Romeo, you'll pay. Capiche?'

'Likewise,' said Barry, standing his ground.

The two stared each other out like a couple of poker players holding royal flushes. Eventually, Delores blinked first. 'I've seen enough of this place. I like you, Barry White. I'll take it.'

'You haven't made an offer yet,' said Barry.

'I'll pay whatever you're asking for.'

'Do you even know the valuation?'

'A quarter of a million English pounds – or thereabouts.'

'So what if I want double?'

Delores knew Barry was testing her. 'Then you'll get it.'

'Valuation's perfect,' said Barry, rubbing his man boobs in self-satisfaction. 'I would have accepted less. Still would, within reason.'

'Is that bar of yours – or should I say mine – open? I feel the urge to say howdy to Dom Perignon to shake on the deal.' Delores began hunting behind the bar.

'We don't have any Dom P. We've got a bottle of Moet, I think.'

'Dandy enough. Mo's a friend of mine too. Though when I'm running this place, we'll offer the good folk of Anghofiedig bona fide Dom Perignon.'

Barry went behind the bar to help search. 'Not much call round these parts for a bottle of fizz that costs three days wages.'

'We'll see,' said Delores.

Barry imagined Delores trying to turn The Dragon into a good ol' American bar and falling flat on her cosmetically enhanced face. She'd swap real ales for glorified gassy lagers and get rid of the popular stouts and ciders. She'd put a chalkboard behind the bar and write up the names of available beers every morning. She'd have a gigantic TV glued to the wall, fixed to the stations of Fox, CBS or NBC via satellite – streaming American football, basketball and baseball to the likes of Uncle Derek and Clever Trevor, who wouldn't have a clue what they were watching. Maybe she'd compromise with a bit of ten-pin bowling for Trev? Tables and chairs would make way for screwed-down wrought iron stools lined up against the bar. Solid fixtures that didn't budge or give you any choice over who you might like to sit next to. Or talk to. Prices would go up.

Brighter lights would go on. Shiny silver stainless steel would replace all the red brick and autumnal wood. The place would be cleaner but more sterile. Synthetic. Noisy. And it would attract bellends galore. Golfers and tourists and fake people with fake tans buying fake drinks for fake highs. No one from Anghofiedig would bother with the place.

'What's your plans? Complete overhaul?' said Barry, accidentally holding a Bonnie Tyler bottle opener the wrong way up so it looked like she was doing despicable things with his champagne.

'No way Jose, I'm not gonna change much.' Delores took the bottle opener off him, threw it down and popped the cork with her hands. She tossed champagne around the place like she was a Formula One racing driver on a podium.

'Apart from hiring the services of Dom P, of course. We need his glam. We need his sparkle.'

SIXTEEN
STOP BEING SUCH A GOOFBALL

'Well fuck me sideways with a blowtorch. If it ain't Romeo and Juliet.'

Grenville Grayson hadn't had a winner since Brecon Beacon Boy upset the Cheltenham Festival apple cart and made Barry a million quid in the process.

That win should have put Grenville on the training map. It should have attracted new owners and horses to his off-beat Herefordshire yard. However, it didn't. He had gone from looking after eight horses to six – four of them owned by Delores. Brecon Beacon Boy was still the stable star but his heart was no longer in the game and he was living off his fluke of a past glory – he was a one-hit wonder, the equine equivalent of Chesney Hawkes, only less hairspray. Nowadays Brecon would mess around at the start of his races, not wanting to set off with the others, before idling and pulling himself up.

Another of Delores' horses, Never Been Kissed, had shown plenty of promise as a four-year-old but was now deemed to possess the same questionable attitude as Brecon and regarded as a bit of a waster. Same with Delores' other two jumpers, Spotty Muldoon and Causeway Boy. They were too stubborn and self-opinionated to let any ability they had shine through. Just like their trainer, who alienated horses and people wherever he went.

To make ends meet, Grenville had gone back to wheeling and dealing in scrap metal as a sideline. It meant his yard had become a health and safety hotspot, with knackered old cars strewn around randomly, threatening the life and limbs of knackered old horses.

Grenville had his head under the bonnet of an old car when he heard his visitors arrive. 'What do you two clowns want?'

'His girlfriend would like to ride out if that's all right,' said Romeo.

'Well, it's fucking not. Unless you're gonna pay me a grand like last time.'

'We're not going to do that,' said Romeo.

'Bugger off then and take fat boy here with you so the sun can come back out.'

'You watch your mouth and apologise immediately...'

A big booming American voice crashed over Grenville's shoulder like a Florida storm that he didn't see coming. He turned around to find Delores standing there, scowling with arms folded, next to Diana.

'Oh hello, Mrs Hamilton, ma'am, just having a bit of fun with the fellas.'

'Not much fun from where I'm standing,' said Romeo.

'Nor here in the shadows,' piped up Barry.

'Sorry, lads, you know me, always joshing.' Grenville followed the trail of his own words with his eyes as they scrambled out of his mouth and landed like bricks by his feet.

Delores surveyed the yard, unimpressed. 'We need to talk, I wouldn't keep pigs in this swamp, let alone racehorses.'

'Shall we schedule a meeting, Mrs Hamilton?'

'Yes. How about your office, thirty seconds from now?'

Delores marched off towards Grenville's unloved portable cabin. She stopped to whistle over one of the Dickensian-looking street urchins who worked in the yard and told him to saddle up Brecon Beacon Boy for Diana to ride.

'What about these two misters, they riding out too?' said the grubby underfed assistant.

'No, not today.'

'They dressed up as jockeys last time. Proper funny they were,' said the assistant.

Delores shoved a couple of crisp fifty-pound notes into the urchin's top pocket, then summoned Grenville to catch her up. When he got close enough, she grabbed him by the arm and began escorting him towards his office. The beaming young assistant instructed Diana to follow him to the tack room.

'You ridden a horse before, Miss?'

'Yes, lots, used to have my own. Not a racehorse, mind you.'

'Brecon's been a bit nervy lately – fallen out of love with the game if you ask me,' said the assistant.

'Bless him, I'll be gentle with him.'

'That's what he needs, there ain't a lot of gentleness to be found around these parts.' The assistant pulled a beetle out of his own hair.

'Why do you stay?' said Diana, staring at the large bug.

'For the horses. And cos I don't want to let Miss Delores down.'

Delores tore several strips off Grayson and turned the South Walian air Yankee red, white and blue. She said she'd be back in a week's time to personally inspect the yard again and if it wasn't 'A1 all over' she'd remove her horses immediately. She inspected the whole place, shouting orders and instructions to Grayson as she went. He scribbled everything down on a notepad best he could. She told Grayson she wouldn't tolerate the slightest mistreatment of any of the horses – or staff – and even insisted on going through his paperwork, including the wage and feed bills. He pleaded poverty but agreed to all of her changes. He knew he'd be a damn sight poorer without Delores' horses and her incoming direct debits. For all his faults, he realised he'd got lazy and needed the wake-up call.

Delores then turned her attention to Barry, who was watching Diana having a ball aboard Brecon Beacon Boy. Diana laughed and giggled like a carefree schoolgirl – encouraging Brecon to fly around the gallops, leaping small hurdles as they went. Brecon looked much more relaxed than usual, relishing the soft voice and even softer hands cajoling him. His nostrils were more rounded, his lower jaw drooped and he was dribbling. The whites of his eyes, that so dominated his features, could hardly be seen at all. He pawed at the ground and flicked his ears back.

'He likes you, Miss, not seen him this happy in ages,' shouted the assistant, from the middle of the gallops.

Diana responded with a grin and a thumbs up sign.

'So Barry White, what's going on with you and your lady?' said Delores.

'Nothing much.' Barry knew it was a bad answer.

Delores kicked the ground. 'When was the last time you saw her laugh like this?'

'Months.'

'You gotta make more effort. Relationships take work. Women want to be appreciated. Just like racehorses.'

'How do I do that, give her a lump of sugar?'

'You put her first. And you let her know she comes first.'

For all Barry knew, Delores might as well have been speaking Russian. 'Righto.'

'Does she come first?' pressed Delores.

'Yes.'

'Well show her. Stop being so goddamn British.'

Barry watched Diana some more, her hair bouncing up and down on shoulders that were free of their invisible weights for once. 'Can she ride out here more often?'

'Anytime she wants. The way she's getting a tune out of Brecon she'll be doing me a favour. She's a natural horsewoman.'

'She is, isn't she?'

Delores leant against the rails sideways, facing Barry. 'Have you told her about all the money you're going to get from the pub and barbershop?'

'Not yet.'

'When are you going to tell her?'

'Don't know. Need to pick the right moment.'

'Stop being such a goofball and tell her tonight.'

'I will.'

Delores grabbed Barry by the shoulders and wrestled him to face her. 'You want to keep her, don't you? Then be straight with her. Tell her what you're up to. What's inside your head. Give a bit. Share a bit. You trust her, yeah?'

'Of course,' said Barry, hoping Delores would let go of his arms soon.

'Then shower her naked with your honesty.'

'Not heard that one before. Does Romeo do that to you?'

'Not exactly, but you two boys are works in progress. You're emotional hobbits, like ol' Grayson there. And the rest of your sorry species.' Delores released her grip and turned to face the man shovelling horse shit some seventy-five yards away.

'Grenville, how about some English tea and cookies? Say, I like them Hobnobs you gave me last time. And I want your very best Wedgewood china. And wash those shitty hands first...

'And where in the name of Humphrey Bogart is my little old lover boy Romeo hiding? I've got a nice surprise for that hunk of beef.'

The mood in the rugby club bar was upbeat after the day out at Grayson's stables. Diana couldn't stop talking about Brecon Beacon Boy and Barry loved seeing her this happy – oblivious to the fact that several moons ago, the man she now lived and shared her life with had won a colossal fortune by drunkenly gambling on this rank outsider to win at the Cheltenham Festival. She was also oblivious to the fact that Barry was about to get a sizeable chunk of this fortune back.

Despite Delores' little pep talk, Barry couldn't bring himself to tell Diana any of this. Not just yet. Part of him wanted to unload it, but in his limited experience sharing the inner contents of his mind was a surefire way to land himself in trouble. What Diana didn't know couldn't hurt her, right? Or him. He didn't want to face a barrage of questions and moral judgements. He didn't actually need any second opinions, not even hers. It was a terrible admission to have to make to himself, but it was the truth. He was a crap boyfriend. Perhaps he was just a crap human being. Every decision he made and every road he chose was the one that led to the quietest life. It had always been so. Avoiding conflict was his number one goal, which was one of the main reasons why he made such a terrible rugby player. He'd never considered himself a brazen liar before, but Delores had got him thinking. He didn't go around saying things that were patently untrue. But he did go around saying little – or nothing – to dispel things that he knew not to be true.

He'd done this kind of passive lying all his life – letting the likes of Ma, Uncle Derek, Aunty Ruth and his bosses at work believe all kinds of rubbish. He let Ma think he was a hard worker. That he didn't actually drink that much on his nights out in The Dragon or down the rugby club. That he had ambitions for his life way beyond lying in bed with a doughnut in one hand and a TV remote control in the other. Sometimes, usually in church, he used to deliberately pull pensive faces to make Ma think he was contemplating deep philosophical stuff such as the meaning of life or the beginning of creation. However, behind the manufactured expression lay a big fat empty vacuum of nothingness that could keep him occupied for hours at a stretch.

No one else knew the village pub was about to change hands into American ownership, apart from Delores and Romeo. The latter was cock-a-hoop and drinking champagne out of a glass rugby boot on account of Delores' little surprise – the gift of a horse, Never Been Kissed.

'Can you believe it, I'm an actual bona fide racehorse owner – me! I'm Anghofiedig's JP McManus.'

'No I can't believe it, but life's been weird for a while now, hasn't it?' said Barry.

'You counting me in that reckoning?' Diana had been listening in.

'Of course not, my love,' replied Barry, realising straight away that he'd just spouted an out and out untruth, as opposed to his more regular 'say nothing' kind of lie.

Eddie turned up at the rugby club around seven, just as Diana was getting ready to leave. Because she was in such a good mood, she told him he could stay with Barry for a couple of Cokes as long as he was home by 8.30pm. Barry promised they wouldn't be late but the beers were sliding down his throat pretty easily. By the time Uncle Derek and Aunty Ruth rocked up he'd lost all sense of time and place.

'Beer, Uncle Del Boy?'

'Muchos Gracios.'

Whilst they were alone, Ruth confided to her nephew that they'd had a couple of rough days and she was struggling to cope with Derek's depression. She said his emotional flare ups were harder to manage than his physical ones – that he would be easier to handle if he 'was in a wheelchair but had all his marbles'.

This morning, he'd shouted a load of abuse at John John in the mart and called him a Nazi because he didn't have the latest copy of *Rugby World*. In the afternoon they'd gone to see a specialist and Derek had struggled to get any words out for a good forty-five minutes. Lately, he'd been crying a lot, for no apparent reason.

'He's kicked a big chunk out of the living-room wall in sheer frustration,' said Ruth, sipping a vodka and tonic.

'Is he violent to you?'

'Not to me. Just around me.'

'Anything I can do?'

'Come round a bit more?'

'Sure,' said Barry, feeling guilty for having to be asked.

'It gives me a break when you call in. Even if it's just for a cup of tea, he always perks up around you. Finds a bit of his old self. Me? I just seem to bring out the worst in him.'

Ruth told Barry that his uncle was now on antidepressants, along with a whole chemistry set of other pills and potions. Derek had told the doctor he wouldn't be going back to hospital as an inpatient because he didn't want to live in a filthy kennel with a pack of dying, mangy dogs who did nothing but piss, shit, eat, sleep and fart. He'd also started watching old children's TV programmes most afternoons, *Hong Kong Phooey*, *Robinson Crusoe*, *Top Cat* and *Banana Splits*.

Barry didn't let on that occasionally he would watch them too.

'It's frightening to see him go backwards so fast. He says he has so many voices in his head he doesn't know who to trust,' said Ruth.

'Do you think he'd do something stupid to himself?' said Barry, concerned.

'I don't know.'

Ruth said some days were darker than others. Derek had told her on one of his more lucid days – when 'the wifi wasn't playing up' – that he would never take his own life because he wasn't sure it would take his pain away. He said he envied the kind of faith that she possessed. He envied her certainty of an afterlife.

'There's nothing we can do to change things but he just needs to know we're there for him come what may,' said Ruth.

'I get it,' said Barry, holding Ruth's hand.

'Ere get your mucky fingers off my missus, she's spoken for,' said Derek, sliding back into his seat. 'And where's that pint you promised me?'

'Coming right up...'

Barry got up to go to the bar but was distracted by the sight of Llewellyn Davies pushing through the double doors, holding Eddie by the ear.

'Sort your lad out will yer, just caught him smoking in the disabled bogs.'

'Er, will do, Llewellyn, thanks.'

Derek started to snigger, encouraging Eddie to do the same.

'It's not funny, Eddie, why do you keep letting me down like this?' said Barry, angrily.

Eddie's grin fell from his face.

'I'm going to have to tell your mum what you've been doing. I can't carry on keeping secrets from her. We've both got to change, you hear? You and me.'

Barry had barely finished his sentence when he noticed

people running from the bar and loud anxious screams coming from the vicinity of the toilets.

'QUICK ... GET OUT ... NOW ... GET OUT, RUN ... THERE'S A FIRE! EVERYONE OUT ... RUN ... DO YOU HEAR? ... RUN ... THERE'S A FIRE.'

SEVENTEEN

EVERYONE WANTS A BLOODY LEGACY

Eddie had barely come out of his room in a fortnight and was refusing to go to school. The smokers in his year group had nicknamed him Torchy and waved their lighters in his face whenever they saw him, like they were at a seventies rock concert. Even Mr Rogers, immature teacher of French and geography, joined in a few times.

The fire service got to the rugby club pretty quickly to ensure no one was hurt. They even managed to save the clubhouse from burning down. In reality, it was Anghofiedig RFC's best result for many a season but few saw it that way.

The toilet block was a write-off, though. It would need to be demolished and rebuilt. It would cost the kind of money the club didn't have. Portable loos seemed the most likely solution. Another step backwards for the club but raising money – and the necessary bodies to commit to months of unpaid building work – was a struggle no one had the heart for. The club's flame for a fight had been dowsed long before the fire service's jets steamed in. Off the pitch as well as on it.

The atmosphere within 76 Cerys Matthews Heol, days after the fire, was combustible. Another tinderbox likely to erupt and cut down lives at any moment. Diana blamed Barry for getting her son into more trouble and for the soot stains that now blackened his name and character. Barry felt unfairly victimised. He had no more idea what Eddie had been up to in the toilets than she did. Diana's assertion that he 'always set a bad example' seemed harsh because he didn't even smoke. The fact that Diana assumed he had somehow masterminded and encouraged the whole thing, like some kind of despicable supervillain, spoke volumes about them and the current state of their relationship.

Trouble seemed to be following Barry wherever he went. First, the pub riot. Now this.

He needed something to take his mind off things. Then he remembered he already had it, an on-the-run man of the cloth, wanted by Interpol, who just happened to be hiding in his pub cellar. Reverend Hill was probably munching his way through the out-of-date salted peanuts by now, on account of the fact that Barry had forgotten to feed him or take him clean clothes for the past couple of days.

Sergeant Sargent rarely set foot in The Dragon, not socially at any rate. So when he sidled in wearing his unfamiliar old man brown and grey civvies, asking if he could have a 'quiet word', Barry felt the blood rush to his cheeks and his stomach muscles stiffen. Barry showed the sarge through to the kitchen, half expecting a bunch of muscly boys in blue to come storming straight through the front door to flood the pub with weapons, noise and chaos and nab Hill from his cellar hideaway, just feet from where they currently sat.

Sergeant Sargent was probably close enough to smell Hill. Were he a sniffer dog. With sharper senses.

Barry's guts churned over with anxiety. His head felt light and his fingers tingled with pins and needles.

'So what's this all about, sarge, have you had fresh sightings of the reverend or summat? Where now? Montevideo? Amazon Rainforest? The road to Damascus? Rhyl? Or is this about the skittles brawl? Wait, don't tell me those two cocky detectives want to come back to interview me again. Is that it? I told them everything I know already. You were here. You heard me.'

'Sit down, Barry, please. I'm not supposed to be here, but there's something I felt you should know.'

'About what?'

The sarge patted the chair next to his and insisted Barry use it. 'It's about the fire down the rugby club. We're pretty sure we know how it started.'

Barry thumped the table. 'Please don't arrest him. He's only a boy. He didn't mean no harm.'

'It wasn't the lad,' said the sarge, clasping his hands together.

The sarge had a pal in the fire investigation team who told him the blaze most definitely started in the rugby club kitchen, not the disabled loos where Eddie had been caught smoking.

The char patterns – the fire's footprints – began at the cooker where a man had been seen trying to boil water on a gas hob just minutes before the fire broke out.

Sergeant Sargent coughed to clear his throat. 'We've got a witness, a reliable one, who says they saw this man lighting the gas hob with a flurry of matches. They tried to stop him because he kept tossing lit matches into the sink. Apparently, he claimed he was making a cup of coffee for his wife. Our witness tried to point out to the man there was a kettle right next to the cooker, but he just swore and told them to mind their own business. He said he'd do it his way. The proper way.'

Barry paused to think. 'Wow. Eddie never even went in the kitchen.'

'There's more,' explained Sergeant Sargent. We're one hundred per cent certain this man was the last person to use the cooker before the fire started. And we're sure the fire's origin was the hob. You've seen *Silent Witness*, right? On the telly? Every crime scene tells a story. There are always clues everywhere if you know what you're looking for. Well, my mate's an expert in all this stuff. A proper rubber-gloved Hercule Poirot. He knows what a cooker looks like after it has burnt through. Not just that, he can tell from the thickness of the surrounding ash how hot it was in there. That determines where the fire began. None of this is speculation. We know the alarm in the kitchen was the first one to trigger.'

Barry got up and poured himself a glass of champagne from the bottle Delores had left behind. He was relieved Eddie was in the clear. Maybe, just maybe, his home life would return to normal. Whatever that was.

Sergeant Sargent might not be the brightest button on a constabulary uniform but he could detect Barry wasn't reading the room right. The sarge hadn't come here to put his or anyone's mind at ease.

'Just hang fire on the celebratory champers,' he said, holding up a hand like he was back directing traffic on market day.

'But you said it wasn't Eddie?' Barry put his glass down on the kitchen counter and returned to his table seat.

'Correct, Edward Fenwick did not start the fire.'

'So who did?'

'Derek White.'

'Derek White? My uncle Derek White?'

'One and the same.'

All his life, Barry had never been bothered about creating a legacy. He had no desire to leave a mark on the world, lasting or otherwise. He didn't want to fill the valleys of Wales with the pitter-patter of tiny Barrys, huffing and puffing their way up cobbled streets with their bellies and shirt tails hanging out. Sure, he'd come into a tonne of cash but he didn't want any of it. He considered his new-found wealth a bloody hindrance. A handicap that was ruining his life. He didn't dream of being famous. Quite the opposite. How awful it must be to have strangers bothering you day and night, asking for signatures and selfies. Either telling you you're greater than God or that you're a piece of lowlife shit. Acting like they own you. Setting benchmarks you can't even see, let alone live up to.

He gained comfort from the fact that no one would remember him for long once he departed for the great Millennium Stadium in the sky. He liked the idea that the small ripple of his existence in life's pool would disappear in a heartbeat. As if he'd never been there.

Now Ma had gone no one would mourn him for long. Certainly not Diana. She'd probably be glad to be rid of him and the aggro, bad luck and inconvenience that followed him – and now her – around. Eddie wouldn't miss him for long either, he had youth as his shield. Pretty soon he'd start thinking he could conquer the universe and never grow old. Until decades later when his clock had ticked around to late afternoon and he began to think about his own demise and what imprints he might leave on this crazy lost raft called earth floating aimlessly through the universe's ocean.

Aunty Ruth might wish he was still around. For a bit. Uncle Derek? He would forget the quickest. He would forget the most.

Barry didn't give a damn about his own epitaph or the abbreviated story of failure it would tell. He rocked up, he fucked up, he blew out.

Yet here he was, about to lose everything he had. For legacy.

He had lied to the police and incriminated himself in the process by refusing to come clean about how he won his money and how he gave it away. He'd probably end up in prison for these lies and deceits, but why? Because he wanted his poxy tinpot village – full of people he didn't care that much about – to think the best of Ma. He wanted them to think that she had left them a small fortune in her will because it gave him a strange comfort that he was prepared to go to jail for. For *her* legacy. So that people thought well of her and remembered her longer into the night. Her sacrifices. Her goodness.

It was also legacy that drove him to keep accepting failure on a rugby field. Despite Derek's many protestations, Barry knew his uncle gained a few crumbs of satisfaction from seeing the White name on the Anghofiedig team sheet in the 21st century. Like it or not, Barry was part of the White rugby story. And, like fine wine, or Llewellyn Davies and his committee room cronies, he'd get better with age. His rugby career would peak when he finally stopped playing and those who actually witnessed him in action, or rather inaction, died out. Then he'd take the plaudits his name afforded him. History was kind that way.

It was legacy, too, that made Barry decide in an instant to carry the can for the rugby club fire. He couldn't possibly let his uncle's hard-earned reputation in the village – and the wider rugby community – be tarnished by a pathetic dementia-driven lapse that he actually knew nothing about. Uncle Derek had given everything he had to this bloody rugby club and its people, including body, mind and senses. He deserved to be remembered fondly for that. How dare anyone try to take this away from him now. Barry wouldn't let it happen. Legacy might not matter much to him, but the legacies of those he loved the most, his family, meant the world to him.

And for that – and them – he'd forgo relationships and even his own liberty if he had to.

———

Liberty had been on the mind of Reverend Hill a lot lately too. He'd been contemplating giving himself up, walking out of the pub cellar and strolling into a police station to take whatever fate was dished up to him. God would stand by him. He was already in prison as it was; a revolting one, with solitary confinement. Except for creeping rats and cockroaches. No daylight. A bog that didn't flush. A sickening foul stench of hops and yeast that made you feel giddy and half drunk all the time. A proper prison would be an upgrade on this cellar. He'd get three meals a day, regular as clockwork, and an hour's exercise outside in a yard. He'd have light to read and pray by. He'd be able to study. Make some noise. Listen to Radio Four. Christian Premier Radio. Fist Full of Metal Radio. A small television, maybe? And because he'd given Black Caracal all the money they had demanded, they'd look after him. Keep him safe inside. Wouldn't they?

Reverend Hill got so hungry he devoured the out-of-date peanuts in one sitting. So too the remnants of a jar of old eggs, probably pickled around the time Barry sat his GCSEs. Reverend Hill's constitution was obviously strong. By the time Barry pitched up with fish and chips and a litre of cheap lemonade he was already full. He pushed the food aside but changed into the clean clothes supplied for him – another tracksuit or rather, this time, a shell suit, circa 1989, rustling polyester in neon pink, green and gold. Designed to light him up under any disco ball. The shell suit was much too small for Reverend Hill but with no other options, he put it on anyway.

'Snug,' said Barry, grinning.

'Do you think this is appropriate clothing for someone trying to avoid police capture?' enquired Reverend Hill, sarcastically.

Barry did a limp body pop. 'It's not so bad. You look like you're in Goldie Lookin' Chain. Minus the gold.'

'I just need a back to front cap, Reeboks and sunglasses and my disguise is complete. Barry, I feel ridiculous.'

'Sorry.'

'And why did you have to give me underpants with elephant ears on?'

Barry blushed. 'They were Romeo's. I borrowed them and never gave them back.'

'But elephant ears? Swinging either side of a trunk? For me? Really? I'm still a reverend for heaven's sake.'

'They're lush though, proper toasty on cold days. I've worn them loads. Sad to see them go if truth be told.'

'Please, Barry, don't torture me anymore. I can't take it. I'm going to give myself up. Hand myself in.'

Reverend Hill explained he'd had enough. He was ready to take his punishment, whatever that looked like. 'What do you want me to do, Barry? How do we end all this?'

Reverend Hill admitted that when he gave all that money to Black Caracal he was convinced he'd get it back somehow. He felt sure the Lord would provide providence for him.

'But I can't and he hasn't.' Reverend Hill adjusted his elephant ears.

'I've been through so much but I've been a coward. No more.' The elephant ears were really annoying him so he pulled down his shell suit bottoms and ripped off both ears simultaneously with a grunt. One of the elephant's eyes also came away inadvertently, leaving the poor thing half blind. He threw the ears with all his might and an even bigger groan across the cellar. There was a pause as his rage subsided.

'Did I tell you they found the escaped bear?' said Barry, picking up the elephant eye from the floor and stealing a chip off the reverend's plate in the same movement.

'No, you didn't.' The reverend hitched up his trousers to make himself decent again.

'Turned up at the village hall cos he wanted a dance with Dot. She said he was lighter on his toes than Derry Lee. He's gone home to France now. Loads been happening lately. Clever Trevor Peacock's been charged with ABH. Can you believe it, eh? Greg's on the run, same as you. They say he knocked out three coppers but I don't believe that. Pricer's missus kicked him out so he's staying here for a bit. I told him to stay out of the cellar but Pricer's all right, even if he found you he wouldn't dob you in. Pricer's missus is loving the single life by all accounts so won't be having him back. He'll be better off in the long run but he's a bit mopey at the minute. What else? Oh, Romeo's rich girlfriend, Delores, has given him a racehorse. Never Been Kissed. That's the horse. Not Romeo.'

The reverend sat on a box closer to Barry. 'How are you and Diana getting on?'

'Not good. There was a fire at the rugby club see, and everyone thinks her lad accidentally started it.' Barry got up and walked away. 'Trouble is, it was me. I caused the fire. I left a hob on. Bit of paper or something must have fallen into it.'

The reverend got up and stood directly in front of Barry, trying to make eye contact.

'Are you sure you know what you're saying?'

Barry walked away once more. 'I'm going to sort it. Make it right. I'm selling this pub to Delores. And I've already got shot of the barbershop. The rugby club will get the money to fix things up. I'm going to sort everything.'

'I think you're lying to me.' Reverend Hill opened his bottle of lemonade and started swigging from it, trying not to burp too loudly. 'Why are you hiding me here? And why didn't you give me up to those detectives? I stole from you, yet you're the one defending me and helping me avoid capture? It doesn't make any sense. I've been racking my brains about it non-stop. And you know what I think?'

Barry grabbed a big handful of chips off the reverend's plate and started gorging himself in a frenzied search for instant comfort. 'Come on, Sherlock, give it to me...'

'I think the money never belonged to Pearl in the first place. But you wanted people to think it did.'

Barry didn't know what to do. He didn't want to lie anymore. He wanted to spill everything to someone and right now, he figured Reverend Hill was as good a bet as anyone.

'I won it gambling, okay.'

'What? All of it?'

'Yes.'

Reverend Hill put the lemonade bottle down and made Barry sit next to him. 'So you did lie to me? And your family? And the police? And everyone else? For what? So they'd think Pearl was some kind of village saviour?'

Barry rubbed hard at a grease stain on his shirt sleeve, caused by the chips. 'That's part of it.'

'And the rest?'

'I never wanted to be rich. I didn't want people looking at me differently. Treating me differently. Being fake nice to me. That's why I gave it all away. I didn't want the bloody money. None of it. Still don't.'

Reverend Hill was struggling to understand his most complex parishioner in a village full of human Rubik's Cubes.

'But Barry, people, by and large, with a few exceptions, generally treat you like you're an idiot, even though you're obviously not. Don't you want that to change?'

Barry pondered hard. 'No.'

Reverend Hill pondered harder. 'My friend, you really are an idiot!'

Barry grabbed the lemonade bottle and started to drink defiantly. He let out an almighty belch with enough unadulterated pride to make the reverend jump. The roar temporarily took him back to his woodland stand-off with Napoleon the bear.

'I just want things to go back to the way they were,' said Barry, still dribbling gas like a slowly deflating balloon.

Reverend Hill wiped something unpleasant off his shell suit top and was pleased it was waterproof. 'That can't happen.'

'I know.'

'So what are we going to do?'

'I need more time. To think.'

Reverend Hill realised he was now in a much stronger bargaining position than he had been before Barry, fish and chips and elephant undies turned up at his cavernous door. He fingered the crucifix around his neck and waited for the right words to come to him.

'Okay, I'll stay down here for one more night. But that's all. The ball's in your court. Either turn me in or turn me loose. I think that's fair. Don't you?'

EIGHTEEN
CORFU, HERE WE COME

The proverbial was beginning to hit the fan. Romeo's big gob had dumped Barry in the brown stuff so many times over the years but this was probably his finest hour. He didn't even know what he'd done. He'd run into Diana in the chip shop and within a single minute had changed the direction of her life. Not to mention the lives of Eddie and Barry. Lives ransacked, if not exactly ruined, in less time than it takes to fry a fishcake.

Romeo assumed that by now, his best friend would have mentioned over morning cornflakes how he'd come into fifty grand following the sale of the barbershop. Applying the same logic – that men and women living together actually conversed with each other – he also assumed she knew about the forthcoming sale of the pub, which would line Barry's pockets with a further quarter of a million quid. Even when Diana stormed out of the chip shop, the penny never dropped. Romeo put it down to a sudden loss of appetite, or maybe the fact that there was no cod on the menu tonight, only haddock.

Around eleven, Barry sauntered in from his shift down the Dragon, hoping for a bit of peace and quiet and an episode of *Only Fools and Horses* on UK Gold before bed. Bizarrely, Diana was waiting up. More bizarrely, she had all her clothes on. Including her leather jacket. Eddie was perched on the sofa next to her, his big puppy dog eyes screaming silently. Three big suitcases sat by the living-room door.

Barry's heart sank. He knew what this was. No words were required but the charade still needed to be played out.

'Here he is, home at last, Elon Musk.'

'Come again?'

'The billion dollar boy.'

'Who told you?'

'Romeo.'

'Ah right. Bigmouth strikes again.'

Barry thought about fighting to try to make her change mind. Make her see his point of view. But to be honest, he wasn't sure he understood it well enough himself. He did love her and wanted her to stay. Not just for what she did for him, but for who she was. And the ways she made him a better, more grown-up person. He liked being around her, being in her company, just not all the time. He needed his space sometimes. Quite a lot of times. He enjoyed sharing, just not everything. Anything he owned was hers. The stuff in his head? Well, that was harder to disentangle. He'd convinced himself he needed room for 'man things'. Drinking. Eating. Scratching his balls. Watching telly. Watching Netflix movies. Watching sport. Thinking about sport. Playing rugby. Socialising after rugby. Napping. Reading his *Racing Post*. Laughing with people who shared his sense of humour (Romeo, not her). Chilling. Watching videos of Chico. Daydreaming. Just sitting, thinking and doing nothing, maybe contemplating life's big questions every so often, such as how do budgies stay on their perches when they're asleep? Or, if a man punched himself really hard and it didn't hurt, is he weak or is he strong?

These were proper pastimes in their own right that required

serious effort and focus. Wasting time was his actual hobby, which meant of course, it wasn't a waste of time.

Diana didn't understand. Her idea of a fun night out was cornering him alone so she could describe to him in great detail how she was feeling – for hours on end, with curved tangents galore that he couldn't follow. His preferred method of geometry was straight lines. Short ones. She'd complain that all she wanted him to do was listen to her a bit more and be attentive. But how could he? When she spoke for twenty minutes at a stretch without pausing for breath and Llanelli versus Cardiff was on the big screen right behind her head.

He'd have happily told her all about the money coming his way. Coming their way. He'd have given her the lot. The thing he had a problem with was the painful 'let's talk about it' bit. The discussions that he thought weren't needed but she, and to be fair, most other people on the planet, not just those with two X chromosomes, regarded as pretty bloody necessary.

'Where are you going to go?' Barry thought he'd bypass a whole load of 'pretty bloody necessary' and cut straight to the chase.

'Aren't you even going to ask why I'm leaving?' Diana started to cry.

'I know why. Cos of me. What I'm like. I should have told you about all the money. It's yours if you want it. You know that.'

'Yes, you should have told me – but it's not just that, is it?'

'No.'

Eddie was upset, watching and listening to everything. His presence ensured Diana chose her words carefully and made her determined to stay in control of her emotions. She didn't want to emerge from this the bad guy in Eddie's eyes.

'We're gonna visit my mum and Christos in Corfu for a couple of weeks. It's school holidays. It'll do us all good.'

Barry looked at Eddie and felt a real sense of loss. 'And when you get back? What then?'

'Not sure.'

'Okay.'

Barry didn't want them to go but he understood. He'd want to run away too if he had to live with himself. He wanted to give them a parting gift though. Something uplifting to prove to them he wasn't all bad. Something that showed Diana he did have the capacity to talk and share. Something to make them feel better right now.

'I've some other news, about the fire. Eddie, you didn't start it.'

Eddie sprang forward. 'What?'

'The investigators know for a fact that it didn't begin in the disabled loos. It started in the kitchen. From a hob on the cooker. Which I accidentally left on. It was me. I caused it.'

Eddie didn't know whether to laugh or cry.

Diana looked horrified. 'And you never mentioned this before because...? You let people accuse Eddie of all sorts, knowing what you'd done? You watched him shrivel up inside himself? You let him hide in his bedroom, torturing himself for weeks? And you never thought what you've just said was relevant or worth mentioning? Not even in passing? You didn't consider this snippet of information important? Aaggh...'

Diana screamed. Barry and Eddie watched and waited for it to stop.

Finally, Barry thought it was safe to speak. 'I'm sorry.'

Eddie shrugged. 'That's all right, Uncle Barry.'

Diana couldn't control herself anymore. She pulled Eddie up by the hand and pushed past Barry knocking him over onto the sofa.

'I hope you and your three hundred thousand quid are very happy together. Come on, Eddie, let's get out of here. I feel sick.'

Eddie tried to mouth a sympathetic message to Barry but his mother – tears streaming down her face – thrust two suitcases in his hands and had him out of there in seconds, slamming the front door as she went. Barry heard more shouts and screams outside before there was a flurry of slamming car doors and the thrust of a loud revving engine pulling away at speed.

Then there was silence. Complete and utter silence.

Barry flicked on the telly and stared into it vacantly. Del Boy and Rodney Trotter were up a ladder in some stately home, shouting instructions to Grandad in another room, who was waiting to catch an expensive-looking chandelier in a big tarpaulin. Grandad hit the pin holding the chandelier with a hammer. A different chandelier fell to the ground and smashed into thousands of pieces.

Barry had laughed at this episode hundreds of times before, if not thousands, almost without fail.

Tonight though, it just wasn't funny.

'You're such a pathetic specimen, I would have loved to have come up against you on a rugby field. I would have owned you. Dragged you around the pitch on a dog lead. You would have been my bitch, begging for mercy. You wouldn't have got any. I'd have destroyed you for the fun of it. And that old man of yours, hiding behind that counter, ogling my missus, plotting and planning? You're just like him. It's plain as day now. Except you're a lot fatter. Less cunning. More stupid. You think the same way though. You hide in plain sight the same way.'

'Dad? Is that you?'

'I ain't your dad. I ain't nothing to you.'

'Why are you here? What you doing?'

'Stop making up bullshit lies about me being in the pub

cellar, okay? With no head. And a rugby ball under my arm. You're taking the piss. I won't have it, you hear? You stop, or you see if I come back to haunt you or not. Understand?'

'Yes.'

'You've really gone and done it now with that nurse, haven't you? She's got out just in time if you ask me. Had a lucky escape. That boy of hers too. He's better off without a dad rather than having you as a supersub. You really are a walking disaster, aren't you? Everything you touch turns to dust. You don't even know what to do with a million quid. You're not a man. You're nothing. I'm glad I wasn't around to watch you grow up. That's what hell is. For me.'

'But, Dad?'

'Fuck off...'

A bottle of empty rum lay by Barry's side. The telly was still blaring more repeats of *Only Fools and Horses* on UK Gold. Barry rubbed his eyes, still half asleep. He unplugged the TV and trudged up the stairs to bed. Alone.

There was no way he was going to sleep tonight. Too much on his mind. His dad had seemed so real.

Barry looked around his bedroom and tried to remember what it was like when it was Ma's room. He imagined her sitting in this same bed not long before she died. Hiding her pain. Trying not to make a sound in case it woke her precious son across the landing. She wouldn't have wanted to disturb him because he had work the next day. People relied on him. He needed his rest.

This was also the room where he had been conceived. John John's naked, pale white arse had actually flapped around in here. Bet he kept his socks on throughout the lust.

And Ma had fallen for that? How bad things must have been for her.

He'd have liked to have had a proper grown-up relationship with her. He'd like one now. She always thought the best of him. She understood that he messed things up, but that his intentions were usually good. She didn't doubt his motives like everyone else. She was the only one who properly believed in him and didn't put him down. Sure, she held him back and stifled him, because she couldn't bear a life of her own without him. Fair enough. He understood that too. It was forgivable.

He picked up her photo from the bedside table and held it close to his chest.

'Goodnight, Ma, sleep well.'

He hoped that she would come to visit him in his next dream instead of the old man.

He thought about the things the vision of his dad had said earlier, about owning him, making him his bitch and giving him no mercy.

'Dad, if you can hear me, I'm gonna tell a whole load more people tomorrow that you're strolling around the pub cellar with a rugby ball for a head. I'm going to tell them you keep bumping into things cos you're a stupid bastard with no sense of direction who can't stop himself from going the wrong way. I'm gonna tell them you're lost and clueless, so they'll have nothing but sympathy for you. I'm gonna tell them you're being tortured for eternity by the sound of ringing Nokias from the back of your lorry after your dumb crash.

'I'm gonna make them pity you.

'I'm gonna tell them you're still my dad. But I'm really the son of Pearl.

'I'm stubborn as a mule, see. A chip off the old block.

'I'm gonna tell them I'm Barry White. With as much right to the name as you.'

NINETEEN

DOLLY PARTON IS USUALLY RIGHT

Chepstow Racecourse was Romeo's favourite racetrack in the land – though he'd only ever been to three. In his opinion it was better than both Cheltenham and Ffos Las, but he generally preferred places he knew his way around. He'd visited Chepstow regularly since he was a kid, not just for horseracing but also for market days and car rally stages. It was local. And built on a hill, which made viewing the horses around the course pretty easy.

It was therefore no surprise that Romeo chose Chepstow for his horse's first outing under his ownership. On paper, Never Been Kissed looked well out of his depth in a fairly hot three-mile handicap contest, but no matter. Romeo revelled in being a VIP for the first time in his life – mixing in circles he'd only seen from afar before. And the horse was running in *his* colours: white, with royal blue cross belts and a royal blue cap with white spots.

Feeling guilty and semi-responsible for causing Diana to run off to Corfu – and because Delores had other commitments – Romeo invited Barry along as his 'plus one'.

Walking around the parade ring, half an hour before the

race, Romeo kept stroking his owner's badge and looking around for security guards, expecting to be chucked out. Nerves were getting the better of him and Barry wondered if his pal – a committed maladaptive daydreamer – would flee to his fictitious haven of Feelgood for a bit of therapeutic pacing in order to relax himself. Thankfully, for Barry at least, Romeo resisted this urge to make a public spectacle of himself.

'I don't feel like I belong here,' said Romeo, rubbing his badge once more for luck.

'You look like you do,' said Barry, marvelling at Romeo's race day attire of green and pink check shirt, brown corduroy trousers, green tweed jacket and pink cravat beneath a brand-new Barbour coat, cloth cap, and brown suede boots with silver buckles.

Barry and Romeo watched the horses enter the ring. Neither were able to pick out Never Been Kissed in a crowd, but they spotted the Dickensian urchin from Grayson's yard – whose name they still didn't know – leading him in. Grenville Grayson followed close behind, in conversation with jockey Phillipson Montague.

'All right, lads,' said Grayson, sheepishly.

'What no insults?' said Barry, poking the bear.

Romeo smiled. 'His card's been marked by Delores. Ain't that right, Grenville old boy?'

Grayson gritted his teeth as his already gammon-boiled cheeks turned pinker.

'I heard him promise Delores he'd be a good boy, isn't that right, Mr Coochie Coo.' Romeo playfully squeezed Grayson's cheeks as if he were a baby.

Grayson reacted spontaneously. 'Go fuck yourself, else I'll lamp you one. And I don't give a shit if you tell Ivana Trump what I just said.' He looked around nervously just to make sure she wasn't there.

Phillipson Montague stepped in to calm the trainer down, pulling him away and getting the topic of conversation back on to racing.

'I figured we'd just pop out at the back of the field and let Never jump around on his own today,' said Phillipson, tapping his whip confidently on the side of his thigh as he spoke. 'No point doing much else in this company. Best we save ourselves for another day. Agree?'

Grenville nodded wholeheartedly. Romeo, however, looked like he'd seen the headless ghost of Barry White Senior charging straight at him with both fists sticking out.

'Oh Phillipson, no, no, no, no, no.'

'Come again?' Phillipson did not expect to have his race plans challenged by someone who looked like he'd just won a trolley dash in *Outdoor and Country*.

Romeo took his cap off and began tugging at his hair for reassurance. 'Now here's the plan... I want you to go like the absolute clappers from the off. I want you to run like the wind, howling as you go. Let's get a massive early lead, as big as possible. I expect the full monty, Monty. Think Charge of the Light Brigade. Full pelt. Cannons to the left of you, cannons to the right, but you keep going, hell for leather, come what may, okay? I want to see them long legs of yours pumping and flapping and that tight arse of yours clenching like a welder's vice. I want you to put as much distance as you possibly can between you and all the other horses right from the start, from the moment the tape goes up. You got that, me old mucker?'

Phillipson's face wrinkled and contorted. Grayson clenched his fists tightly by his side. He stood so straight he looked like an Apollo rocket, with enough pent-up gas inside to speed him to the moon in minutes. Barry laughed and lit the fuel to send him on his way.

'So to recap, the instruction is run, Forrest, run! You understand?' Barry did his best to sound like Forrest Gump.

Grayson was beaten. He sat down in the paddock, in full view of all the other owners, jockeys and trainers and began to chew his race card.

Romeo punched Phillipson on the arm. 'You can do this, I know you can. Barry here thinks his missus, or rather ex-missus now she's buggered off to Corfu, knows more about riding horses than you, but I have every faith in you. That's why I told Delores I wanted you to keep the ride today. But mess up and I might think again.' Romeo looked towards the young assistant, still patiently holding on to the reins of Never Been Kissed with his mouth hanging open.

'Ere, workhouse, what's your actual name?'

'William.'

'William what?'

'Sykes.'

'Fancy riding my horse in his next race if old Phillipson fucks up today?'

'Okay.'

'Deal.'

Romeo punched Phillipson on his other arm, much harder than before. 'There you go, Phillipo, a bit of extra motivation for you. But listen, you've got this. *We've* got this. We can win. We've just got to believe in each other. Now let's go to work. And remember, you get yourself a big old fat lead and you hang on for dear life. Understand?'

Barry walked off towards the betting ring on his own, in need of a bit of space, quiet time and sanity. He'd only walked a couple of dozen steps when he spied a familiar face, standing on a box, shouting the odds in a thick Yorkshire accent.

'Peter? Honest Pete Redfearn?'

The bookmaker recognised Barry immediately and almost fell off his box.

'Well I'll be damned. If it ain't the Brecon Beacon boy.'

'Long way from Pontefract, ain't it?' said Barry, offering a hand. The bookmaker held back from shaking it.

'No offence, but I ain't taking no bets off you today. Try one of the other bookies, all right?'

Barry smiled. 'Don't worry, Pete, I'm off proper gambling.'

'How come?'

'Cos I'm scared I might win again.'

Barry updated the bookmaker with the abbreviated snakes and ladders story of his life since his mega bet had come in at the Cheltenham Festival. Honest Pete tried to look interested but had little time for a sob story from a man who had taken him to the cleaners in one fell swoop.

Barry eventually realised how pathetic he sounded and turned the focus of the conversation around. 'Anyway, enough about me, I thought you'd quit this game and got yourself a job on the Homebase tills. Didn't it work out?'

The bookie put a pair of binoculars to his eyes and looked out across the track to see the horses jostling for their positions at the start of their race.

'I missed the buzz of all this. Dolly Parton was right. Working nine to five ain't no way to earn a living.'

The bookie remained transfixed on the horses. 'Say there's a crazy animal just sprinted like a mad banshee to the first fence and come an almighty cropper. Jockey is on the ground doing his nut, stamping up and down like a spoilt kid. Ha! Never stops surprising you, does it, this funny old game?'

Barry's heart sank. 'Is the horse all right?'

'Oh aye, it's up and bolting on like a crazy firework, thirty lengths ahead of the field. Just ain't got no rider on top.'

Honest Pete got down off his box. 'Listen, I will shake your hand cos I do owe you. The day you wiped me out, you told me to keep twenty grand for myself. To help me start again. Remember?'

'I remember.'

'Well, that's the reason I'm back here today. Still doing what I love. So thank you. I mean it.'

Barry felt himself welling up inside because it had been a while since anyone had thanked him for anything and genuinely meant it.

'No problem, Peter. I hope you stay lucky.'

'So do I,' said Honest Pete, his mind already fast-tracking as he calculated that the last race had just earned him a clear profit of two hundred and seventy-seven pounds and seventy-four pence – more than enough to get his little Nissan Micra back up to Pontefract, with the added bonus of a tacos or noodles supper at one of the more upmarket service stations en route.

TWENTY

MRS DOUBTFIRE'S BIG REVEAL

Delores had agreed to meet her Romeo in The Dragon at seven. She got there early, knocking back vodkas like a Siberian soldier, with her phone switched off to save her ears from the expletive-ridden moans and groans of Grenville Grayson.

'I know you're sweet on the bloke, but it's gotta be said, he's not right in the head. The stuff he ordered us to do, he could have got the horse killed, ma'am. And Phillipson with it. He's a fucking lunatic if you'll pardon my French, m'lady.'

Delores was seriously thinking of removing her horses from Grenville's yard because there was just too much aggravation. However, there was one big problem: Never Been Kissed was no longer her horse. She'd given him to Romeo. Even though she was still paying all the bills. She regretted her rashness but had wanted to do something extra special for her beau.

When he rocked up at The Dragon, Delores escorted Romeo out the back for a discreet private chat. She wasn't afraid of causing a public scene when she had to – she was American, after all – but she also knew how to do business. She was streetwise and sassy, not stupid. The couple returned to the bar after twenty minutes or so, holding hands and still loved up. 'Did yer get a dressing down?' whispered Barry, whilst the two friends stood side by side at the bar waiting to be served.

'Kinda,' said Romeo. 'But her hands were warm.'

Barry admired how Delores had navigated a potential relationship fork in the road so skilfully. She knew she couldn't avoid having a difficult conversation with Romeo after the way he had behaved at the races, but she still considered his feelings and spared him any public humiliation. She tackled the problem head on, but not in the middle of the pub, in front of everyone.

Barry felt sure that in her shoes he'd have just shirked the issue completely, said nothing and let his own resentment fester. Maybe that's why he was here, drinking alone, and Diana was sunning herself in Corfu. For a man who had spent most of his working life in communications, he was a crap communicator.

Barry was equally in awe of how Delores switched persona so easily, according to whatever the situation demanded. She was now back to being her big, brash 'normal' self, holding court in front of a handful of pub regulars including Rupert Baird, Terry Truman, Rex Blunkett, Lazarus Taylor and Clive Clementine, regaling them about the ghost of Barry White Senior, who walked the Dragon's cellar in the dead of night, with no head, and a rugby ball under his arm. Barry wished she'd shut up. He wished he'd never made up the ridiculous story in the first place.

A few weeks ago he'd have put Delores' big mouth down to her being crass and American, lacking any subtlety or tact. Now though, he knew different. She was shrewd. And this was clever marketing ahead of the announcement that the pub was hers. People would come from far and wide to hear, or maybe even see, the ghost of Barry White. She'd see to that. She'd turn him into a tourist attraction.

'Shh, listen. What was that?' said Lazarus, putting down his pint glass gingerly.

'What was what?' Rupert gripped the edge of the table with both hands as if he was at a séance.

'I heard something. Sounded like a snort. Or a sneeze. From down below.'

'It's him, I tell you – it's Badass Barry on the prowl.' Delores lowered her voice to create more atmosphere. 'He's restless.'

'Let's go look,' said Terry.

'Yeah.' Rex Blunkett, a man who could lose his spectacles on the end of his nose, was surprisingly keen to go hunting for ghosts. Not just any ghost either, but one notoriously partial to a bit of casual violence.

'Wait, you can't,' yelled Barry, getting up from the table so quickly he knocked Terry's pint into his lap. 'Have some respect, will yer? That's my father you're talking about as if he's some circus freak sideshow. He's just Barry, okay? Not Badass Barry.'

'Sorry,' said Terry, wiping his wet groin with a bar towel extremely vigorously. Bizarrely, Rex was helping him.

'Come back tomorrow night when Junior ain't here. I'll take you down the cellar for your own personal guided tour,' whispered Delores to the group, fully aware that Barry could hear her and also fully aware that this baloney ghost story had originated from him.

Bugger, thought Barry, looking like he'd seen a ghost.

'Why do you keep doing this to me? It's your way of exacting revenge, isn't it? C'mon, be honest about it. I wouldn't mind so much if some of the stuff you make me wear actually fitted.'

Barry tied a headscarf belonging to Delores around the

reverend's head to complete his outfit and cover his beard. Most of what he had on belonged to Delores, a biggish woman, but certainly not as big as Jacob Hill. She'd left an overnight bag behind in the pub so Barry decided to make full use of it. Her expensive sunglasses, her handbag and gloves, her sparkling long black dress now looking like a mini skirt stretched around the Reverend's beefy torso. Her mink coat, which fortunately covered most of Reverend Hill's decency, apart from some hairy lower legs. He wore his own grubby trainers.

'It's not safe to stay here no more. And you wanted out anyway, didn't you?'

Barry filled a black bin bag with rubbish and the reverend's meagre possessions. It was important not to leave a trail behind. He didn't want to leave any clues for amateur ghost sleuths.

'Where are you taking me?' asked the reverend.

'My house, you're coming to stay with me for a while.'

'Won't Diana mind?'

'Nope. Not one bit.'

'I feel like Mrs Doubtfire.' Reverend Hill held up a beer bottle to check his reflection. 'Make that Sam Smith.'

'Needs must, reverend. It's not far. You can put your dog collar back on when you get to mine.'

Barry ushered Reverend Hill up the cellar stairs and out through the back door of the pub. They loitered in the car park, behind a tree, whilst Barry dumped the bin bag in a wheelie bin and made sure the road ahead was clear. Then they tottered off down the street, arm in arm as if they were an everyday 21st century couple out for a nightly stroll through Soho.

They made a spectacularly odd sight in the backwaters of Anghofiedig. But fortunately, there wasn't another soul around to see them.

Next day, Reverend Hill was in his element playing house. He looked and smelt amazing. He wore some of his own clothes for the first time in ages and felt clean and comfortable. Almost relaxed. He wasn't looking over his shoulder after every slight noise. He even managed to sleep for eight consecutive hours unbroken. He'd vacuumed throughout the house and done two loads of Barry's washing. He'd sewn up the splits in the groin area of two pairs of trousers and two pairs of shorts. He'd baked a loaf of brown bread and some granola cookies and read the entire book of Philippians from the New Testament. Next up he fancied a nice podcast, maybe a classic Desert Island Discs? The selections of someone wholesome like Shirley Ballas, Delia Smith CBE or maybe Bono? And a strong Nespresso coffee. Feet up. Time to snooze.

A few streets away down at the Dragon pub, Inspector Craig Willard rubbed his chest hair inside his purple shirt, whilst his colleague from the Serious Crime Squad, Detective Sergeant Duncan Burrows, played with the curly hair on his head. The pair had pitched up, warrant in hand, to turn the pub over in their continuing search for Reverend Jacob Hill, following an anonymous tip-off.

They were joined by around a dozen armed colleagues in riot gear, who ripped the joint apart as if they were disgruntled alcohol-infused skittles players.

'Not a sausage down here, guvnor, apart from some random bloke with a mohawk wandering about in a dressing gown,' said Detective Purple Shirt into his radio.

'This whole case is seriously getting on my tits,' protested Detective Curly Hair to Pricer in the pub's kitchen, which no longer had a door.

'You gonna clean your mess up before you go?' enquired Pricer, flicking on the kettle to make himself a brew.

Detective Curly Hair shrugged. 'Sorry about that, not our department I'm afraid. But I'd love a coffee if there's one going. I'm properly parched. Raids always give me a thirst.'

Pricer pulled one cup out of the cupboard and poured a splash of milk into the bottom of it.

'Sorry, no can do. Not my department, see. Try the Silver Spoon café, about three miles down the road. Heard they do a wicked Mellow Birds in a paper cup for £4.50.'

TWENTY-ONE

BE SURE YOUR SINS WILL FIND YOU OUT

Barry hadn't visited the rugby club since the fire. Few had. All training sessions and matches had been cancelled and no one seemed to miss it much. It would have made an appropriate, if not fitting, demise for the once-great club if things just tamely petered out like a slow dripping tap – each drip getting smaller, with longer intervals between drops, until no more.

Barry had publicly confessed to accidentally causing the fire and no one in the village knew who the real culprit was, save for the sarge. Barry expected a big backlash for such an admission, a tirade of abuse and unfair demands from Llewellyn Davies and his cronies, but he got nothing. No one seemed surprised or bothered. No one seemed to care about the club anymore.

The one exception was James. He'd contacted half of the village in an attempt to get bodies at the ground for tonight's resumption of training. And he'd also exhausted his book of contacts to cajole four potential new recruits from LesCargo Logistics into giving the club a go.

He told the newbies that 'the ashen waste of the former toilet block would allow the club's phoenix to rise'. They had no idea what he was talking about, but came anyway because of his childlike enthusiasm. And the promise of beer and chips afterwards.

Barry got to the ground early, hoping to find James alone.

'All right, El Capitano?'

'Ah Barry, so pleased you made it. Listen, I've had a word with the chaps. None of them hold any grudges against you. It was just one of those things. Everyone's relieved that no one got hurt. You're still welcome here. It's business as usual from my perspective. This is still your club.'

Barry wished he was more like James. He wanted to smother him with a big dollop of platonic kisses just for being so thoroughly decent. 'I'm going to put things right,' he said.

James nodded, hardly paying attention as he flicked through the messages on his phone checking through the late drop-outs.

'I transferred fifty grand into the ruby club bank account this morning. There's more on the way. I want to pay for all of the rebuilding work. I want things to look even better than they did before. Will you sort it all out? With the powers that be and all that?'

James dropped his phone and stared at Barry. 'You serious?'

'Yeah. Money's all there.'

'Wow, I don't know what to say. Barry, you really don't have to do that. In fact, I don't think you should. I know you probably feel guilty but you've got a family now. Other responsibilities.'

Barry took two steps towards a rugby ball lying idly on the ground in front of him and shaped to punt it as hard as he could, past the flattened area of the clubhouse where the toilets used to live, towards the road-end goalposts, now cordoned off with black and yellow tape. He slipped on the wet turf and fell in a heap. James tried to help him up but Barry pushed him away.

'Decision's made,' said Barry, gruffly. 'I keep telling people but no one will listen. I caused all that damage so I'm gonna fix it.'

It was the same Basildon Bond notepaper that Ma had used to write to Dot all those years ago. To tell her friend about her moment of madness – or perhaps, joyful clarity – with John John, respectable retailer and, surprisingly, lover extraordinaire. Father of her only child. More of a man than hard-nut Barry White any day. Why? Because his sperm were the like the SAS. They got in quick. Got the job done. On their first and only mission.

Barry got out Ma's best fountain pen and began to write.

Dear Diana,

This house seems very empty without you and Eddie. I miss you both walking about the place in your dressing gowns, you making do with his because he reckoned yours was comfier.

Every day I wish you were still here, but I understand why you're not. If I could run away from myself, I think I would. I know from personal experience what a nightmare I am to live with.

There's quite a lot you don't know about me – big things, I suppose – but I don't reckon any of it really changes who I am, or who you think I am.

But I'll try to explain...

Just before I met you and Ma died, I won a load of money on the horses. We're talking thousands. I didn't really know what to do with it all and I didn't want my life to change. So at the Cheltenham Festival, with my few sensible brain cells pogoing around on Guinness, I lumped most of the money on another long shot, probably hoping it would lose and my problems would end. Unfortunately, the bloody thing won at massive odds. Leaving me a millionaire. I was pretty peed off for a while, I can tell you.

I tried giving it all away: I bought the pub for the village, a barbershop for Romeo, did up this house from top to bottom to help out Angharad. I also gave Reverend Hill £100k for his special projects. I told everyone this money came from Ma's will because I wanted her to get all the praise and all the attention. I wanted everyone to remember her. And I was still afraid of what people might think of me if they knew I was rich. Including you.

Things keep going wrong. The money keeps coming back to me like an annoying boomerang. Romeo's repaid some of the cash from the barbershop and I've just sold the pub to Delores for more than it's worth (or I want) cos I'm sick of it. Reverend Hill blew his hundred grand on gangster debts – but the police think he stole it from Ma. He really didn't. I gave him the money. But they're chasing him hard and I've not told anyone the actual truth cos I'm a coward. Call me Old Yellow!

Now Reverend Hill is hiding here. Right now, he's sitting opposite me reading one of your John Grisham books and wearing your slippers. Blimey, those things must fit all sizes. No dressing gown, though. The man's not one for lounging about in his night-time attire. We look at each other across the room, smile, wonder what the other is thinking and contemplate our own guilt.

I think that's everything. Apart from the rugby

club fire. Eddie didn't start it and neither did I. It was Uncle Derek. But I'm still telling everyone it was me cos I don't want people to think bad of him. Like Ma, he deserves better.

I'm sorry it looked like I was hiding behind Eddie when everyone thought the fire was down to him. I wouldn't do that.

I've rambled on and still not said the bits I want to say. I'm a better person when you're around. I wish you would come back to me but I think you'd be daft to ever do so. You're better off staying away and so is Eddie. Things go wrong around me. I'm sorry for all the lies and letdowns. With you at least, I should have been more honest but it's hard to break the habit of a lifetime and let someone inside your head and inside your life, especially when you've always occupied those places alone. Also, I don't think the inside of my head is a particularly nice place to wander around in the small hours without a chaperone.

So for your sake and Eddie's, I won't ask you to come back.

I'll just ask you to forgive me.

And not forget me.

Thank you for giving me the best year of my life. You opened a window to a world that I never thought I'd see. I'm so grateful to you for showing it to me. At least I can now say I know what it looks like.

Yours,

Barry xxx

Barry got up and walked across the living room towards the sideboard. He put the letter inside an unsealed envelope and slid it towards the back of the middle drawer. He knew Diana would never read it.

Writing the letter had been therapeutic. Barry vowed to burn it in the morning. Making extra sure he didn't set fire to the house in the process.

A loud knock on the door disturbed Barry from his sofa slumber. The second knock came more quickly than anticipated.

'Who's that?' hissed Reverend Hill in a panic.

'Might be Jehovah's Witnesses. Wanna talk shop with them?'

Barry waved at Reverend Hill to go and hide and went to answer the door.

'Oh, evening, sarge. You're out and about late. Anything wrong?'

'Can I come in?'

Barry thought about saying no but realised it might look incriminating. 'Sure.'

Barry led the sarge into the living room, hoping the reverend had found a good place to conceal himself and his feet weren't sticking out from underneath the curtains. The coast looked clear.

'So what's up?'

'I'm sorry for the raid on the pub earlier. Beyond my control I'm afraid.' The sarge picked up the Bible lying on the arm of the sofa and examined its cover.

'What raid?'

'You mean you don't know?'

'Nope.'

'Serious Crime Squad received an anonymous phone call that our friend Jacob Hill was hiding in the cellar of the Dragon. They turned the place over.'

'Oh dear,' said Barry, feeling like he needed the toilet urgently as his insides turned over. 'Did they find anything?'

'No, but you knew they wouldn't, didn't you?'

Barry gulped. 'Did I?'

The sarge was still holding Reverend Hill's Bible. He tapped the cover twice. 'Been seeking spiritual guidance, Barry?'

'Always.'

The sarge put the book down. 'Why do I get the feeling you're not being completely honest with me about something?'

'Dunno. Maybe you're tired. In need of a holiday.'

'No, it's copper's instinct. Rarely lets me down.'

'Is this an official visit, Sergeant Sargent?'

'No. It's just two friends talking.'

'Then why do you think I'm not being straight with you?'

'Because I know you gave the rugby club fifty grand to cover the fire damage. Lot of dosh that. And I know you've been going around lying, saying you started the fire, even though we both know it was your uncle Derek.'

Barry leant forward and felt a button pop on his shirt. 'Am I in trouble? Police trouble?'

'Not for the fire. We know how it started and who was responsible. We know it was accidental. Some people will want to speak to you though.'

Barry grimaced. 'Purple Shirt and Curly Hair?'

'No. Different people. But just like them. Don't worry. It's only a formality.'

The sarge got up and walked towards the window. He pulled back the curtains abruptly. Barry was relieved to see no one standing there.

'Cup of tea, sarge?'

'Lovely. Milk, one sugar, please.'

Barry went off to the kitchen, his heart racing faster than Lewis Hamilton around Silverstone. Whilst the water was boiling, he crept upstairs to scout around for signs of the reverend. He couldn't find any.

In the living room, Sergeant Sargent made the most of the alone time. He began opening cupboard doors and looking under cushions. Flicking between magazines and checking under tables. Searching for clues. He could hear Barry walking around upstairs, going from room to room like a baby rhinoceros. He knew he was hiding something. Copper's instinct. The same instinct that told him most people underestimated him as a policeman. He didn't mind that. Playing the Welsh Columbo worked a treat in Anghofiedig and helped him keep the crime rate down. It also helped him control his patch without the likes of the Serious Crime Squad stepping on his toes too often.

He looked across at the sideboard and something caught his eye. The middle drawer was slightly open. Nothing unusual in itself but all the others were tightly closed. Copper's instinct again. He opened the drawer wider and rummaged around, working from back to front. From bottom to top. He found the letter and pulled it out. The ink was freshly smudged. He could hear Barry coming downstairs but knew he had enough time to read the letter because Barry would go to the kitchen first to make the tea. He'd get out proper cups, not mugs, and apologise for taking so long because he'd got distracted. Maybe he'd say that he'd needed the toilet? But there had been no sounds of a flush. A policeman's brain was always ticking. When the tea arrived there was sure to be chocolate biscuits on a side plate. You didn't need to be Serious

Crime Squad to work that one out. Not in Barry White's house.

The sarge read the letter. He leant against the sideboard but by the time he got to the end, he had to sit.

He knew Barry had been lying all along. However, he hadn't known why, until now. He felt sorry for him. He wanted to help him. But the law was the law. Justice would need to be served. Due process would need to happen.

When Barry returned with a tray bearing two teacups and three different packets of biscuits, the sarge didn't even try to hide what he had in his hand.

'What yer got there, sarge?'

'It's a letter.'

'Who off?'

'You?'

'Who to?'

'Diana.'

'Bugger.'

The sarge folded the letter and tucked it away in his inside jacket pocket.

'That's mine,' said Barry, defensively.

'Not anymore. It's evidence.'

'You can't do that.'

'Think I can.'

'It's all made up. I was just messing around.'

'Where's Reverend Hill? It's time to come clean. Stop all this lying and pretending.'

Barry shoved three biscuits in his mouth simultaneously, giving himself a few more precious moments to think because he could not speak. Sergeant Sargent sat patiently, waiting for him to finish, watching his mouth and brain work overtime. He noticed Barry looked like a cow chewing the cud. He half expected him to regurgitate the biscuits back up and start chewing them all over again before recycling them to one of his three other stomachs.

'What if I choose not to say anything? I've seen them TV programmes where they sit with their arms folded, saying "no comment" over and over again.'

'That's your prerogative.' The sarge took a single custard cream off the tray and broke it in two. He delicately put the smaller piece into his mouth.

Barry fidgeted. 'I could do a runner.'

'Yes, you could. But I reckon you're the only man in the village I could probably catch.'

'That's a bit harsh.' Barry shoved two more biscuits into his gob.

'So where's Reverend Hill?'

'Don't want to say,' mumbled Barry, spitting half-chewed biscuits all over the lawman.

The sofa on which Barry sat started to move. Barry lurched forward unexpectedly, spilling his tea. Out of the side of the settee popped a head. Followed by a pair of shoulders.

'Hello, Sergeant Sargent,' said Reverend Hill, grinning as if he were meeting parishioners at the entrance to the church on a lazy Sunday morning.

'Good day, Jacob, mighty pleased to see you,' replied the sarge.

'How did you get there?' said Barry with ridiculous mock surprise.

'Game's up,' said Reverend Hill.

'He's right,' said the sarge.

Reverend Hill pulled the rest of his twisted frame out from behind the sofa and sat next to Barry. He helped himself to a biscuit.

'What happens now?'

The sarge handed Jacob Hill his Bible. 'We sort this mess out.'

'Will we go to prison?' asked Barry, noticing he'd now lost a second button off the front of his shirt.

'Not my call,' said the sarge. 'But we'll all need to go down to the station. There's a fair bit of music to be faced.'

Reverend Hill nodded in agreement as if seconding a nomination for a new churchwarden. He put his hands behind his back, readying himself to be handcuffed.

'Don't think that'll be necessary,' said the sarge, gently laying a hand on his shoulder.

Barry pulled a face, showing strain and agitation. 'I seriously need a poo before we go.'

The sarge pushed him forwards towards the front door. 'Have one down the station, lad. You'll be glad of something to do while you're whiling away the time in your cell.'

TWENTY-TWO

FOR THE BENEFIT OF THE TAPE

Barry donated fingerprints, saliva and oral swabs and had his belt and shoes taken off him. His trousers kept falling down and he had holes in both socks. His Ma would never have let him go out in such a state. Things like that mattered to her. 'What about standards?' she would say.

Barry had also been photographed for a mug shot. He'd smiled a cheesy grin and shouted 'rabbits' at the camera. It hardly endeared him to Detective Inspector Craig Willard and Detective Sergeant Duncan Burrows from the Serious Crime Squad, who were keen to remind him this was serious.

Willard, AKA Detective Purple Shirt, played around with a cassette machine in the interview room, trying to stop the spools from sticking. Barry wondered why the Serious Crime Squad was still using old tape machines in this day and age. Burrows watched, but largely ignored his colleague's struggles as he drank black coffee from a Manchester United mug with a worn-out red devil on it.

Barry felt an overwhelming urge to empty his bowels right there on the spot but resisted. He had indeed had plenty of time to use the loo whilst waiting around in his cell for hours on end but the lack of a toilet seat, razor sharp loo paper and a security camera fixed upon the wall completely put him off. He needed privacy to do his business. He wasn't an exhibitionist.

Burrows reminded Barry that he had the right to remain silent during his interview if he so wished. He reminded him he was there voluntarily but that anything he said could be used in evidence against him if charges were subsequently brought. Barry nodded and declined the offer of a solicitor.

'So, the last time we spoke, you told us that your mother, Pearl White, deceased, had given Reverend Hill 100,000 pounds in cash to develop a number of church projects. Is that true?'

Barry squirmed. 'Yes.'

'Can you speak louder, please? For the benefit of the tape.' Detective Curly Hair sucked lead from a well-chewed pencil.

'Do you mean yes, you said it? Or yes, it's true?'

'Yes, I said it.'

'But is it true?'

'No, it is not.'

'Then we have a problem. Don't we?'

Barry leant forward and silently mouthed 'is it recording?' to Detective Curly Hair. The officer nodded.

'What my colleague really means is that you lied to us.' Detective Purple Shirt massaged his own eyebrows as he spoke.

'Did I actually lie?'

'Yes you did,' said Detective Purple Shirt, flicking through the notepad he'd bought from WH Smiths. 'You said your mother won a small fortune gambling on the horses sometime during the 1980s.'

'You did tell us that,' said Detective Curly Hair, spitting out more bits of pencil.

'Turns out, however, this small fortune was all yours. And it wasn't small at all, it was larger than your capacity for spinning yarns to law-abiding policemen going about their daily–'

Detective Curly Hair touched his colleague on the arm to stop him. 'It was you who gave 100,000 in cash to Reverend Jacob Hill, wasn't it?'

Barry looked around the room and noticed a poster on the wall telling him that he could join Heddlu De Cymru (South Wales Police) today and have a wonderful career. He said nothing.

'Are your pants on fire?' enquired Detective Purple Shirt.

'Pardon?' enquired Barry, half wondering if he'd emptied his overflowing bowels without realising it.

'Are your pants on fire?'

'No.'

'But you've told us so many lies. They must be on fire.'

'Gotta be smouldering down there at least. I'd say burning. Just like that rugby club fire you reckon you started. Another big fat lie.' Curly Hair tossed his pencil on the table.

'I'm an honest fella,' said Barry, unable to remember what he'd said to the officers during his previous informal interrogation.

Both officers began flicking through their notepads. They took it in turns to jog his memory.

'You said your mother won a fortune on the horses donkeys years ago.'

'You said she was a big fan of Red Rum back in the day.'

'And she pumped a load of money into saving the Dragon pub.'

'Even though she didn't drink. Or go out that much.'

'You told us it was her who gave a hundred grand to Reverend Hill for special church projects.'

'Her dosh, not yours.'

'And the reverend stole it for his own purposes.'

'His purposes, not hers.'

'Special projects, I guess, but not churchy ones.'

'You said your ma didn't trust banks.'

'So she insulated her loft with fifty-pound notes instead.'

'You told us you didn't know where Reverend Hill was hiding.'

'Yet he turns up behind your sofa.'

'Strange that.'

'I think I would spot a clergyman hiding down the back of my settee, wouldn't you, Detective Inspector Willard?'

'I'd back myself to do so,' replied Detective Purple Shirt, smugly.

'Do you think you have to be a copper to identify a man of the cloth hiding behind furniture in your living room?' said Detective Curly Hair to his colleague, ignoring Barry as if he wasn't there.

'Wouldn't reckon so. I'd say a blind man would know there was something afoot. Sticking out.'

'What say you, Barry?' The detectives turned their focus towards Barry but he was barely listening.

'To what?'

'To what, he asks,' said Detective Curly Hair, laughing like a psychopath in a Hitchcock movie.

'Man's a genuine goldfish. Gotta memory span of no more than seven seconds,' said Detective Purple Shirt.

'You two should be on the stage.' Barry remained defiant.

'Hear that?' said Detective Curly Hair.

'I do,' replied Detective Purple Shirt. 'He thinks we're Ant and Dec.'

'Do you think we're Ant and Dec?'

'Wish we had their money.'

'Say, you've not got Ant and Dec's money, have you?' Curly Hair spat the words out along with a dollop of phlegm.

'Are you two clowns going to charge me? It's all very simple. I got confused before. I panicked. I didn't know what I was thinking. Or saying. I was under duress. You didn't properly explain who you were or what you were doing. But now I'm sure of myself and my own mind. I'm sure of the facts. It was all my money. To spend how I liked. And I gave a big lump of it to Reverend Hill. To spend how he liked. Really simple, see? How I earn my money and what I choose to do with it is actually none of your concern. So, boil it all down and what have you got here? No crime has actually been committed. By anyone.'

The two officers bristled.

'What about this letter you wrote?' said Detective Curly Hair, waving a piece of paper in the air. 'Want me to read it to you? It's fascinating stuff. All in your own handwriting.'

'We're really sorry your girlfriend left you for the sunshine of Corfu and all those lean, tanned hunks,' said Detective Purple Shirt, smirking.

'Explains a lot, this letter.'

'Sure does.'

'It's like one of Jacob Hill's Bibles.'

'The Book of Revelations.'

Barry waved a dismissive hand at the officers. 'It tells you diddly-squat. It tells you no crime was ever committed, that's what it does.'

'Listen to that, eh, Craig? He's getting brave. And he's a lawyer now too.'

'That's right, Duncan. No wonder he doesn't need a solicitor. He's a genuine Ally McBeal. Or maybe he's more of a Saul Goodman – *Better Call Saul*. Lying to the police and wasting their time ain't a crime anymore, did you know that? It's official. Cos no crime was ever committed. Ain't that right?'

'You learn something new every day in this job. Don't yer?'

'Every day's a school day.'

'Say, Mr Lawyer Man, seeing as you're the font of all legal knowledge and an expert in the criminal justice system all of a sudden, tell us something else we don't know.'

Detective Purple Shirt folded his arms and rocked back in his seat. Detective Curly Hair nodded his head and tilted it to the side expectantly.

Unlike the toilet in the grim police station cell, Barry sensed he was holding a royal flush in this game of poker.

'Okay, I got something new for you, something that you don't know but I think will really interest you,' said Barry, eagerly.

'Go on.'

'This old cassette machine of yours – the one you're using to record this interview. Well, the wheels aren't going around. In fact, they never have been. So am I free to go – cos I desperately need a shit – or must we go over all this again? For the benefit of the tape and all that.'

Outside the police station Jacob Hill savoured the fresh air and the simple joy of light raindrops on his skin. It was good to be free and not have to run or hide. Sunlight was such an undervalued gift. No one was watching him so he smoked the cigarette his detective interviewers had offered him and watched a group of boys kick a football about in the park opposite. They were playing World Cup: four strikers shooting into the same goal past the same keeper. Last one to score is knocked out until there's only one boy left standing. He stubbed the cigarette out abruptly when he saw Barry trudge out through the front door, his right hand holding his beltless trousers up and his shirt tails flapping.

'How did it go for you?'

'Good.'

'You?'

'I'm a free man.'

'Me too.'

'So is it really over?'

'Yes. Think so.'

Barry received a caution for wasting police time. Purple Shirt and Curly Hair were too embarrassed to push for anything more, having taken so long to find Reverend Hill behind the sofa in his front room. They were getting terrible stick off the rest of the Serious Crime Squad and it was starting to annoy them.

'Wanna go for a pint? I'm gagging for a beer.' Barry swallowed hard.

'Yeah, sounds good.' The reverend told himself that a few jars wouldn't hurt. He'd pick up the road to righteousness again tomorrow.

'I'm sorry for letting you stew so long. In the woods. And in the cellar. I should have told the truth earlier and got you out.' Barry looked at his shoes, sheepishly. He still needed to thread the laces back in.

Reverend Hill shrugged. 'I'm sorry for blowing all your money.'

'Are you really?'

'Yeah, I am. Though I'd do it again. To save my brother.'

'So what now?'

'Pub.'

'After that?'

'I'm going to get the church going again.'

Barry nodded. 'Village needs that. Village needs you.'

Reverend Hill kicked the fag butt he'd stamped out through a grille as if he was one of the innocent boys playing World Cup in the park over the road, dreaming they were Kevin de Bruyne, Harry Kane or Mo Salah.

'Nah, village don't need me. Village needs Jesus. Let's go get those beers. It's your round cos I'm brassic, remember?'

They chose a little spit and sawdust pub in the wilds of the Forest, hoping they'd be the only ones there. Finding Angharad and John John sitting alone at a corner table was most disturbing. Barry hated the fact that he couldn't go anywhere without being seen by someone who knew him. Anghofiedig could be stifling. Suffocating. That was one of the things he loved most about his trip to Europe, no one had a clue who he was or what he did.

Angharad was crying. Lately, that seemed to be the norm for her. She used to be such a happy soul with an infectious laugh. Where had that giggly girl gone? Barry had always thought she was the prettiest butterfly around – but here she was – sat with Mr Butterfly Collector, and her wings looked creased and colourless. Almost mothlike. The only emotion Barry felt for her now was pity. What a fall from grace, eh, from school prom queen to being pitied by none other than Barry White Junior?

Just as Barry was shocked to discover Angharad and John John huddled away in a clandestine corner of a seldom-used pub, Angharad and John John were equally surprised to see Reverend Hill – on the run from the police and public enemy number one in these parts – stroll in bold as brass and order himself a pint of stout with a whisky chaser.

The reverend had to reconnect with his flock sometime. Might as well start now. Without being invited he sat next to John John. Reluctantly, Barry plonked himself beside Angharad.

'Why you crying?'

John spoke for her. 'She's had a knock back.'

'What is it this time?' Barry knew at once his words sounded unsympathetic.

'I thought me and James were getting along great. I thought it was time to move our relationship on to the next level. I did something unexpected that freaked him out. He ran out of the house. Told me I'd got things all wrong. Again.'

'You weren't naked when you did this something unexpected were you?'

'Almost. Apart from tassels.'

Barry laughed. The dam holding back Angharad's tears broke and sent further floods across the table.

'I'm pathetic, aren't I? I'm old and wrinkled and pathetic.'

'You're not that wrinkled,' said Barry.

'She needed someone to talk to. I agreed to meet. Our families go back a long way,' John John said, just to make it clear to Barry and the reverend that he wasn't the latest rebound target in Angharad's desperate game of pinball love search.

'Of course,' said the reverend, savouring his whisky chaser.

'James will come around. He's a good friend. A top bloke. A modern man of the world. He'll understand.' Barry put a hand on Angharad's back then quickly removed it in case she got the wrong idea.

Angharad stopped snivelling and looked up. 'Anyhow, what's he doing here?' She looked directly at Reverend Hill.

'He's having a drink. With me.'

'Does the law know?'

'Shouldn't think so.'

'I don't want to get in trouble.'

'You won't.'

'I'm a free man in a free country,' said Reverend Hill, grinning. 'All that police business was a simple misunderstanding. It's sorted.'

'So you didn't steal any money?' enquired Angharad, sniffing.

'Er... Barry, care to answer that one?'

'No, he didn't.'

John John sipped his lemonade. 'None of that money ever belonged to Pearl, did it? It was all yours wasn't it, son?'

Angharad choked on Barry's pint, which she had helped herself to. 'What do you mean, son?'

Barry moved quicker than he had ever done in his life. 'It's just a figure of speech. Ain't that right, John John?'

'Yes,' said John John, looking forlorn.

'And you're right. Ma didn't leave any money to anyone in her will. She didn't have any money. But I wanted people to think she did.'

John John pursed his lips together. 'So how did you come into so much cash?'

'I won it. Gambling.'

'And there's me working all hours, 24/7, trying to build a business and a life for myself. Who's the fool here, eh? Tell me, who's the biggest village idiot around this little table of ne'er do wells?' John John looked agitated. It wasn't about the money; he was still sore about Barry's public rejection of him minutes ago.

Angharad contemplated John John's question and told herself that the answer was her.

Reverend Hill also considered himself to be the biggest idiot in the room. How could he ever expect to win back people's trust after everything he had done? He hadn't just betrayed Ma and Barry; he'd betrayed all those who needed his help and dropped their guards to let him provide it. God surely worked in mysterious ways. But it would take an awful lot of prayer and Holy Spirit interventions to put things right again. Not to mention time.

'I've got an idea, let's all get pissed. I don't mean let's have a few. I mean let's get properly shitfaced.' It appeared Barry was coming with a late charge down the inside rail in his quest to defend his champion village idiot crown, which had long been undisputed (providing you discounted Romeo).

The other three looked at each other.

'Count me in,' said Angharad, finishing Barry's pint.

'What the hell, though I might need a sub.' Reverend Hill looked for some divine intervention in the nether regions of his wallet.

John John looked shocked. 'I'm seeing another side to you, Jacob.'

Reverend Hill found a tenner in a side pocket of his wallet and beamed. 'Then Peter came to Jesus and asked "Lord, how many times shall I forgive my brother or sister who sins against me? Up to seven times? And Jesus answered not seven times, but seventy-seven times." That's Matthew 18, John John.'

'What about you, John John, fancy something a bit stronger than lemonade and chocolate cake?' said Barry. 'Go on, let your metaphorical hair down for once. Have an afternoon on the lash with me, Bridget Jones and the runaway vicar 'ere.'

Barry patted John John's bald head affectionately. This was him reaching out, trying to make amends for humiliating and disowning his biological father earlier. This was who he really was. John John would find out much more about his youngest son by trading pints with him over several hours, until they fell over in a messy heap, than he ever would eating prawn sarnies and clapping cover drives at Glamorgan County Cricket Club.

John John put on his coat and scarf. 'You know what, I think I'll pass. I ought to be running back to the shop, got a big delivery of frozen foods coming from the wholesaler in half an hour. Have a pleasant afternoon though, won't you? I'm glad you're feeling more optimistic about the future, Angharad. And I'll see you in church on Sunday, reverend, yes? I'm so pleased to have our services back. Go steady with the drinking though. You might not think so, but public appearances matter in our positions. People expect better of us. We have to be the ones to set standards and we have to make sure people see us setting them. I hope I'm not speaking out of turn here, Reverend Hill, but despite your interpretations of Matthew's gospel there are only so many chances a man – let alone a God – can give a prodigal child. You understand. I know you do.'

When John John left the pub, everyone sighed with relief.

'Hey, did I tell you that Greg's in custody? They picked him up in a metro station somewhere near Paris. He was harassing random women, so no change there, eh?' Angharad wiped a small tear from the corner of her eye.

'He's happy to be in jail by all accounts. When they arrested him he was dazed and confused and didn't have any shoes on. He reckoned he wasn't even hassling women, made out he was trying to cadge some money for the Eurostar ride home. He told the French police he hadn't fled the UK on purpose – said he'd been kidnapped by strangers wearing tuxedos with embroidered waistcoats and wide-brimmed hats, and a friendly bear had nicked his shoes. Honestly, how on earth did I ever end up married to that?'

Barry was a glutton, for food, drink and punishment. Yesterday's session in the pub with the vicar and Angharad had left him with a raging hangover, which was unusual as he rarely suffered from them. It was an indication that perhaps, pints had exceeded hours in the last twenty-four-hour whirling lifecycle of the clock.

Angharad had been the first to go home, in a taxi booked and paid for by Barry. She had drunk way too much and was slurring but on the plus side she had stopped crying. Reverend Hill didn't last much longer. He really was a man in turmoil, waging war with himself and his own demons. Barry sensed he wanted to get smashed and cause carnage. The gangster within was desperately trying to get out, to run amok and rip someone's head off in a pointless fight. However, the reverend succeeded in keeping this dangerous figure under wraps in the cellar of his soul. He was desperate to triumph over himself and make amends; to do good things and please his Lord. So he drank five more pints of stout and walked back to Barry's to rest and pray and think.

Barry kept going. When he'd exhausted all his welcomes in

the Forest's pubs he went back to the Dragon and carried on drinking there. The faces in front of him kept changing until it was time for him to throw himself out.

Now, it was Saturday afternoon and he felt terrible. It didn't help that he found himself in the stinking, cramped away team's changing rooms about to run out for a match with old foes the Wye Ziders. Playing rugby was the last thing he really wanted to do today. He thought he might throw up. He never listened to a single word of James's pre-match team talk. Still, at least they had sixteen players, affording Barry the luxury of being sub.

'Barry, I want you to start the game at tighthead prop. Okay?' James smiled as if he was doing his friend an enormous favour with this latest misplaced vote of confidence.

'Ooh, you sure about that? My hamstring's a bit tight again.'

'Nonsense. You're in. I've got every faith in you.'

Things got a whole lot worse for Barry when he ambled out onto the pitch and heard the menacing tones of former school bully and longtime adversary Psycho Daniels.

'Well looky here, if it ain't Barry no balls, come to get his head kicked in for old time's sake. I've phoned ahead to the A&E. Got you a bed ready. You don't need to thank me.'

'Hello, Huw, how's tricks?'

'Go screw yourself.'

'Oh Huw, aren't you tired of all this silly trash talk? I know I am.'

'I ain't even started yet, Sherriff Fatman. But you just wait...'

So many cheap threats and insults. Barry wondered how life had been so cruel that this was the sum outcome of Psycho Daniels and his life, aged forty-five. Had he really found no greater joy than abusing others since his schooldays? Was the thrill of bullying gentle misfits and social outcasts, or people with minor disabilities such as limps, lisps and trusting natures still his number one pastime? Was this as good as it was ever going to get for him? How sad.

'I'm 'aving you today, Whitey. No mincing. No messing. I'm gonna kill you. After I've made you eat dog shit first. Brought my own with me. It's in my pocket, see?' He delved into his pocket, pulled out a plastic bag and waved it in the air.

Barry shook his head. 'You'd better be quick then cos we've actually got the luxury of a sub and tell you the truth, I don't plan on being out here long. Bit of a long session yesterday with the vicar and my friend Angharad. Say, why don't we have a quiet beer together after the game? Put all this childish hostility to bed once and for all? What do you say, Huw? Will you smoke a pipe of peace with me? Let bygones be bygones? Bury the hatchet?'

'I'll bury the hatchet in your skull.'

'Oh Huw. Predictable as ever.'

'Stop calling me Huw will yer? I'm Psycho. Got it?'

'No, I left Psycho behind in the schoolyard all those years ago. You're Huw Daniels, middle-aged, going grey at the temples too by the looks of it. Listen, the way I see it we're just a pair of old rugby vets enjoying their last few hours in the sun. Let's just savour the fact that we're still breathing and enjoy some good clean rugger to work up a Saturday night thirst. How does that sound to you?'

'Sounds like you're still fucking loopy, White. Like your Uncle Derek. I hear he don't even know who he is no more. Good enough for him, I say.'

Barry couldn't quite believe what he had just heard. He froze on the spot and didn't know what to do. The sound of the referee's whistle to start the match slammed him back to reality.

Barry played the rest of the game in a daze. On autopilot. He dreaded every scrum because each one brought him back into direct conflict with Psycho. Barry knew how to take a

beating and he was used to being bullied by Psycho Daniels –
both physically and verbally – because he'd endured it, on and
off, most of his life. However, this was a new kind of warfare.
Psycho had expanded his artillery and worked out that he could
hurt Barry the most by ridiculing his Uncle Derek's dementia. It
made him the worst kind of troll imaginable. And it left Barry
feeling lost, isolated and vulnerable.

McQueen got wind of what was happening.

'Whitey, it's okay, I've got your back.'

'Thanks, McQueen.'

'No, Whitey, really. I've got your back. He can't be saying
that stuff. It's not right.'

'No it's not. What you gonna do?'

'Not me. Us.'

'What we gonna do?'

McQueen scrunched up his face and spat out his words like
he was Johnny Rotten imploring God to save the Queen in the
silver jubilee year. 'Right, here's the plan. When anyone sees
Daniels standing on his own, we get the ball to James so he can
launch it high above his head. Then the rest of us will charge
him. We'll all pile into him at once as he catches the ball. You lot
can join the dots from then on.' McQueen was oozing real blood
having bitten his lip in excitement.

'Not sure about all this,' said James, ever the diplomat.

McQueen venomously fired a clot of blood from his mouth,
which landed like a dart between James's feet.

'The plan is the plan,' he snarled.

Barry was relieved to have the old McQueen back. Sure, he
could be mean and a bully, just like Psycho Daniels, but he was
different. He was more like a 1960s villain, he had his own
moral code and his own red lines, they just weren't always easy
to fathom out. And he had a strong sense of right and wrong,
even if, more often than not, it was a bit fucked up. When the

chips were down and people on his side needed someone to fight their battles for them, he would step up. Just like Uncle Derek always used to do. They were hard men, but they understood natural justice.

McQueen spotted his opportunity when Psycho slipped and failed to run upfield with the rest of his pack. He threw the ball to James, who delivered the perfect up and under, high above Psycho's head. Psycho steadied himself to catch the ball.

'Charge!' yelled McQueen, like a crazy frontline general going over the top with no reasoning why.

Most of the Anghofiedig team followed and piled in on Psycho Daniels just as he took the ball. McQueen and Jonah got there first, quickly disappearing under a melee of bodies. The wind hissed out of Psycho's body. The Wye Ziders players rushed in to help one of their own, drawn to a good old-fashioned dust-up like moths to a night light.

The referee tried to ignore what was happening. James ran forward with his teammates but held back from jumping in on Psycho. Instead, he caught his own kick on the bounce and threw a pass to Barry – the tortoise to McQueen's hare – who was simply too slow and too far from the action to get to Psycho in time for the 'shoeing'.

It was then that everything froze. The punch-up taking place on one side of the pitch became incidental as the referee continued to turn a blind eye to all things illegal and waved play on. Barry found himself with ball in hand and a clear and open pathway to the try line.

'Run, Barry, run!' yelled James.

The heads of several Wye Ziders poked out from the cyclops of arms, limbs and torsos.

'Get him!' yelled the Wye Ziders captain, realising they'd been duped.

Within seconds, the whole of the Wye Ziders team, save for

Psycho, who sat on the grass watching new stars circulate around his orbit, pulled themselves to their feet and began chasing after Barry.

'Take the handbrake off, Whitey!' screamed McQueen, no longer wearing a shirt because it had been ripped from his back in the ruckus.

'I've hit altitude!' shouted Barry, getting his excuses in early for the inevitable cock-up that was sure to follow.

The try line was getting closer but so was the fastest Wye Zider. With twenty yards to go, a muscular blond youth of about eighteen got to Barry and looked destined to pull him to the ground.

James groaned. McQueen swore. The rest of the Anghofiedig team rubbed body parts that hurt and contemplated the meaning of life: what's it all about and why the bloody hell are we here?

However, Barry wasn't done. When the hit came in from behind, he wobbled like a newly born fawn but didn't go down. He advanced several yards more. Two more defenders got to him and jumped on his back but still he kept rolling forward like an unstoppable tank.

Only one man stood between Barry and the line – Elvis Evans, the Wye Ziders captain: big, ugly and sixteen stone of muscle. Incredibly, with two large men still riding on his back like he was Brecon Beacon Boy flying around Cheltenham racecourse, Barry kept going. In his head all he could picture was Uncle Derek's face. He could even hear his uncle's voice urging him on.

'Go on, son, I knew you had it in you somewhere.'

Barry sidestepped Elvis with a deft shake of his own pelvis and crashed over the line for an unbelievable score.

He could no longer breathe but he rationalised that if he was about to die, this was a good way to go.

It was his first try of the 21st century and the score that won the match.

Being a bona fide matchwinner, Barry had every right to plonk his chair in the centre of the clubhouse lounge and demand his peasant subjects bring him free drinks all night. He'd long dreamt of such an occasion, holding the magic flute that held his champagne moment to drink over and over again. He'd get fleeter of foot with each retelling of his story and the distances he had to travel to get to the line would grow too. The men he carried on his back would become Goliaths and those he sidestepped around would be transformed into nimble ballet dancers. There would be many more thwarted defenders on the field by the end of the evening. They'd reproduce and multiply in Barry's head like randy bugs before squeezing their way into the new legend he was in the midst of creating.

However, none of this actually happened. Barry drank a single pint of weak lager, paid his match fees, accepted a few congratulatory slaps on the back from a handful of relatively contented teammates, then left. He still felt uncomfortable about the whole business of the fire and didn't want any stupid run-ins with unfriendly committee members. He was sure that would happen if he hung around, laughing and playing the hero. In Anghofiedig, if you were up, someone always wanted to knock you down. And matchwinner or not, Barry was still the reason why – in most people's eyes – they had to walk out of the clubhouse and across the cold car park to take a piss in a smelly portable loo.

As he made his way out of the club's main gates, Barry spotted a sad figure sitting alone on a low wall.

'All right, Huw, how's the head?'

'Doc said I had mild concussion. Fine now.'

Barry was surprised not to be sworn at. 'Sorry about what happened out there. But you kinda asked for it.'

Huw nodded and said nothing.

'What you doing sat here on your own?'

'Waiting for a lift. Missus is picking me up.'

'Ah right. Go steady.'

'Yeah.'

Barry didn't know if Psycho was still concussed or whether he'd genuinely had the stuffing knocked out of him, but he'd never seen him so mellow. Maybe Doctor Humphreys had pumped him full of sedatives? Barry almost felt sorry for his old adversary. In a masochistic sort of way, part of him even wanted his old nemesis to spontaneously jump off the wall, grab him menacingly around the throat – squeezing hard enough to cut off the supply of both air and blood – before pronouncing, 'Hey, Barry no balls, wanna eat some more dog shit?'

'Hey, Whitey, wait up.'

Barry paused and watched Psycho walk slowly over towards him. He stopped just inside Barry's personal space. Barry waited for the sound of fist on cranium but it didn't come.

'Your Uncle Derek. He's all right, by the way. I shouldn't have said that stuff.'

'Aww, thanks, Huw.' Barry stuck out a hand for shaking.

'Nah, screw you, fat boy. He might be all right but you're still a prick.'

And with that, Huw 'Psycho' Daniels jumped in a speeding Nissan Micra that blew in on the wind out of nowhere, spitting gravel as it went. And as quickly as it appeared, it was gone.

On his meandering walk home, Barry called in at John John's Mart and bought himself a bag of cream doughnuts, a pork pie and a can of Fanta. Outside the shop he bumped into Olly the barber, who was waiting for the bus to his grandad's new bungalow in Reardon Avenue.

'Watcha, Olly, want a cream doughnut?'

'No ta. Grandad's doing me tea tonight. A nice nut roast.'

'Nice one. How's life back in the hair trade?'

'Bit slow. But good all the same.'

'Better than the slaughterhouse, I bet?'

'Oh much. You wouldn't believe what goes on inside those places. I'm full-on veggie now.'

Barry hid his pork pie behind his back. Olly saw him do it but wasn't bothered.

'Say, why don't you drop in on Monday – you look like you could do with a haircut.'

Barry's eyes bulged out on stalks but he tried to conceal his anxiety. 'Er, got a fair bit on next week, Olly lad. Another time maybe?'

Olly moved in closer and began talking in hushed tones, as if he were selling cocaine on the street corner.

'I'll give you my latest thing, fab it is, it'll make you look like Liam Gallagher. It's great for OAPs like you, well, them still with hair any roads. It's a rocking feather cut, long at the back with a short straight fringe. Spiky too. It's the dog's bollocks. Real popular.'

'Sounds like the old classic mod cut,' said Barry, wincing.

'Yeah, it's modern all right. Justin Bieber had one a while back.'

'Did you do his?'

'Nah. But I could've done it. It's already my signature style and I ain't long learned it. Secret is to make it extra long and pointy down the sides. And to snip the fringe real high and real straight. I use a ruler for exactness.'

'Ooh, a ruler, eh? You sure you don't wanna doughnut, Olly? You look like you've lost a few pounds. Them trousers of yours are slipping right off yer arse. You'll be half naked by the time you get back to your grandad's.'

'I don't want a doughnut, thanks. And as for the trousers, that's fashion, Bazza.'

Barry cooed. 'Baggy trousers and feather cuts. You're the man round here, Olly!'

Olly looked pleased with himself. 'That's me bus coming. Don't forget to come and get your Liam G, will ya? When you're not busy, like...'

Barry somehow pulled the ring on his can of Fanta clean off and slurped hard on his pop. 'I won't.'

Barry couldn't resist calling in to see Uncle Derek to tell him about the day's rugby exploits. He walked straight through the front door without knocking.

'Hey, Uncle Derek, you'll never guess what happened today.'

'We're up here.'

Barry followed the voice and found Derek and Ruth sitting on their bed looking at old photo albums.

'Hello, lad, how did rugby go?' said Ruth, warmly.

'We won, Aunty Ruth, and you'll never believe it but I scored the winning try.' Barry beamed like a proud schoolboy, expecting his Uncle Derek to congratulate him and ask for a blow by blow account.

'That's nice,' said Derek, disinterested.

'It's all right, love, it's just a tide out kind of day.' Ruth flicked Barry a knowing look. 'That's why I thought it might be nice to take your uncle down memory lane.'

Ruth held up a picture of the three of them at the seaside. Derek looked young, athletic and tanned in just a pair of tight blue speedos, flexing his muscles as if he were Wales's answer to Arnold Schwarzenegger. In the photograph, Barry was on the ground making a sandcastle, not looking at the camera. His moat appeared to have flooded his castle because half of the walls had subsided. Ruth was sitting on a deckchair, smiling and holding a Jackie Collins paperback. She wore a big straw hat and large sunglasses.

'Remember this? Anglesey 1987, I think. You came away in the caravan with us. It gave your ma a bit of a break. Wasn't long after your poor old dad died.'

'I remember.'

Derek snatched the photo and stared at it, hardly recognising himself. A different man in a different world. 'We wanted a son. Nearly had one, didn't we, love?'

Ruth pulled the photo out of her husband's hand and placed it back inside the album it had come from. She closed it and put it to one side.

Barry frowned. 'What do you mean, Uncle Derek?'

'Oh shush, love, he don't know what he's saying,' said Ruth, keen to change the subject.

'I bloody do,' said Derek, grabbing the album once more. 'We didn't think we could have kids. Same as our Barry. Then out of the blue, both Ruthy and Pearl got pregnant within a fortnight of each other. We were all happy as larks. I know I was. And so was our kid. We felt like proper men. I remember that holiday away with you cos... well, I felt like a dad. I got to imagine what it would have been like to have a real son. One of my own.'

Ruth turned her face away from Barry's gaze.

'Aunty Ruth, is this all true?'

'Course it is, I ain't completely senile yet!' snapped Derek.

'Aunty Ruth?'

'Yes, it's true. I carried our baby for seven months and two weeks but then we lost it. You came along just after.'

Barry sat on the bed next to his aunty, who was now crying.

'Why didn't anyone tell me?'

'No point. Not going to change anything is it?' said Derek.

'But I deserved to know.'

Derek got up and tossed the album onto a chair. Lots of the photos fell out onto the floor, so Ruth got down on her hands and knees and began to pick them up and place them carefully back in their rightful places in the album.

Derek watched her and tutted before turning to Barry. 'You didn't deserve to know anything. We weren't even sure you were Barry's kid.'

Ruth screamed, 'Derek! Stop!'

'Only saying what we all thought. Boy reckons he's got a right to know things so let him hear it.'

The colour drained out of Barry's face.

'Ignore him, love. It's the dementia,' said Ruth.

'Don't lie, Ruthy. I know what I'm saying. We all wondered. Me, Ruth and most of all, our Barry. Why you didn't look like us. Act like us. Think like us. You were always different. It was obvious.'

'That true, Aunty Ruth?' Barry grabbed a different photo from the 1987 Anglesey holiday out of her clutches. In this one, Derek was holding a rugby ball and they'd marked a little pitch out in the sand.

'We wondered, that's all. But you were a gift to each of us. Pearl especially.'

Barry got up and rubbed the back of his leg.

'Aunty Ruth, I've been reading up on things we can do to

help Uncle Derek. It's important we get him to stick to routines and write lots of lists to remind him of things. We need to find things he likes doing and then do them at the same time every day. We gotta keep things consistent.'

'That's right,' said Ruth, wiping her eyes with a handkerchief.

'And we've got to keep reassuring him that we understand. These photos, we need to get them out of their albums and put them up on the walls – everywhere – so the house feels familiar and safe for him. So he's always got reminders of the things he can remember.'

'Sounds good.'

Barry bent down and held his uncle's hand.

'Guess what, Uncle Derek, we beat the Wye Ziders today with a last minute try and I ran half the length of the pitch to score it.'

Derek smiled, every line of his face fading away. 'Did you? That's amazing, lad. I always told people you had it in you. You're a White see, one of us. Ain't that right, Ruthy?'

Ruth laughed and sobbed in equal measures.

'Yes, my love. He's a bloody White all right.'

Reverend Hill stood behind the curtain as if he was a rock star settling his nerves before running out to salute his crowd and receive their adulation. However, there was unlikely to be much adulation in these pews today. He could tell without looking that there was a sizeable congregation from the easy murmurings and noisy chatter. He couldn't see a soul save for Barry, who was on the organ banging out 'Old Rugged Cross' way too fast as usual. He was out of practice and it showed. His pacing was way off. He was thumping the keys too hard, as if he was trying to fend off Psycho Daniels on a rugby field. Still, all that was the least of the reverend's problems today.

Jacob Hill clasped his hands together and recited the Lord's Prayer under his breath. By the time he got to the power and the glory bit, he was ready to go out and face the music. However, he knew that a restless church was no place to start a comeback tour.

He walked across the room towards his pulpit in total silence. He stood quietly for just a few moments, though it felt like an eternity.

In his head, he couldn't shake off the words 'Hello,

Glastonbury!' He wanted to smile and pump a fist but he knew he had to show more contrition and accept his fate.

Let's get this over with, he thought to himself. *Lord, give me the right words.*

'Church, standing before you is a pitiful sinner. A sinner who has let you down. I am a thief. And a liar. I stole 100,000 pounds from you all – denying you of the good things you were promised.

'Am I sorry? Yes. And no. I see your faces and I can feel your anger and contempt for me. I feel terrible for selling you out. And yet, I did not use any of this money for personal gain. I used it to save the life of my brother from gangsters who know nothing of God and wanted to hurt him badly. Maybe even kill him. I used to call these same men friends of mine in a previous life. They used to embrace me as one of their own.

'I have learnt these past few months that the genuineness of our faith is only revealed through trials and tests. We will all be severely tested in life. Why? Because God wants to see if our faith is real or not. The Devil will tempt us and try to destroy us. Our God drops us in fires to see if we can stand the heat and – if we can – he'll watch our faith grow as he pulls us away from the flames.

'I have spent months running away from so many things: Justice. Policemen. You. And myself.

'Locked away in a dingy cellar for so many long days and even longer nights I read my Bible and prayed constantly. In my cellar, I discovered one true friend, Jesus. No, that's not entirely correct, I found two friends, because Barry White also stood by me. It might surprise you to know that I actually believe me and Barry White aren't so different. I know it surprises me to hear those words said aloud. We both want to change. But don't know how.

'I am bad but I want to be good. As long as I walk this

miserable earth, I will remain bad. That's how I'm made. I am broken. I will fail and let you down over and over again. Just as you will fail yourselves and each other. And maybe me too.

'So what else have I learnt from my time in exile? Above all, I now know that I have nothing of any value to give to God except my desire to be better than I am. I need to stand up for that, even if that means standing alone. Like I am now.

'You might choose to attack me once I quit talking, either verbally or perhaps physically. That's okay. I understand I have no authority to stand before you in this pulpit unless it comes from God.

'However, my recent experiences mean I am more qualified to stand here than I was before. With my reputation in shreds and your eyes piercing my sides with hatred, I am a better Christian than the man who stood here several months ago, accepting your praise and admiration.

'People, I have made terrible mistakes, but my time in the wilds was not wasted. I consider it a blessing.'

Reverend Hill dropped to his knees and, with tears streaming down his face, began talking in tongues.

Barry got up from his organ and cautiously approached him. 'You all right, rev? Need some water?' He handed Reverend Hill a glass.

'This is all very touching but what about our over-seventies Teddy Boys Club?' shouted Derry Lee from the back of the church. He was wearing a bobble hat, even though it was boiling hot outside.

'Hey, Derry, wos with the bobbler?' enquired Dot.

'Don't even go there, Peggy Sue,' said Derry Lee, twitching.

'I know why he's wearing it,' exclaimed church treasurer Ralph Kilminster, his hair sticking up on top like he'd just frantically rubbed it with a balloon. Or walked straight off the set of *Quadrophenia*.

Swifty Taylor, also modelling a fancy feather cut with a Rod-the-mod-Stewart spike at the back, nodded vociferously. 'Never setting foot in Kenny Wick's shop again. My missus did a better job during Covid with a broken saucepan and a pair of toenail clippers.'

'Let's get back to business, shall we?' said Helen Ball. 'Reverend, you stole a hundred grand from Pearl White. When are you gonna pay it back?'

'It doesn't seem right that the police just let you off like that. You should go to prison!' yelled local curmudgeon Harold J. Jones, waving his arms about as if he was drowning.

'I'm inclined to agree with Jonesy for once,' said Betty Ford, biting her lip.

'But the boy's sorry. Look at him,' replied Dot, sympathetically.

'That's not tears, that's him laughing all the way to the bank.' Clive Clementine spat on his hands and rubbed them together after speaking.

'Hear, hear, miaow,' mimed Maximilius Percival through the glove puppet of his white cat.

'Lock him up, lock him up, lock him up!' chanted Llewellyn Davies, as if he was Donald Trump at a rally. A few others joined in the chorus.

'Oh please, pipe down, you sanctimonious bastards!'

The church fell deathly silent. Barry wasn't quite sure where those words had come from, but it appeared they had come from him.

'Listen, the reverend is not going to prison because he didn't steal anything. I gave him all that money. Me. Not Ma. Me. See, it wasn't her money, it was mine. All of it. I'm actually quite rich. It's not really any of your business but I won a fortune gambling, mostly on ridiculous long shots that everyone else dismissed as crazy and fanciful. Well, on this occasion, some of them came through.'

Barry paused for breath and surveyed the room. There were so many open mouths it looked like a convention of dentists. He ploughed on regardless. 'I wish I'd never won a penny cos winning all that loot robbed me of any joy I got from betting on horses. And so far, being lucky has brought me nothing but bad luck, but – and you need to listen closely to this bit – I gave that money to Reverend Hill not to the church. Me. I asked him to do something good with it, that's all. The what, why and wherefore was all down to him. Now, his choice of investment is not exactly what I had in mind, but that doesn't matter because he probably saved his brother's life. And no disrespect, Derry Lee, but in a game of Top Trumps that beats you having a bells and whistles rock around the clock with your teddy boy guys and gals once or twice a week, doesn't it?'

Barry took a big gulp of water from Reverend Hill's glass. 'One more thing. It was also me who bought The Dragon for this village. I thought it would bring everyone closer together but I was wrong. The good news is the pub's going to stay open. However, the bad news for you lot is that you no longer have any say in the running of it. Because you all behaved like total arseholes and left me to carry the can for most things, I've sold up and sold out. Basically, cos I was fed up.'

'Who you sold to?' asked Clever Trevor Peacock, secretly wondering if there might be a reprieve for the skittles team.

'Delores Hamilton.'

'That rich Yankee woman who's got her claws in that lunatic pal of yours?' cried Harold J. Jones, his voice attempting to emphasise every syllable.

'Yes, sir, the very badger.'

'Guess that makes you pretty rich again,' said Frankie Spencer, spinning her beret in her hands.

'Technically, at this precise moment in time, I suppose it does. But by this time next week I'll be as skint as you. And to be completely frank, Frankie, I can't bloody wait.'

Outside the church, Angharad found Barry sitting on the bench where they'd shared many a Sunday morning confessional together. Angharad squeezed out Clever Trevor – who was updating him on his likely court dates – and made it clear she needed to talk.

'Barry, listen up.'

'Okay. What is it?'

'I'm leaving.'

'Leaving who?'

'Leaving Anghofiedig.'

James had helped Angharad land a new job with a reputable property company in Cardiff. He'd pulled a few strings (one of his posh mates was a director) to get her the fresh start she desperately wanted. The job came with a smart flat as well as a sizeable salary; a stepping stone towards fulfilling her ultimate dream of becoming a property tycoon in her own right.

'James really is a sweetheart. Just a shame I'm not twenty years younger, eh? Where's the time gone, Barry? When did we get this old?' Angharad held Barry's arm, acting out the point that they were a senior couple, sitting on a park bench, watching the world go by and putting it to rights.

'Ma used to say I was born with old bones. She reckoned I'd come into my own when my body caught up with the rest of me.'

Angharad laughed. 'You're such a twat sometimes.'

Barry said nothing but couldn't help thinking that he wasn't

the one persistently throwing himself at people on the rebound
from a spectacularly failed marriage.

'What's happening between you and Diana anyhow?'

'Not much.'

'Don't let her slip away. You'll regret it.'

'She's already slipped.'

'What d'you mean?'

'She's in Corfu.'

'Holiday or longer?'

'She didn't say.'

Angharad sighed. 'Oh Barry, why are you so crap with
women? Even my wacky brother is putting you to shame in that
department and he's a man who visits imaginary planets ten
times a day to hang out with imaginary people.'

Barry had no answers. These past few days and weeks he'd
come to realise just how much he enjoyed having Diana in his
life. He wanted her to come home but didn't feel he had much
to offer her. And he still reasoned that letting her go was better
than letting her down.

'Do you want to be loved?' said Angharad, kicking her heels
back and forth like she was twelve as she looked up at the sky.

'I do.' Barry's gaze was directed at his feet. He noticed he
was wearing one black sock and one red one.

'Then go after her.'

'What, fly to Corfu? On my own?'

'If you have to. Do whatever it takes to win her back. Show
her you really want her. Women want to be chased.'

'Is that the real reason you're going to Cardiff? Do you want
James to come running after you?'

Angharad laughed. 'I want to be loved too. Anything wrong
with that?'

'Course not. But don't act like you're needy. It puts men off.

And it's okay for you to be on your own for a bit. It's probably the best thing for you.'

Angharad kissed her friend on the cheek. 'You're a box of surprises, Barry White. One minute I think you're the biggest knobhead on earth and the next you're all wise and protective.'

Barry blushed. 'No problem.'

'Pearl would be proud of you. You're legacy enough for her.'

Barry blushed some more, his skin tone switching from dark red to purple. 'I'll miss you when you're not around. I'll miss this.' He slapped the bench where they sat.

'Cardiff isn't very far. Learn to drive. Come and visit weekends. Give up rugby. Come and stay.'

'Might do that.'

'You won't.'

'No, I won't.'

TWENTY-FIVE
MR WHITE, WHAT MAKES YOU UNIQUE?

Walking back through the swinging main doors was like walking back in time. Everything was deep red and gold, even the carpets. There was shimmering glass and mirrors everywhere, moving around the place, you had to keep your wits about you. Everything was so clinical. Clean. Swiss-like. As if you were about to receive private knee surgery. Or worse, get euthanised.

Barry couldn't believe he used to come to this place every day, 8.30am until 5pm, five days a week, with an hour for lunch, as part of the LesCargo comms team. Harder to believe was the fact he was here now, about to be interviewed for a job he didn't want that would see him make the biggest U-turn known to man since his poor old dad realised he was driving his juggernaut the wrong way down the M4 at 75mph.

Angharad wasn't the only one being fixed up for work by James. The initial offer came out of the blue, over a lazy Sunday lunchtime beer. After Barry had told James he was selling The Dragon to Delores and didn't have any immediate plans for his own future.

Before the day was out, James had arranged for Barry to be interviewed for a temporary six-month position in LesCargo's logistics planning department, managing thirty-, sixty- and ninety-day forecasts to identify lines at risk of going out of stock and recommending actions – which James said was always, without exception, to get more stock.

'Look, it's dead easy and you can work from home three days a week,' said James, enthusiastically.

'All sounds a bit dull.' Barry was unimpressed.

'Not at all, there's something hugely satisfying about managing algorithms so effectively that you can see your successes visually, laid out in front of you on well-stacked warehouse shelves.' James got more excited the longer the sentence went on, just like he used to do when explaining rush defence tactics to baffled faces down the rugby club.

'It all sounds fucking abysmal if you excuse my French. Besides, I hate working with numbers. I'm a wordsmith.'

James refused to be beaten. 'Nonsense, you need something to get you up in the morning. Look, I know you can do it. I read your supply chain dexterity piece last week, the one you did with Douglas McAllister, the Inverness boss. Most impressive it was. Full of pertinent stats. You clearly understand logistics in its true art form.'

Barry rocked his head back like he'd just been poked in the eye with a pencil. 'Has that piece only just been published? I wrote it over a year ago.'

'Well no, it landed on my desk for my input and approval but it's nearly there. Only four or five more managers to go.'

Barry cursed the world of LesCargo in more home-cooked French, not wasting a single syllable to ensure James understood exactly how he felt. Barry's words took James from A to B along the fastest available route, in the quickest possible time.

'Oh come on, give it a go,' said James, persisting. 'It's just a six-month contract to tide you over and keep you out of mischief. You'll be doing me a personal favour. I'm lead recruiter on this one and I need someone I can trust who can start straight away. The job will be yours if you apply, I promise. There will have to be an interview, of course, but it will be a formality. Between you and me we've only had two other applications so far, one from a Nigerian prince who plans to commute from Lagos a couple of days a week and the other from Don the Bastard. At the moment, I'm leaning towards the prince, but I'm in a bit of a hole.'

Now, sitting before Barry at the interview was James and his operational sidekick, Mary Hopkins. Like James, she was part of the new breed of go-getting managers brought in by the company to replace the dinosaurs, refresh strategies and modernise processes and thinking. She reminded Barry of Liz Truss in both looks and mannerisms.

Surprisingly, Mary led the interview, with James taking the back seat role. Barry sensed immediately that she didn't rate or even like him. Her questions came thick and fast but he fended them off as best he could, usually with lies, damn lies and a few more statistics.

'Mr White, what do you consider your main strengths to be?'

'I'm a team player who's quick on his feet.' *Did you see my try on Saturday against the Wye Ziders? Well, did you? Out of this bloody world it was.*

'How do you handle stress?'

'With deep breathing exercises and by breaking things down into smaller deliverables: the things I can control and the things I can't.' *And if that doesn't work, I drink a bathtub of beer and get rat-arsed.*

'What makes you unique?'

'Without doubt, my ability to see the big picture, to distinguish the wood from the trees.' *What makes me unique? My capacity for booze is pretty special. Also, I can take a hiding and bounce back for more. Pretty useful I'd say, especially if I'm gonna be working around you. I'm also uncannily good at tucking away hamburgers. Fifteen is my personal best. And sleeping. I can pretty much kip anywhere. Including LesCargo warehouses. Even when they're busy and noisy and people won't leave me alone.*

'Are you currently applying for any other positions?'

'Yes, I'm looking to broaden my horizons and widen my net, so I wouldn't expect to be on the job market for long.' *Am I looking for work? Really? Do I look like a psychopath? Hell no!*

Mary Hopkins didn't seem convinced by anything Barry had to say for himself.

'Mr White, I must say, I have some concerns about your suitability for this position based mainly on your company history which, it seems, is best described as chequered. Tell me, why do you want to come back to LesCargo?'

Barry flicked James a 'help me, I'm desperate' look. James fired back with a 'you know how to bullshit' stare.

'Well, Mrs Hopkins, I've discovered lots about myself these past few months and it's made me realise the grass is not always greener on the other side.'

Mary paused, looked at James, then switched her attention back to Barry.

'On the other side of what?'

Barry stuttered. 'Er, the LesCargo fence.'

Mary carried on reading Barry's work file without even looking up. Barry watched the muscles in her neck twitch. James leant back even further and pulled another anxious face of encouragement from behind her back.

'Mr White, what have you discovered about yourself since leaving your last position with us?'

Barry fidgeted in his chair. 'Ooh loads.'

'Tell me one thing.'

'Well…'

'Yes…'

'Well, I've discovered I blooming love logistics, I do. And that I'm not entirely sure I can live without it.'

James hit his own head with the back of his hand and made out he was rubbing an itch. 'I think what Mr White means is, he now feels he made a mistake leaving LesCargo. He regrets his decision and if he had the opportunity to turn back the clock he'd take it. Isn't that right, Mr White?'

'Spot on, Jamesy, you're so good at this malarkey. Nice one.'

'So why the planning department? I mean, you worked in communications previously. Planning is quite a departure, if you'll excuse the pun.' Mary began laughing at her own joke, a joke no one else in the room understood.

Barry leant against the arm of his swivel chair and almost toppled out the side.

'I've always been a planner, me.'

'What have you planned?'

'Ooh loads of things.'

'Tell me one thing.'

James sat back rigidly, praying that Barry wouldn't say 'piss ups'. Or 'ma's funeral'. Or 'the concealment of a fugitive vicar – on the run from the law – in my pub cellar'.

Barry sighed.

'Listen, can we stop all these silly games? Truth is I don't care much about this job or the company and I care even less about logistics or trying to impress you. But that bloke next to you is a good friend of mine and he said he was in a fix and needed a favour. So here I am, I suppose to help him out. And when I've done that I'll be off, hopefully to never set foot in this place ever again. It's really that simple. Jamesy begged me to come here today and he reckons I can do a job for him. I've got my doubts, like you, but to be honest, his judgement is usually a lot sounder than mine in most things so I'm prepared to give it a shot for a few months if you are. How does that sound?'

Mary Hopkins smiled for the first time that afternoon.

'Mr White, that all sounds most agreeable. Welcome to LesCargo. We're glad to have you back on the chain gang. The *supply* chain gang.'

James cringed. Barry feigned a smile, the kind a hostage would throw his or her captor in a bid to avoid a beating. And Mary Hopkins – looking and sounding more like Liz Truss than ever – put her pen down squarely on the table and folded all of her papers away feeling mightily pleased with herself.

'Just one more thing, your starting salary will be slightly lower than when you left us previously but after a few months should increase to a more reasonable level.'

Mary Hopkins's head went lopsided, forcing Barry to stare a little too long before replying.

'Thanks for letting me know. I'll adjust my performance, attitude and efforts to match all that.'

TWENTY-SIX
WHEN WORLDS COLLIDE

It was just like old times. Barry sitting in bed at an obtuse angle, supported by pillows, with a laptop on his knees – moving the cursor around every so often so his Teams light stayed green to show the powers that be he was 'active'. His television was on, loud and blaring – a rerun of *Minder*, with his all-time favourite actor Dennis Waterman starring and also singing the theme tune. 'I Could Be So Good For You'.

It felt good in some ways to be back amongst the nine-to-five brigade. Downstairs he could hear hustling and bustling in his kitchen, the spit of the frying pan, the sizzling of fat sausages.

He opened an email from James, welcoming him to the company and requesting his presence at an induction meeting at the LesCargo offices, tomorrow at 9am.

Bollocks to all that, thought Barry, as he plotted an imaginary 24-hour stomach bug to keep him away from offices, warehouses, people and all things red and gold.

He sat back to watch his programme: the episode where Terry's friend George Palmer escapes from prison with only three months left on his sentence. His eyes started to close until the buzz of his mobile phone brought him back into the morning.

'Whatsupp....'

'Hey, Romeo, what you doing?'

'Watching *Minder*. You?'

'Same.'

'How's work?'

'Good. How's Delores?'

'She's good too. You coming to the opening night later? Should be special.'

'Yeah, wouldn't miss it.'

'Nice one. I'm helping Delores get the place ready. She's got me hanging balloons and bunting all day. Red, white and blue 'uns with stars and stripes on 'em. If you're not too busy come down and help me out. I could do with some of your gas to fill them up.'

'Sorry, I'm flat out. First day back and all that.'

'Ha! You don't change, you lazy bugger.'

'Catch you later, dude. Sesh on, yes?'

'I'm up for that. Been ages since I had a proper blow out.'

'Ciao for now, dog breath.'

'Yeah, ciao, dick brain. Give them LesCargo bosses hell for me, won't yer?'

Barry settled himself back down amongst his pillows, pulling the duvet up to his chest when he heard a knock on the bedroom door.

'Is it all right to come in? You're not naked or nothing?'

'No, I'm decent.'

In walked Dotty, carrying a large tray bursting under the weight of a full English breakfast that Chepstow café owner Harry would probably call the mega Tarbosaurus or the all-conquering Leptoceratops.

'There's tea and toast as well, but I'll have to go back down to fetch it cos I couldn't fit it all on one tray and I couldn't carry two,' said Dot, out of breath.

'Thank you.'

'Well, it's the least I can do. I know Pearl would want me to look after you and help you keep your strength up now you're back doing proper work. I'll push the hoover around if you like but then I've got to go. I'm meeting Derry Lee at eleven, we're practising our jitterbug and our bunny hop. We've entered another comp at a fete in Coleford next week. I reckon we've got a good chance of coming home with the cup this time.'

'You gotta keep dancing, Dotty.'

'Will do, my love. I'll be back same time tomorrow to fix your breakfast. Nine o'clock isn't too late for you, is it? I can get here sooner if it helps. You're probably busy, though, first thing: going through emails, giving people orders and doing all your computer stuff.'

'Nine's just fine. Don't think my diary is overly busy tomorrow.'

'Anything else I can do for you before I go?'

Barry pondered. He contemplated asking Dot if she wouldn't mind learning how to keep an eye on his laptop, watching the Teams light until it changed from green to white with a red cross in the middle – for absent – then giving his cursor a little nudge to make it go back to green.

'No, can't think of anything off the top of my head,' said Barry cheerily, filling his face with a forkful of egg and mushrooms.

Dotty's training session to become a qualified, semi-automated mouse jiggler could wait until another day.

Aunty Ruth didn't go anywhere without her face on and even made sure she looked her best when nipping to John John's Mart for a bag of sugar. Barry couldn't remember ever seeing her unmasked before and it shocked him to see how old she looked. He could see her facial lines and her grey roots shooting through, close to her skull.

'Wondered if you were coming down The Dragon for Delores's opening night? Looks like it's going to be a good one. And I wanted to check everything's all right with Uncle Derek. And you. Is it?'

Ruth barely looked up from the magazine she was reading. 'It's never going to be all right again, is it?'

Barry didn't have any words or crumbs of comfort to offer her. It was little wonder she was depressed. He'd be depressed if he was walking around in her tiny size five shoes. Usually, he was able to find some kind of emotional raft to lend people when they were feeling down but this was different. She and Uncle Derek were flapping around in seriously choppy waters, drowning slowly, and there was nothing he or anyone else could do to save them.

'It was Derek who started the fire down the rugby club, wasn't it?' Aunty Ruth's piercing blue eyes snapped tightly on Barry's face like immovable crocodile teeth.

'Yeah.'

'And you took the blame for him?'

Barry shrugged.

Derek walked into the lounge from the kitchen as if he was a zombie, sliding his slippered feet along the ground so they squeaked and holding his hands out in front of him in case he fell. He looked directly at Barry but said nothing.

'Hello, Uncle Derek.'

Derek looked across at his wife, then back at Barry. 'Who's this lump of lard?'

Barry's mouth dropped open. Ruth tried to act calm and reassuring but she was unable to pull it off.

'What d'you mean, you soft old fool? This is Barry. Your bloody nephew.' Ruth got up and helped Derek into his favourite armchair.

'Never seen this man before in my life. Didn't even know I had a nephew. Where've you been hiding him?'

Ruth started to get cross. 'Oh for goodness' sake, it's Barry. You know who I mean. Barry!'

Barry stroked his aunt's back. 'It's all right, Aunty Ruth, honestly.'

He turned to face his uncle and knelt down beside him. 'Nice to meet you, sir, I'm Barry Junior. Your brother's boy.'

Derek peered into Barry's eyes. 'Well I'll be damned. Our Barry had a son, eh? He kept that quiet. Where you from?'

Barry smiled. 'Australia.'

'Ha, a bloody convict in the family, eh? That would be right. An Aussie too. Who'd have thought it?'

Uncle Derek began to laugh. Barry did the same and the two fell apart, giggling uncontrollably over nothing in particular. Aunty Ruth couldn't help but join in. She'd not seen her husband laugh like this in months.

'Ruthy, be a love and get the kettle on for our guest here and make the lad some tea, will yer? Don't bother with the biscuits, he looks like he's been fed enough. Say, whatever your name is, would you rather have a beer? I've got some cans of ale out the back. Proper stuff, none of your weak as piss Aussie lager. Won't have it in this house.' Derek began laughing hysterically all over again. It's warm beer. Tastes better.'

'No worries, mate, she'll be right,' said Barry in a shockingly bad Australian accent.

Derek was laughing so much he had to wipe tears from his eyes.

'Our kid always was a dark horse. Still, it's lovely to welcome you into the family. I'm made up. Really I am.'

Barry hugged his uncle like he'd done a thousand times before. 'Me mam's called Sheila. Sheila Bassey. She came here on holiday in 1980 and had a fling with your brother. She took me home to New South Wales with her few bits of hand luggage, she didn't even know she had me inside her until she started throwing up a few months later. She raised me on a sheep farm with her seven brothers. And their seven brides. We're a big family but we all get along just great.'

'Well how about all that, eh?' said Derek, shaking his head incredulously at the living wonder that had walked into his house, seemingly from the other side of the world.

Ruth got up to go to the kitchen and make tea. Barry followed her. 'Say, Ruthie, how's about we throw some shrimps on the barbie and get this party started?'

Ruth playfully threw a tea towel at Barry's head. 'You're a silly sod. How do you think up nonsense like that on the spot?'

Barry threw the tea towel back. 'Just comes naturally. It's a gift.'

'It was lovely to hear him laugh again. Thank you.'

'It'll be fun getting to know Uncle Derek with a clean slate,' said Barry, going to the fridge and helping himself to a can of cold beer. 'I'll be whoever he needs me to be. If that's Barry White, great. If it's someone else completely, that's dandy too.'

***

Barry drank three cans of beer as he sat with his uncle for around an hour. They casually chatted about all kinds of everything, the great Wallabies rugby teams of the seventies and eighties, Ashes cricket, the *Crocodile Dundee* films and sheep farming in the valleys compared to sheep farming in the outback. They also discussed giant spiders, the Great Barrier Reef, Kylie Minogue's love life and the upsides and downsides of too much sun.

When his uncle started to tire, Barry made his excuses and said it was time for him to go.

'You're not flying back to Walkabout Creek tonight are you, boy? You're welcome to stay here. I will see you again, won't I?'

'Sure, Uncle Derek. I'm going to be around for quite a while. You're going to see a whole lot of me. We're going to get to know each other properly.'

Derek beamed. 'Fantastic. Go steady, Aussie lad.'

Aunty Ruth walked Barry to the gate.

'It's scary all this, isn't it? I'm not sure I'll be able to cope when it's me he no longer recognises.'

'You'll cope, Aunty Ruth. You always do. And he's still Uncle Derek. It ain't no one else in there.'

Barry shut the gate best he could as the latch didn't fit properly, and sauntered down the road whistling Kylie Minogue's 'Can't Get You Out of my Head' to himself.

He'd gone around to his aunty and uncle's wanting to share important news. It could wait. It would have to, under the circumstances. There were only so many shocks and surprises his aunty could handle on any single day. Perhaps his news would register when she went shopping in the morning or tried to pay a bill online. She would surely shake and tremble and imagine there had been a terrible mistake. Then she might reflect for a bit longer and work it all out for herself. Barry hoped she'd be grateful, if not entirely happy. Relieved, if not jumping for joy.

He certainly felt much better in his own skin knowing that the £250,000 Delores had paid him for the pub was now gathering interest in his aunt and uncle's joint bank account, rather than his own.

The way things were going Derek would need every penny of that money in the weeks, months and hopefully years to come.

Ruth might not have much to laugh about right now, but at least she had things and people to be thankful for.

TWENTY-SEVEN

SORRY ISN'T THE HARDEST WORD

There wasn't a Welsh dragon in sight. Delores had promised that The Dragon would remain a typical British boozer rather than an American themed bar – but that didn't stop her going all in with a big dollop of patriotism for her opening night.

Trays of complimentary champagne lined the bar, Dom P of course, one for each guest on arrival. Chilli dogs, giant hamburgers, tacos, fried chicken wings and chocolate doughnuts were being served from a large table with a red check tablecloth by two people wearing face masks.

'Howdy, pardner, what's it to be?' said Britney Spears, cheerily.

'Chilli dog, please.'

'Thought you'd ask for the lot in one enormous trough, you fat bastard,' said a belligerent Lady Gaga with a voice full of sarcasm.

Barry peered into the eyes of the woman serving him, trying to work out who would be so rude.

'Hello, Grenville, glad to see Delores has a found a proper

use for your talents.' Barry turned his focus to Britney, squinting closely for a better view. 'Sorry, I've no idea who you are.'

Britney's head dropped. 'It's William Sykes, sir. Workhouse... from the stables.'

Despite Grenville Grayson's insults, Barry was determined to enjoy himself and it seemed like most of the village had turned out for the occasion, or rather, the freebies. There was no room for Barry to sit and eat his dog so he swallowed it in several large gulps, like a jungle snake feasting on a small mammal, whilst walking around. When indigestion struck, he found an old log to sit on in the beer garden – where Delores was about to introduce the first of the night's entertainment, a young illusionist called Magic Mike. The poor lad had barely started his Chinese linking rings routine when angry middle-aged women – expecting a performer wearing nothing but baby oil rather than a long black cloak and Harry Potter-style rimmed spectacles – began pelting him with plastic beer glasses and pairs of warm knickers.

Sidney 'Elton' John came 'all the way from the mediterranean' according to the compere, Pricer, albeit off a cruise ship. Sidney tottered onto the temporary stage like a seven-year-old trying on his mother's shoes for the first time. His elaborate outfit comprised of a rainbow feather headdress and a glittering red, white and blue American striped suit with white stars spangled all over the arse. His ill-fitting garb was unbuttoned to the waist to show off his paunch and a surprisingly thick chest carpet that fleetingly made Barry mourn the loss of Chico. He wore large red fake spectacles with no lenses and knuckle dusters on each hand, one saying 'Elton' and the other 'John'. He took his place at the mini electric keyboard, grinning from ear to ear. For the first time in his life, he felt like his own village was accepting him for who he really was. Or if they weren't exactly accepting him, they were refraining from throwing things and showering him with inappropriate insults.

Sidney leant forward to speak into the mic perched on top of his organ.

'It's lovely to be here with you this evening, Anghofiedig, so gadewch i ni barti! (let's party!) I'd like to dedicate my set tonight to my wonderful father, your friend and mine, John John. Without his love and patience, I don't think I'd be here with you now, certainly not in all my sensational shimmering sexual glory. Daddy, I love you, man. This one's for you.'

John John bowed his head in embarrassment, hoping no one would notice he was there – or that the ground would swallow him whole, like Barry eating a chilli dog. When people started whooping, hollering and shouting his name, he feigned a smile and flashed an acknowledging hand in the air for no more than two seconds, before sinking as low as he could go into his wobbly deckchair.

Sidney's musical tribute to his father was 'Your Song'. John John turned a funny shade of green, which didn't subside until his son had stopped warbling. Elton – or El Sid as Delores called him – then followed up with 'Rocket Man', 'Sorry Seems To Be The Hardest Word', 'Someone Saved My Life Tonight' and 'The Bitch Is Back' before leaving everyone speechless with his performance of 'Don't Go Breaking My Heart', which he sang as a duet with himself. He turned from side to side, taking his glasses off and swiftly putting them back on again for each part, changing the pitch of his voice accordingly. It wasn't supposed to make people fall about laughing but it did. He won the crowd back with a stirring version of a local favourite 'Saturday Night's Alright for Fighting' before going full-on cabaret with his big finale: a rendition of 'Yankee Doodle Dandy' from the eponymous 1940s Hollywood movie. During this song, Sidney slowly took off most of his clothes. By the end of it he was wearing nothing but big shoes, the rainbow headdress and a pair of American flag Y-fronts, as he proudly declared himself to be 'the original Yankee Doodle Boy'.

Barry looked across to where John John had been sitting, but he was gone.

Sidney Elton John was certainly a hard act to follow, but the Parisian Prancers pulled it off. It was with some trepidation that they returned to these parts after their miserable previous experiences. In their Gallic minds, Anghofiedig was a danger zone, right up there with Port-au-Prince and Kyiv. Still, they badly needed the work and Delores didn't mind digging extra deep into her pockets to pay them more for a single performance than they had been paid for all their gigs combined throughout the rest of the year.

Napoleon the dancing bear had thankfully recovered to full health and moved around the small stage with the grace and lightness of touch of a young Anton Du Beke, accompanied by his pretty, delicate raven-haired dance partner, Veronique. He looked so happy doing what he loved most, waltzing on the tips of his pads.

It was quite a night for the Foresters in the pub too, especially the older ones, who never thought they'd see the day when a dancing bear felt safe enough to return to this neck of the woods without fearing what the locals might do to him. Napoleon's troop leaders happily got drunk on a river of free red wine and swapped jokes and stories with pubgoers once the show was done and they knew Napoleon was sleeping safely in his cage – minded by guards with guns (two of Delores's nephews, who had flown over for the week) – and dreaming of newly mastered steps, whilst blanketed in the warmth and adoration of the love of his new-found English fans.

By nine o'clock, The Dragon had thinned out enough for Barry to take his place at an inside table next to Romeo. There was plenty of Dom P left over so the pair were steadily filling their boots.

'Say, why's your missus got a statue of Queen Victoria's head on the bar? I reckon she's been watching too much *EastEnders*,' said Barry, frowning.

It ain't Queen Victoria, it's Tina Turner. Delores bought it off some council worker who reckoned Banksy made it. Council bod only wanted fifty quid for it. Bargain, eh?'

Romeo was oblivious to the fact that this was the head of Ma, from the statue he had commissioned months back. Barry failed to recognise even a passing resemblance to his own mother, though he was pretty damn sure it wasn't Tina Turner.

Their feeble discussion of modern art was disturbed by the unexpected entrance of Sergeant Sargent, who surveyed the room and made a beeline for Barry's table.

'Been looking for you, boyo,' said the sarge.

Barry's face went white.

'What have I done wrong now?'

'Did I say you'd done something wrong? I just said I've been looking for you.'

The sarge whistled like he was calling a dog to order and in bounded the most excitable puppy on two legs you could imagine: Eddie. He ran in and threw his arms around Barry, knocking him over the table, sending champagne glasses flying.

'Steady on, son, let's not breach the peace,' said the sarge.

'I've missed you so much,' said Eddie, clinging on to Barry's ample waist. 'Corfu's too hot for pale Welsh lads like us, Uncle Barry. Might as well live on the sun, you go outside and your skin falls off in seconds. You gotta wear suncream indoors. There are stray dogs everywhere. And flies. And loads of greasy blokes who Mum called sharks. I think she was flattered by all their attention at first, but then she got fed up with them sniffing around her wherever she went. She got fed up with Grandma even more. They argued so much. Grandma and Christos argue a lot too. Uncle Barry, did you know they eat pies for breakfast over there? Just like you.'

Barry was struggling to take it all in. 'Where's your mum now?'

'I'm right here,' said a voice from across the room.

Diana walked towards Barry and hugged him; less enthusiastically than Eddie, but every bit as warmly.

'Missed you, pilgrim.'

'Missed you too.'

Out of the corner of his eye, Barry could see Sergeant Sargent standing over him like a peeping Tom.

'What are you doing here, sarge?'

Diana held Barry by both hands. 'The sarge is the reason we came back. He messaged me. He forwarded the letter you wrote.'

'What letter?'

Sergeant Sargent produced a piece of paper from his top pocket and handed it to Barry. 'This one. The one I found in your house, the day I discovered the reverend down the back of your sofa. The letter I said I was keeping as evidence. Remember?'

'You should have told me the truth,' said Diana, snuggling her nose into Barry's cheek.

'Which truth?'

'All of it. About the money. And Reverend Hill. And the fire. I thought you were trying to blame Eddie just to save your own neck. I didn't know you were covering for your uncle. You should have told me. You should have trusted me. How is he?'

'He thinks I'm Australian,' said Barry, stony-faced.

Diana tried not to laugh. 'Let's go home.'

'Which home?'

'Our home.'

'You mean we're still together?' Barry's brain was struggling to keep pace with all the things Diana was saying and the stuff she wasn't saying but seemed to be implying. He realised he understood feminine body language less than he understood Greek. Or Parisian Prancer French. Or even bear.

'You do still want us, don't you?' Diana pulled back slightly and leant against Eddie's shoulder.

Barry smiled. 'I do.'

Everyone in the pub clapped and cheered.

'Hang on a moment, I know I said "I do" but we're not getting married or anything like that.' Barry was now sweating like a strong French cheese.

'We could get married,' said Diana, provocatively. 'If you wanted to.'

'Really?'

'What's it gonna be, stud muffin?' said Delores, cackling like a witch. 'You gonna stick or you gonna twist?'

Barry picked up two full glasses of champagne from the table where Delores was now sitting with Romeo – and drank them both down himself. He could feel the whole pub watching him, collectively holding their breath as one.

'Can we talk about this another time?'

Diana took the empty glasses out of Barry's hands and put them down on the table. She picked up both of his hands again and held them in front of her. 'Of course.'

The whole pub groaned. As if Wales had just lost to England for the umpteenth time.

'You know I don't have any money left. I gave it all away again.'

'Don't care.'

'I didn't think you were coming back. Not to me at any rate.'

'Well, here we are. And we're not going away again.'

Barry realised his inability to make important spontaneous decisions meant another golden opportunity to transform his life had just slipped through his grasp. But he also knew it didn't matter this time. That there would be other chances. Better ones. Ones that would probably feel more right. He grabbed another champagne, stood on a chair and raised his glass high, calling upon the whole pub to join him in a convoluted drunken toast to Diana and family, and Anghofiedig, and The Dragon pub. And to honesty. Villagers hoisted their own glasses shoulder high and slopped booze over each other as if it was New Year's Eve. No one minded the showers. Their toasts were genuine and the grins real, save perhaps for Diana's. She was pleased to be home once more with Barry, but she felt bad for raising a toast to honesty, knowing she had a positive Greek pregnancy test hiding at the bottom of her handbag. She was ninety per cent sure she understood the Greek wording well enough, however, she wanted absolute certainty. Maybe two blue lines meant something else in Corfu? And one of the lines did seem a bit fainter. She didn't trust it. Or herself. Not completely. She reasoned she had already made a fool of herself once, with a pathetic, spontaneous proposal that came out of nowhere. So she opted to keep mum, even if that meant lying to herself, Barry and everyone else for a bit longer.

'Uncle Barry, if you and Mum do ever get married are you going to adopt me? And will I be able to start calling you Dad?' Inexplicably, Eddie was now sat on Delores' lap, swigging on a glass of Dom P.

'Edwardo Dougal White... It's got a certain ring to it, don't you think? Unlike Mum's third finger on her left hand, eh. It's not as good a name as Barry White Junior, obviously, but it's definitely not bad. Say, Delores, this drink you call shampoo is quite tasty, isn't it? Can I wash my hair in it? It's tonnes better than that fiery potato juice you tried to kill me with. Did you know that in Corfu they drink ginger beer with lemons in it? Spicy it is. And Christos drinks something called ouzo. He gets through bottles of the stuff every week. Mostly when Grandma nags him, which is like all the time. Get this, Delores, he told me that he once went three whole weeks without even speaking to Grandma. Three weeks! Mum can't go three minutes without speaking to someone about something or other. I asked Christos why he went so long without talking to her and he said "because he didn't want to interrupt her". Women, eh? You can't live with them, and you can't live without them. Ain't that right, Uncle Barry? Or should I start calling you Pop now? Just for practise...'

The End

ABOUT THE AUTHOR

Rob Harris grew up in the Forest of Dean but now lives in Oxfordshire with his wife and daughter.

Rob's first novel, The Absurd Life of Barry White, was published July 2024 by Bloodhound Books.

Rob previously wrote a memoir about the rare highs and frequent lows of being a committed but ultimately frustrated village cricketer - called Won't You Dance for Virat Kohli?, which was published in 2021 by Pitch.

For more information about the author go to www.robharrisauthor.com

A NOTE FROM THE PUBLISHER

Thank you for reading this book. If you enjoyed it please do consider leaving a review on Amazon to help others find it too.

We hate typos. All of our books have been rigorously edited and proofread, but sometimes mistakes do slip through. If you have spotted a typo, please do let us know and we can get it amended within hours.

info@bloodhoundbooks.com

www.ingramcontent.com/pod-product-compliance
Lightning Source LLC
Chambersburg PA
CBHW050609190726
48283CB00007B/2347